THE
MASKED
FAE

SHARI L. TAPSCOTT

ROYAL FAE OF ROSE BRIAR WOODS
BOOK ONE

ALSO BY SHARI L. TAPSCOTT

FANTASY FICTION

Royal Fae of Rose Briar Woods

The Masked Fae

The Gilded Fae

Crown and Crest

Knight from the Ashes

Forged in Cursed Flames

Fall of the Ember Throne

The Riven Kingdoms

Forest of Firelight

Sea of Starlight

Dawn of Darkness

Age of Auroras

Silver & Orchids

Moss Forest Orchid

Greybrow Serpent

Wildwood Larkwing

Lily of the Desert

Fire & Feathers: Novelette Prequel to Moss Forest Orchid

Eldentimber Series

Pippa of Lauramore

Anwen of Primewood

Seirsha of Errinton

Rosie of Triblue

Audette of Brookraven

Elodie of the Sea

Genevieve of Dragon Ridge

Grace of Vernow: An Eldentimber Novelette

Fairy Tale Kingdoms

The Marquise and Her Cat: A Puss in Boots Retelling

The Queen of Gold and Straw: A Rumpelstiltskin Retelling

The Sorceress in Training: A Retelling of The Sorcerer's Apprentice

ALSO BY SHARI L. TAPSCOTT

CONTEMPORARY FICTION

27 Ways Series

27 Ways to Find a Boyfriend
27 Ways to Mend His Broken Heart
10 Ways to Survive Christmas with Your Ex: A 27 Ways Novella

Glitter and Sparkle Series

Glitter and Sparkle
Shine and Shimmer
Sugar and Spice

Stand-alones

Little Lost Love Letter
If the Summer Lasted Forever
Just the Essentials

The Masked Fae
Royal Fae of Rose Briar Woods, Book One
ISBN: 9798791300683
Copyright © 2022 by Shari L. Tapscott
Editing by Z.A. Sunday
Cover Design by Covers by Juan
Special thanks to Christine Freeman and Leah Feltner

ALICE

The air smells like the rose water Grandmother kept in a cut crystal bottle on her dressing table when I was young. And yet, it's not quite the same. This fragrance is sharper, fresher, more...pink.

It isn't the deep crimson scent of bouquets brought by suitors, nor is it the sunny yellow smell of the lollipop-shaped rose tree topiaries beyond the library's glass doors.

This is sweeter, with hints of apples and clover. It's a gentle floral, pleasing without being cloying.

But there is something about it that concerns my sleep-hazed mind. I dance on the edge of consciousness, in those precious moments before dreams give way to reality.

Cold air caresses my bare arms and neck, making my skin prickle with goosebumps. Even once I'm awake, with sleep and dreams fading, it takes me several moments to remember where I am.

Wild roses, scented like cool summer mornings before the sun chases away the dew.

Rose Briar Woods.

My eyes fly open with a start. A velvet curtain pillows my cheek, and my shoulder presses into the sidewall of Gustin's carriage—a carriage that should be moving.

Gustin.

My brother's name stirs up both anger and anguish, and I sit up as the strong emotions clear my head. Why have we stopped?

I push aside the scarlet curtain and peer into the growing darkness beyond the window, hoping to find we've arrived at Lord Ambrose's estate. Perhaps his staff took pity on me when they found me asleep and left me at peace for a few minutes.

But my chest tightens when I see nothing but dense, dusk-cloaked trees. The undergrowth is thick with raspberry bushes. The berries are small and not yet ripe. They fight for territory under and around the evergreens, their adversaries the wild roses that grow only in this spring wood.

The leggy, heavily thorned rosebushes bloom in froths of blush. Like holiday garlands, their long canes venture up the dusty fir trees, wrapping around the trunks and heavy boughs like true vines.

Roses don't behave like that outside the wood. Even to grace an arbor, they must be trained and tied, pruned and coaxed.

But things don't follow the natural rules here, because here is *there.* A Faerie wood—beautiful, wild.

And dangerous.

An arched bridge marks the border between our land and the Fae's. It's a grand example of ancient architecture, built of gleaming white stone, spanning a river that protects the West Faerie border like a moat of old—keeping humans out, keeping the creatures of Faerie in.

Not that our people don't mingle. We do. The high Fae come into Kellington, the westernmost city in the kingdom of Valsta, to visit our shops and sell their strange, magical wares in our market. Some brave humans even venture into their nearby village of Corrinmead.

But only the very bold, or the very foolish, enter into a contract or agreement with their kind. And no one, foolish nor bold, ventures past the boundary after nightfall.

Yet, here I am, on the wrong side of the bridge well after the sun-kissed afternoon hours, serenaded by the persistent warning of a raven. The bird's repetitive, throaty cries do nothing to allay my growing fears.

"Mr. Anthony?" I call tentatively from the false safety of the carriage, my voice sharp.

The coachman doesn't answer.

My pulse quickens, and my palms grow clammy.

Knowing I have no choice but to venture outside, my hand settles on the handle. It takes several moments to work up the courage to shove the door open, and I stop short when the smell of the rosy forest greets me at full force.

The gentle fragrance twines around my senses, soothing like a lullaby, promising I am safe and welcome.

It lies.

"Mr. Anthony?" I call again at a whisper, desperately hoping the coachman only excused himself to tend to personal needs.

Fallen evergreen needles rustle under my feet, too loud in this familiar but foreign world. My gown brushes the ground, a smidgen too long for the slippers I chose this morning. A week ago, my maid would have chided me for sullying the skirt, but I have no one to chastise me for dirty lace now—nor do I have anyone to wash it.

The raven continues to crow, agitated on her perch high in a weeping spruce, and the noise further frays my nerves. But it's not until I round the carriage that genuine fear lodges itself in my throat.

Not only is my coachman missing, but the pair of horses as well. The carriage sits in the middle of this empty dirt road, alone and abandoned. I stare at the surreal scene before me, unable to make sense of it. Each beat of my heart thrums louder in my head, until I fear it must be audible for miles.

After several panicked moments, a strange sound catches my attention—and it comes from not far away. Perhaps I would have heard the odd noise sooner if it weren't for the raven's incessant cries...or maybe my brain was simply too addled to process it.

Either way, I now focus on the shuffling and snorting. It sounds like a dozen pigs rooting through the undergrowth. Twigs snap, and bushes rustle. Something tiny squeals as if suddenly snatched from the safety of the ground by a predator.

My instinct to flee is strong, but where would I go? I could run in the opposite direction, into the forest on the other side of the road, but what new danger awaits me there? I stand frozen like a spooked rabbit as my eyes dart around me, first looking for protection and then a weapon.

I'm just leaning down to pick up the largest rock I can hold when I'm snatched around the waist and pulled into the brush behind me.

Before my mind can wrap around my predicament, my abductor briefly presses a hand over my mouth. "Don't scream."

I'd defy him if I were capable, but the shock has stolen the air from my lungs. I'm tugged to the ground, made to crouch precariously between the roses and raspberries, barely able to avoid either's wicked thorns. The position is awkward, especially since it puts me so close to the man who snatched me from the road.

Dressed in black, he wears a mask over his eyes like a thief. His wide-brimmed hat is black as well, and it further shields his features in the fading light.

He yanks at my layers of skirts, which have caught above us in the brambles, tugging them out of sight. The sound of ripping fabric makes me cringe, but my dress matters little right now.

I suck in a strangled gasp when the bushes on the other side of the road shift as the owners of the strange noises reveal themselves.

Goblins.

I nearly say the word aloud, horrified to discover they're *real*.

Pinkish-gray like pigs, with patches of coarse hair and snouted noses, they wear rags over their thick, stout bodies. Their eyes are beady black and too small for their deeply wrinkled faces.

With snorts and cackles, they surround the deserted carriage.

A particularly ugly one, the tallest of the bunch and about as tall as a five-year-old child, climbs the carriage rack and hoists the largest of my trunks over his head. The others crowd around, squealing with glee.

I cry out when the vile creature throws the trunk to the ground, but the man's gloved hand presses over my mouth once more, muffling the sound.

"Shhh," he murmurs into my ear before dropping his hand. "You don't want them to find us."

"Can they hear that well?" I ask, feeling faint at the thought.

"It doesn't seem like the best time to test their abilities."

I glance at the man, and my attention latches onto his eyes. They're shadowed under the brim of his wide hat, impossible to make out in the growing night.

Filled with dread, I turn back to the goblins. Silken gowns, lacy petticoats, stockings, and hair adornments scatter over the road, trampled by the creatures in their haste and greed. They claw at my belongings, fighting over them, ripping the fabric and awkwardly fitting their newly won treasures onto their bodies.

One tugs a corset over his fat torso, and another plops a hat onto his head. They raid my jewelry box and drape necklaces over themselves like drunken pirates.

It's a disturbing sight and so ridiculously absurd, so darkly amusing, I almost laugh. But the hysterical giggle catches in my throat when they move on to the last piece of luggage.

"No," I murmur, struggling against my rescuer's grip, determined not to let the monsters get their hands on the contents of my second trunk.

"They'll rip you limb from limb," the man whispers impatiently, holding me firmly in place.

It's too late anyway. A goblin throws the trunk, and the latch breaks as soon as it hits the ground. Precious tins of paint scatter with brushes, waxes, oils, and all my other supplies.

I breathe in a heartsick gasp that draws the man's attention.

He studies me, but my eyes are on the goblins. The wretched creatures poke and prod my most cherished possessions. They jab their grubby fingers into my prepared tins of paint and then slather it over their bodies, snorting gleefully. They snap my brushes and dump colorful, powdered pigments onto the ground.

A particularly stealthy goblin shuffles to the side of the road and tucks my palette into his new corset while the others aren't looking.

I turn away, feeling ill, hiding my eyes against the stranger's shoulder.

"Be thankful it's not you they're pulling to pieces," the man points out in a bare whisper.

"I almost wish it were."

What am I without my supplies? How will I save Gustin now?

Amused, he says, "That's a bit dramatic, don't you think?"

Though reluctant, I crane my head back to look at the man. Before I can answer, a whiff of smoke catches my attention. I turn toward the road just in time to see the goblins light the carriage on fire. The fabric catches first, but soon, the entire thing is engulfed in flames.

The last remnant of my family's fortune is now ablaze. The monsters dance around their bonfire, many tripping over the petticoats they've bunched up to their chests. One suckles toxic pigment straight from his fingers, and a morbid smile crosses my lips as I imagine his slow, painful death.

"Are you all right?" the man asks. The goblins are too preoccupied with their revelry to hear us now.

Am I? I'm not sure.

With a heavy sigh, I answer, "I will be somehow. They're just things, after all."

Precious things. All I had left.

Absently, my hand drops to my finger to twist my grandmother's ring—and then my eyes fly down when I realize what I've done.

I packed it with the other things, thought it was best to hide it from Lord Ambrose considering the circumstances. And now it's gone—lost with everything else.

"Yes, I figured that." Wry humor laces the masked man's tone once more. "But I was asking if you're growing weary."

Feeling a bit awkward, I primly answer, "It's not my first time crouched amongst bushes."

Though the last was easily ten years ago, and I was playing a game of hide and seek in Grandmother's garden with Gustin—long before I became a nuisance and a burden to him.

"So, you've hidden from goblins before?" he asks skeptically. His voice is dark and rich, fitting his mysterious persona.

"Well…no. This is a first for me." I study him, intrigued despite myself.

Who *is* this man?

"You?" I ask.

"It's certainly not my first experience." He pauses, smiling beneath the shadow of his hat. "But the company is new."

Night falls around us as we hide, and despite my bluster, my muscles grow fatigued. It feels like we wait hours for the flames to die and the coals to dim to a smoldering red. Sensing my exhaustion, the man holds me tighter, supporting my weight with his arm so I don't topple into the brambles.

Despite his nearness, subtle sounds spook me, making me think we've attracted the attention of other, smaller creatures. I swear I see them from the corner of my eye. They're perched far too close in the bushes, but when I turn, there's nothing looking back at me.

Finally, the goblins leave, dragging their treasures with them into the forest from which they came, and the woods fall silent. I stare at the wreckage in a strange sort of shock.

A sudden breeze blows through the trees, only now making me realize how cold it's become in the spring wood. I shiver, and the man shifts as if trying to block the wind.

"I believe they're gone," I say quietly.

Together, we stand. My legs protest after crouching for so long, and my dress catches on more of the thorny twigs.

Even though my rescuer offers his hand, I still manage to trip on a raised, uneven root. I stumble forward, losing my balance.

On instinct, the man catches me. I fall against his chest, and his arms wrap around me in an embrace that could be mistaken for amorous. Suddenly, I'm very conscious of this stranger I'm pressed against.

Things I didn't notice before shift into clear focus now. The man's leather jacket does little to hide his strong, toned build. His arms are like bands of iron, and they held me securely all that time. The thought makes my chest grow warm.

My hand rests on his abdomen, and when he shifts, I feel the toned definition of his muscles under my palm. There's something undeniably appealing about the mystery of him. For a fleeting moment, I wonder what it would be like to paint him.

The thought barely crosses my mind before it races ahead to the romantic scenarios I've read in the copper-apiece adventure novels I began to purchase when Grandmother was no longer around to tell me they are cheap and tawdry. Because of them, I know a hero is supposed to kiss the damsel in distress once the peril has passed.

Will this man expect a kiss in exchange for the valiant services rendered? Would I let him kiss me if he tried?

But that's a ridiculous question—I certainly would.

The rogue thought makes my face heat. I don't even know this man. Yes, he saved me from the goblins, but that doesn't mean his intentions are pure.

Besides, with the way he's dressed, he must be a bandit. Gustin would have my head if he found out I was entertaining these sorts of thoughts about a common thief.

Not that Gustin is a pillar of virtue himself. If he was, he wouldn't be languishing in a debtor's prison in West Faerie after gambling away our family's estate in a game of chance with Lord Ambrose. Only a fool falls into a Fae's trap.

Only a fool would barter with that same Faerie for her brother's life.

Perhaps it runs in the family. Sister like brother, I suppose.

"Why are you in the forest?" the man asks, pulling me from my wayward thoughts. "Don't you know it's dangerous to pass the boundary at this time of day?"

"I have business with Lord Ambrose. I must have dozed off in the carriage, and I didn't realize..."

How *did* I fall asleep on such a short trip? And what happened to my coachman and the horses?

Like a command, the man replies, "You have no business with Lord Ambrose, or any of the Fae. Go back to your side of the bridge, where it's safe."

"I have nowhere to go," I admit, wondering why I'm sharing that bit of information with this man. "And I have come to work off my brother's debt."

"There is nothing you can offer Lord Ambrose that he will want," my rescuer says, almost as if he's growing bored of the conversation. "You're a lovely girl. Go home —knock on the door of any eligible bachelor. Surely he will take pity on you and your plight, and you'll be married in a week."

I bristle, unsure why that statement sounded like an insult but certain it was.

"Do you, *bandit*, have personal insight into Lord Ambrose's desires?" I say hotly. "I am an artist, renowned and respected. People come from cities near and far to sit for one of my portraits. The Fae are known both for their love of art and their narcissism. How dare *you* tell *me* I have nothing to offer?"

The man jerks his head toward the smoldering remnants of my belongings. "That may be, but I imagine it's difficult to paint without supplies."

Though my heart wrenches, I hide my anguish. "That is none of your concern. I'm thankful you saved me, but I ask you to now go about your own business. I can tend to mine."

The man shifts, and though it seems as if it would be impossible for us to come any closer, I now feel as though every inch of me presses against every inch of him. Thankful for the cover of night, I swallow.

"What's your name?" he asks, his tone laced with amusement once more.

Having no intention of answering, I tilt my head to the side, refusing to look at him.

The man chuckles under his breath. "You're willing to involve yourself with a Faerie as cold and callous as Lord Ambrose, but I don't even get your name after saving your life?"

Perhaps it's his laugh that captures my interest, or maybe it's because I've never allowed a man to hold me like this. But no matter the reason, I suddenly feel like a moth drawn to a dangerous flame.

"Alice," I finally answer, hoping he won't hear the hitch in my voice.

"Alice?" He sounds skeptical—as if perhaps he thinks I'm lying. And maybe that would have been wiser.

"That's right," I answer, this time a touch hesitant.

"Very well. I will give you a choice, Alice," he says solemnly after another few long seconds, acting as if we're about to enter into a contract. "I will accompany you back to the boundary, or I will escort you to Lord Ambrose's estate. Take my advice and choose the first. Even wandering the streets without a copper to your name is preferable to making a deal with Lord Ambrose."

"What business do *you* have on this side of the fence?" I ask instead of answering. "Why don't you take your own advice and go home? Surely stealing from the Fae is far more dangerous than stealing from humans."

I can just make out his smile in the night. Amused, he asks, "You have pegged me for a thief?"

"What else could you be in that mask?" I demand.

He leans in. The side of his jaw brushes against my cheek as his words caress my ear. "The only things I've ever stolen are hearts, Alice. Go home before I'm tempted to claim yours."

I jerk back, startled by the bold words, and he laughs again.

"Have you made your decision, fair painter?" he asks. "Where will I take you?"

I stare at the man, my breath shallow and my cheeks warm. I want to pull the mask from his face and look at him in the dusky starlight, but I'm not that brave.

"To Lord Ambrose's estate," I say firmly. "Right now, there is nothing for me in the human world."

He nods, looking resigned to my decision. "Very well."

2

BRAHM

I should have let the goblins eat the girl.

But no, it will be all right. I'll simply turn her away when she requests an audience. She won't recognize me—how could she? She hasn't even seen my face.

I watch Alice from the corner of my eye as we walk down the road. Her long, pale blonde hair shines silver in the starlight, and her dress is torn in several places thanks to the brambles. Even though she has likely never walked this far in her life, she doesn't complain or ask how far we have left to travel.

This girl is that half-wit's sister?

If Alice had any idea what her brother offered me when he realized what he'd lost, she wouldn't be here on his behalf. I shake my head at the thought of any human sending their kin into Faerie—it's unthinkable.

Just as unthinkable as the eldest prince of West Faerie accepting the ridiculous trade.

But Lord Gustin didn't know my true identity when he made his desperate offer, just as his sister doesn't know I am Lord Ambrose. I go by many aliases—so many, in fact, I often forget who I am myself.

And apparently now, I am a thief.

Something small scampers across the road and into the bushes, and Alice jumps.

I peer at her, narrowing my eyes. "If you are afraid of mice, you certainly shouldn't have crossed the boundary. There are far worse things than rodents on this side of the bridge."

"Things like goblins," she murmurs.

"Things worse than goblins. Some would say Lord Ambrose is one of them."

She looks at me, silently scrutinizing me in the glow of the pale waxing moon that has risen over the trees. It shines down on us, fat and nearly round.

Luckily for Alice, it won't be full for two more days. Imagine the trouble she would have found herself in if I weren't scouting the woods tonight.

As it was, I almost didn't leave when the shadows grew long. I had a headache, likely brought on by the message I received from my mother. Dreading her monthly masquerade, I nearly retired to my bedroom, deciding any stray humans could find their own way back to the boundary.

There are always a few caught on our side of the bridge come night, each too careless to pay attention to the sun's position in the sky until it's too late.

For the most part, however, the humans I encounter are rushing for their side of the forest...not heading deeper into ours.

I glance at Alice again, and a scowl tugs at my lips.

A portrait, I scoff silently. The last thing I need is another likeness of myself gracing a random wall.

Narcissistic, she claims. As if this human girl has ever known one of us well enough to make that assumption. And how is it any fault of ours that we're attractive? To deny it would be a lie, and those are far more painful than they're worth.

We're just nearing the estate gates when I realize that even once I turn Alice away, I won't be rid of her. Someone must escort her back to the bridge. She'd never make it alone.

Too many creatures of Faerie are intrigued by her people. They're captivated by humankind's insatiable curiosity or their laughter, the feel of their skin or the taste of their flesh. It depends on what creature finds them whether they become pet or prey, but either fate is dark.

"Let them have their fun," Mother always says. *"There are enough humans in the world—no one is going to miss the few my subjects take."*

Perhaps I would agree, but only if *she* hadn't come into our lives. I think of the girl who's only a hazy memory at this point, dwelling on the past.

When I realize where my mind has wandered, I shake my head to clear it. But again, I glance at Alice, hit with the strangest sense of déjà vu.

Sensing she has my attention, the girl looks at me. "What is it?" she asks hesitantly.

"You remind me of someone."

It's impossible to make out the color of her eyes in the

moonlight, but they're a light shade. Amber, like rich honey, I imagine.

"Whom?"

I stare at her, this strange recognition playing tricks on my brain.

They share the same name.

No, it's not possible. Though the resemblance is uncanny, that girl's hair was sable. And besides, Mother didn't return the child to her family.

A shudder runs down my spine, my body subtly reminding me that things of the past are best left forgotten.

"No one," I say, dismissing the notion. "Never mind."

Golden eyes peek at us from the bracken as we walk, but nothing but the fool goblins would dare challenge me on the road, though certainly not for lack of interest.

These hidden creatures are small and insignificant—wood pixies and mud sprites, florigans with fat bodies covered in colorful hair and faunaweavers with eyes three times larger than their ferret cousins. None are a threat.

Alice, however, senses them. Their eyes wink out as she looks their way, just before she has a good view, lingering in her side vision to spook her. She's unnerved, glancing into the surrounding forest as we walk, unconsciously edging closer to me.

Funny that the girl unknowingly shies away from those insignificant creatures and ends up next to one who's not so benign.

But she thinks I'm human. I almost laugh aloud, morbidly amused by the innocent assumption.

Too soon, we reach the tall, scrolling gates that mark the boundary of my land.

"Iron," Alice murmurs to herself, frowning. She then turns to me. "I thought the Fae…"

"They cannot work the metal themselves, but it makes a decent deterrent against the less savory of their kind. The materials are purchased outside Faerie and then transported here. Human workers install them during the daylight hours."

Alice presses her hand to the gate, giving it an experimental push to see if it's open. I, however, know the gates are locked from the other side, barred with a heavy rod of metal. A chill travels my spine when I contemplate reaching through the bars and touching it with my bare hand.

Contrary to human legend, iron doesn't burn us. But it does send a jolt through our bodies that's not dissimilar to the sensation one receives if someone scratches a nail across a chalkboard. It's unpleasant.

I turn to Alice. "This is your last chance to change your mind."

Looking hesitant, she peers through the gate at the heavily wooded lane that eventually leads to my estate. "Who is Lord Ambrose, exactly? Why does he live so close to humans?"

"He's the marquis of Rose Briar Woods." I cross my arms. "He protects the Fae border."

"From humans?" She looks back as if the notion is startling.

I nod.

"Have you ever seen him before?"

I think of all the times I've looked at my own reflection in the mirror, deciding it's not a lie. "I have."

"Is he as terrifying as rumor states?" she asks, fear finally making her voice sharp.

I smile, pleased with the turn in the conversation. "Even his mother abhors him."

Alice hugs herself, blinking with indecision.

"Let me take you back to the bridge." I coax.

But my words of warning don't elicit the response I was hoping for. The girl stands taller, letting her arms fall to her sides like she's about to march into battle. "I've come this far; I've lost my things and my supplies. I can't turn back now."

"You can," I point out.

She turns, pinning me with those familiar eyes. "But I won't."

The girl is either very brave or very foolish—or she simply loves her brother, though I cannot fathom why.

"Very well." I bow before her with a flourish of my hand. "Then here is where we part."

"You're leaving?" she asks, reaching for me before she thinks better of it. For just a moment, she grasps my arm. Then, just as quickly, she pulls her hand back.

I cock my head to the side. "Let's just say that as a *bandit*, as you so eloquently called me, I haven't endeared myself to the Fae."

That is also true, but only when it's worded carefully. Still, magic makes my stomach squirm, letting me know it doesn't like me bending the truth quite so far.

"How will I get in?" Her eyes are wide, and I'm sure

she's worried she'll end up standing in front of this massive gate alone in the woods all night.

I reach past her, grasp the velvet rope that hangs behind a tree bough, and give it a firm tug. "They know you are here."

She gulps, visibly spooked. "Thank you for escorting me."

"Do not wander alone in the woods again," I instruct her, and then I turn to leave. "And whatever you do, don't initiate a bargain with Lord Ambrose. I will tell you again —Faeries are dangerous."

"Wait!" she calls. "You didn't give me your name."

"I have no name," I respond, which is a form of truth, at least when I am dressed like this. My people call me the Highwayman. I am a shadow cloaked in midnight. Ridiculed or romanticized by most of the Fae, despised by my mother.

"Will I see you again?" she asks.

Instead of answering, I disappear into the woods to wait and watch. Alice loses sight of me, wringing her hands, and then reluctantly turns back to the gate.

A few minutes later, a flickering light appears on the other side of the gate, bobbing through the trees until its owner comes into view. My housekeeper holds a single candle in one hand and dons a thick leather glove in her other. She wears a black gown, forever mourning her husband's death.

I'm surprised my cousin answered the summon herself at this time of night. Regina is not truly part of my staff, but she currently acts as the lady of the house, dealing with the tedious daily affairs I have no patience for.

Regina's face betrays her surprise when she sees the human girl standing on the other side of the gate in the dark of night.

Alice curtsies, looking terrified. "Good evening, madame. I am Alice Gravely, and I have come to request an audience with Lord Ambrose."

Though Regina is only twenty-three, she has a stern look about her. But I know she has a softness for humans, as do so many of us who lived in Mother's household ten years ago. Her expression becomes concerned as she glances down the road we walked. "You traveled alone?"

Alice hesitates a moment, and I wonder if she's going to betray me. Not that it would matter—Regina is one of the few people who know of my evening activities.

"I hid in the woods when I met trouble on the road," Alice says carefully, as if she doesn't want to lie. Strange, considering how easily deception comes to her kind.

"I see." Regina frowns, and then she shakes her head. "Very well. Come inside."

She pulls back the heavy rod with her gloved hand and pushes the gates open. Alice enters the grounds slowly, perhaps remembering my warnings.

"You're safer in here than you are out there," Regina points out.

"Am I?" Alice asks softly, looking unsure.

Without waiting, Regina leads her down the lane. "Come along."

I watch Alice follow the candlelight, and then I rouse myself, knowing I don't have much time. Quickly, I run along the boundary, stopping when I reach the towering willow that arcs a great branch over the iron fence. I leap up, grasping hold and pulling myself on top of it. I walk the sturdy limb until I'm over the fence, and then I jump down, cutting through the dense forest as I head toward the manor. Once I reach it, I climb the lattice on the southwestern side and then crawl over my balcony rail.

As always, I've left the door to my bedchamber unlocked. Quickly, I shed my black clothes for ones appropriate for a marquis. After tossing the hat aside, I smooth my short hair and then walk briskly for the door.

"Brahm!" Wallen, my valet, cries at a whisper when I step into the foyer. "Your *mask.*"

I rip it from my face just as the front doors open and Regina escorts Alice inside.

"I do not believe Lord Ambrose is in right now," Regina informs Alice. "But you may wait—"

"I'm here," I say curtly, subtly handing my mask to Wallen.

Alice turns her eyes on me, and she freezes.

She recognizes me.

No...perhaps not. It's fear in her expression, nothing more. Her hand moves to her stomach as if she's suddenly queasy, and her eyes sweep over me, wide and terrified.

Surely if she realized I was the man who brought her here, she would appear more at ease.

After a long moment, she drops into a graceful curtsy. "Good evening, Lord Ambrose. Please forgive my impertinent visit, but I didn't know how to send you a message, and I am desperate to speak with you."

"Desperate even," I say coolly. "What business, exactly, could one of your kind have with me?"

She slowly raises her eyes to mine—her *blue* eyes. Startlingly blue, like the sky on a cloudless day.

The woman is stunning.

I knew she was beautiful in the woods, but seeing her in good lighting…

And she looks so much like—but no. Her hair, her eyes…they're both wrong.

Gulping back her fears, she lifts her chin. "I have come to ask you to forgive my brother's crimes and request you release him from the debtor's prison."

"Who is your brother?" I ask with practiced indifference, glancing down to adjust the right cuff of my jacket, watching her from the corner of my vision.

Alice pauses, looking as if she's mustering courage once more. Her bravery ebbs and flows like a wave on the shore, retreating and then pushing forward. "Lord Gustin Gravely."

I turn to Regina. "Am I familiar with a man by the name of Gustin?"

She frowns, hating it when I play my part. But another watches as well—and he is loyal to my mother. Ian Treald, Count of Chadelaine, has just wandered into the foyer. He leans against a wall, observing our exchange.

Two more show up behind him—a pair of housemaids that are more trouble than they're worth. They watch with feline interest, their eyes on Alice.

My audience is hoping I will make a fool of this naïve human who dared set foot in my estate at this hour. After all, that's what's expected of me.

"Yes," Regina says to me. "He's the man who wagered his estate in a game of cards two days ago."

I make a bored noise.

"Please, my lord," Alice says, stepping forward, her unsettling eyes begging for mercy. "I do not ask you to return our family home, but if you could find it in your heart to forgive my brother's crimes..."

"Your brother failed to mention the bank owned ninety percent of the property in which he offered. If I had lost, he would have been a great deal wealthier. Don't you believe your brother should be held to the terms in which we set at the beginning of the wager?"

Alice blinks at me. Again, she runs a nervous hand down her stomach, drawing my attention to the dirt-smudged skirt hem and the snags in the once-fine fabric.

"Ninety percent?" she asks softly.

"Your brother is a chronic gambler. I daresay this end was inevitable." Unable to keep my eyes on her heartbroken ones, I look away. "There is nothing I can do."

I begin to turn, waving my hand at Regina to show her I'm dismissing the girl.

"Wait!" Alice commands, making me pause.

I look back over my shoulder and raise an eyebrow.

"The truth is, I paint portraits," she says in a rush. "I'm talented. I had hoped that you would allow me to paint you in exchange for Gustin's freedom."

"Where are your supplies?" I ask, purposely jerking my head to the empty doorway.

She blanches. "They were destroyed by goblins on the way here."

"Shame," I say blandly. "It appears we have no business."

"What if…" She trails off, her face growing pale in the lamplit hall.

"Yes?" I ask curtly.

Alice raises her eyes to mine, making it impossible to look away. "Perhaps I may work for you, in your household, until I can afford to buy new supplies? Then I will paint your portrait, and if you are pleased with it, you may free my brother."

"I have no desire to do any more business with your family." I begin walking again.

"Please, Lord Ambrose!" Alice begs, crossing the hall swiftly, ending up in front of me, her skirts swaying with the movement. She presses her hands together, holding them in front of her heart. Her eyes shine with tears. *"Please."*

"Your brother does not deserve your sacrifice," I say callously.

"I am homeless now anyway, without even a copper to my name. Take pity on the innocent sister who had no part in your wager but was affected all the same."

Against my better judgment, I begin to waver. "And what would you do in my household?"

Alice looks around, frantically grasping for ideas. "I'll become a maid, or a governess if you have children who require teaching. Surely you can find a place for me in a manor this large?"

"There are no children here." I turn to Regina. "And I do not believe we need another maid, do we?"

"We do not." She says the words sternly, but I hear the

strain in her voice. She stares at me, initiating a silent conversation.

She has nowhere to go, her eyes say. *Your night of careless entertainment had casualties. How will you fix it?*

No matter how I argue back, she doesn't budge.

"Find a place for her," I say heavily.

Ian raises a brow, gracing me with a calculated smile that tells me I'm showing weakness. He will be sure to tell my mother.

Regina dips her head with an air of disinterest, pretending she has no opinion on the matter. "Yes, my lord."

"Thank you," Alice breathes, looking like she's going to burst into tears. "Truly, Lord Ambrose, I will forever be in your debt—"

"*No,*" I say before she can finish the careless vow, my voice harsh. "You are not in my debt—we have not struck any sort of bargain. You are simply working in my home for a few months so you may buy new supplies. It has nothing to do with your brother. If you paint a satisfactory painting, I will buy it. With that money, you may attempt to purchase your brother's freedom if you so choose, though the task is not as simple as you believe. You owe me nothing, and I owe nothing to you. If you decide to walk out tomorrow, so be it."

Alice nods, looking timid again. Softly, she murmurs, "I understand."

Looking smug, Ian and the maids leave the foyer, most likely eager to share their gossip.

"I will make room for her in the servants' quarters,"

Regina says to me, already walking toward the left wing of the manor.

"No."

Regina looks startled. "No?"

The idea of sending Alice into a den of Fae—the one place in the house where I have less jurisdiction than I should—is alarming. Too often, she'd be in their company, away from my eyes.

"Put her in the spare room on the third floor."

Regina's lips part with surprise. "But that is where your sister stays when—"

"I am not expecting Sabine to visit anytime soon." I glance at the empty wall where Ian just loitered. "Make it known that the girl is under my protection while she is here, and no one may take advantage of her untethered nature. Spread the word. If someone so much as thinks of touching her, I will not show mercy."

Without looking at Alice again, I stride from the foyer, yanking at my collar, worried I've made a grave error in judgment.

3

ALICE

I step into the room that Lord Ambrose assigned to me, and then I glance back at Regina in question.

The housekeeper is a young woman, with a stony expression and oddly kind eyes. I'm unsure how to read her.

"Are you certain this is the right room?" I ask.

To say it is opulent would be an understatement, and I am no stranger to finery.

A four-poster bed dominates the room, adorned with golden silk curtains that are tied back to each post. Half a dozen fat pillows top the coverlet, and soft rugs dot the polished wood floors. In the corner, a vanity holds a collection of crystal bottles. There are several armoires, a lacquered secretary, a full bookcase, and a plush, upholstered chaise longue is positioned in front of the fireplace. Dozens of fat, white pillar candles are placed in the hearth. Their flames flicker, but the wax is solid, still retaining its shape, making me think they haven't been burning long.

But it's not the room's beauty that troubles me. It's the fact that it appears to be more than a simple guest room in which the marquis's sister occasionally stays when she visits. Her touches are everywhere, from a collection of tiny figurines, to a jewelry box that is so exquisitely crafted, I itch to peek inside.

Something tells me the Fae woman would not be fond of the idea of me nosing about the place, and even less with me sleeping amongst her things.

"This is the room Lord Ambrose specified." Madame Regina turns to me and studies me with eyes that are not as foreign as I expect.

I've never actually spoken with one of the Fae before. I've only seen them from afar, riding on their snowy white horses, looking too radiant to be real.

This woman is beautiful, certainly, but she looks *human*—except for her ears, which are subtly pointed, as tales say they should be.

Realizing I'm staring, I look away and massage my stiff shoulder. "It's more than I require."

"You have no belongings?"

I shake my head. "They were all destroyed with my painting supplies."

"Goblins," she says with a sniff. "You're lucky they didn't find you."

It's her curious tone that catches my attention. Nervously, I meet her eyes. She wears a knowing expression, but if she suspects I had a protector, she keeps it to herself.

"I'm very grateful I arrived in one piece," I say quietly, recalling the evening's events with a shudder.

Suddenly, I remember Mr. Anthony, and my stomach grows queasy with guilt. I haven't thought of him again since the dark bandit swept me off my feet and deposited me rump-first in a rosebush.

Quickly, I explain the strange disappearance to the housekeeper.

"Do you think there is any way to find him?" I ask when I'm finished.

She narrows her eyes, appearing to be just as confused as I am. "Disappeared, you say?"

I nod. "He and the pair of horses. The carriage was abandoned."

"I'll speak to Lord Ambrose about it."

"Thank you," I say in a rush. "I cannot help but think of him out there, all alone in the woods."

Her expression becomes tight. "If he is alive, I very much doubt he is alone."

I draw in a horrified breath.

Regina either doesn't notice, or she's not terribly concerned by my distress. Stepping into the hall, she says, "I'll be back in the morning, and we'll figure out what to do with you. For now, try to sleep."

She shuts the door behind her. My only company is the flickering of the candles, and even they don't make a sound.

I've never felt so alone in my life.

I'm just drifting when a rap at the nearby window scares me half to death. I bolt upright, clutching the sheets to my chest.

The candles still glow in the hearth, lending a cheerful ambiance to the room. I tried to blow them out when I retired, but they resisted my attempts, charmed with some wondrous Fae magic, no doubt. Their light is welcome now.

The knock sounds again, and a whimper escapes my lips. What horrifying beast is out there? Did the goblins realize I escaped their clutches? Did they follow my trail?

Is it something *worse* than goblins?

"Alice," I hear muttered through the glass. "Open the door."

Recognizing the annoyed tone, I rush for the window... and then I pause. Are there Faerie creatures who can imitate voices? With damp palms, I push back the curtain just a smidgen to peep out, keeping myself hidden just in case something dark and scary waits on the other side.

And it *is* someone dark and scary—but a familiar someone. Though the bandit certainly makes a terrifying figure on the moonlit balcony, dressed in black, his face shadowed by his hat and his eyes masked, his presence fills the hollow pit in my stomach.

I pull the drapes away from the door and unlatch the lock.

"What are you doing?" he demands in a whisper, stalking inside the room without an invitation or a proper greeting. "Why are you still here?"

"I told you—I'm going to save my brother."

He's a tall man, taking up a good deal of the balcony doorway. I should be intimidated, but I'm not.

"You have no supplies," he points out. "How do you plan to barter for your brother's freedom?"

"Lord Ambrose has graciously allowed me to take a position here until I may buy some more."

"A position doing *what*?" He paces in front of the door. "You must not stay. Let me take you back tonight. I'll pay for a room at Hotel Dinmont—a night for every day of the month. Surely you can convince a suitor to marry you in that time."

"Why would you do that?" I narrow my eyes at him, wishing I could see him better. The candlelight is too dim, and he's cautious to use that to his advantage.

He pauses, turning to me, his eyes shaded by the brim of his hat. "Because it's dangerous for you to remain here."

I soften toward the small slice of chivalry that remains in him despite his profession.

"Lord Ambrose was a bit harsh, but he wasn't unkind," I say. "I think I'll be all right."

He glances at the wall, frowning as if there is something beyond it.

"What?" I ask warily.

"Your kind Lord Ambrose's rooms are next to yours."

I gasp before I can stop myself. "Truly?"

He tilts his head as if to make a point. "Are you sure you want to be that close to the master of the house?"

The idea is unsettling, but I won't be swayed. "I'm sure I'll manage."

"Don't you wonder why he'd choose to keep you so close?" he asks, sounding frustrated.

"Do you think he means to hurt me?"

The bandit pauses, pondering the question, and then he bites out an answer I don't expect. "No."

It's almost as if he hates admitting it but has no choice.

"But that doesn't mean there aren't others in this house who would wish you harm," he adds.

"I'll lock the door," I promise. "You needn't worry about me—I'll be cautious."

He turns his back to me, looking tense. "Is there nothing I can say to persuade you to leave?"

"I can't think of anything."

"Fine." He opens the balcony door, but I grasp his arm before he steps into the night.

"I do have one question," I say, looking up at him.

He glances at my hand before he removes it with a shadowed scowl. "What?"

"Can I eat the food here? Legend says it will dull my senses and make it so I can never leave Faerie."

He laughs as if delighted to be reminded. "The effect is temporary, not permanent as you've been told. But it *is* true—it's one of the many ways the Fae trick their pets into signing their lives away."

"Pets?" I manage, chilled at the thought.

"That's right, Alice," he says ominously. "Their *human* pets."

My mouth becomes dry, and I attempt to swallow. "You don't think that's what Lord Ambrose has in mind for me...do you?"

"You'd make a lovely prize." He crosses his arms and

studies me with an air of smug victory. "Are you finally ready to let me take you home?"

"I have no home," I say quietly. "And now, when people watch me, their admiration has been replaced with either pity or wicked delight. I can't return without Gustin—I cannot bear to see the looks on their faces without him by my side to take a portion of the burden."

"Alice—"

"Please," I whisper, hating how many times I've found myself pleading in the last few days.

Please, don't take my home. *Please*, not Grandmother's wedding band. *Please*, let me use the carriage just one last time.

I've never felt so small in my life. "If you know a way to avoid eating the food, *tell me*."

"I'll return tomorrow night," the bandit says heavily. "Do not eat or drink anything—not anything—until I see you again. Do you understand?"

"Thank you," I say in a rush.

"Do not thank me," he says sharply. He then glances back into the room as if critiquing the space. Sounding resigned, he asks, "Is it all right? Are you comfortable?"

"It's beautiful," I say, but a bout of sadness hits me as I remember my own beautiful room. I slept in it only days ago, but it's been torn apart now, almost all my things taken to be auctioned to contribute to the debt Gustin accrued with his idiot wager.

"Don't you have any family you can go to?" the bandit asks as a last effort, sounding exhausted. "Someone who will care for you?"

My chest aches when I think of my parents—I barely

remember them now. Just a few tidbits remain stored in my mind, like a painting on the wall. Mother's warm laugh; Father's dark mustache.

They live with my sister and grandmother, existing only in memories. I can only hope Gustin won't join them soon.

"My grandmother was our guardian," I tell him. "She passed away about a year ago."

"No aunts, no uncles?"

"No one except Gustin."

The bandit makes a disgusted noise.

"You'll be back tomorrow?" I ask as he slips out the door.

"Yes."

"You promise?" I persist, trying to make out his eyes behind his mask.

"Honestly," he mutters as if finding my company trying. "Yes, Alice, I will see you tomorrow."

"You said it's dangerous for you to come this close," I say, realizing I've put him in a terrible position.

"No more dangerous than it is for you—go to sleep."

"What's your name?" I ask, repeating the question I asked in the woods.

"There is none I can give you." And with that, he leaps from the balcony.

I gasp, running to the rail, the forest air cold in the night. I just barely make him out as he slips into the trees that come close to the manor, and then...he's gone.

"YOU WANT me to water the plants?" I ask dumbly, sure I misunderstood Regina when she informed me what position I've been assigned. I glance outside the hall window at the estate grounds. Clouds have drifted low, and it's rained on and off all morning.

"Not outside." Her voice is abrupt, but it sounds like she's suppressing a laugh. "The plants in the conservatory."

Slowly, I nod.

"I've summoned a dressmaker from Corrinmead," she continues. "She will be here this afternoon."

"What for?"

The housekeeper looks over as we walk down the hall. "You cannot go around in that tattered gown."

I glance down at my blue and gold dress. Before yesterday, it was one of my favorites, but there is no fixing the snags and small tears in the fabric. The damage has been done.

"I apologize for coming with so little," I say. "It wasn't my intention."

I suppose the money for the clothing will come out of my pay, and it will take that much longer to earn what's needed for new supplies.

As we walk, the two women who came into the foyer when I arrived yesterday pause in the hall ahead, their curious eyes latched onto us. They're both beautiful, likely dangerous as well, considering their lineage. Judging from their long, black dresses and crisp white aprons edged with ruffles, they are housemaids.

They whisper to each other as they watch me, and the

one with the loose, black hair and porcelain skin smirks at something her companion says.

For the first time in my life, I feel vulnerable—like I'm an ugly duckling dressed in rags, begging the master of the house for the scraps of his goodwill. I never realized how much of my confidence came from my family's good standing in society.

It's humiliating, and I avert my eyes as we pass. Regina doesn't bother to introduce us, but I feel the girls' stares until we turn the corner.

"Don't mind them," Regina says when we're out of earshot. "They have the ridiculous belief that Lord Ambrose will someday look upon one of them. Therefore, they see anyone who enters the house as competition for his affection."

"It could happen," I say generously, remembering how lovely they were. Why wouldn't he want one of them for his marquise?

Madame Regina laughs, genuinely amused by the thought. "His mother would never allow such a lowly union."

I know nothing of Fae nobility, but the way she says it makes me wonder if I should know who Lord Ambrose's mother is.

Not wanting to betray my ignorance, I keep the question to myself. I'll ask the bandit tonight when I see him.

My stomach rumbles, protesting its lack of breakfast. I glance at the housekeeper, worried she might have heard. If she did, she pretends she didn't.

I heeded the bandit's warning, skipping the morning meal a kitchen maid delivered on a silver tray. It didn't look unusual—just two soft-boiled eggs, toast, and a bowl of strawberries. But it wasn't worth the risk.

We pass through the doors that lead into the conservatory, and the moment I step over the threshold, it's as if the tension I'm carrying in my back and shoulders eases.

The room is large enough to stroll through. The glass walls are easily two stories high, and they meet the heavily slanted roof—also glass. The space is warm, and the air is heavy with moisture. It smells like earth and life. Short, potted citrus trees grow along the back wall, holding small, just ripening lemons amongst their glossy, dark green leaves.

More potted plants sit upon shelves and line walkways—most are roses. There are so many, all of them in full bloom, each boasting large, peony-shaped blossoms in pink, yellow, white, and crimson. They, too, lend their fragrance to the air.

"It seems Lord Ambrose likes roses," I say, running the tip of my finger along a velvet petal.

"I do not believe Lord Ambrose has an opinion on them," Madame Regina answers. "He rarely comes in here."

"Oh." I turn, looking at them all. "Then why…"

"His younger brother is fond of them," she says, and for the first time, her voice is truly abrupt. "Come with me. I'll show you where to fill the watering can."

I look around, realizing it will take me all day to water this many plants.

Regina walks to a fountain at the center of the conservatory. From its center, water spills into a large raised pool, where white and orange fish swim.

"What are they?" I gasp, certain I've never seen anything like them in my life.

"Koi," Madame Regina says. "Water is fed into the fountain from an underground aquifer. They don't mind the cold temperature."

I watch the fish for several seconds, enchanted.

"The watering can is there." Regina nods toward the small tin container at the fountain's edge.

"This?" I pick it up and give her an incredulous look. "At most, it looks as if it holds two cups of water."

"Do you have something better to do with your time?"

Point taken.

I hold the watering can under the spigot in the raised pool, showing her I'm willing to work.

"I will leave you to it," the housekeeper says, and then she exits the conservatory.

Soon, I slip into my task, deciding there are far worse chores than tending flowers. Grandmother loved her roses—she spent hours fussing over them every day. It brings back pleasant memories.

But by the end of the day, my feet are tired from standing, and I'm feeling every lost minute of sleep from the restless night. The sun has shaken off the clouds, and its afternoon heat beats in through the glass, warm enough I feel like I'm going to wither before the plants.

When Regina finally comes to fetch me, I gladly leave, dreading the moment I must return tomorrow.

"I've instructed the dressmaker to go to your room," she says as I follow her out of the conservatory and into the dry, cool manor. "Let's not make her wait long."

I hurry to keep up, stifling a yawn behind my hand.

"Regina," a man says when we turn the corner, eyeing me as he smiles at the housekeeper. He's tall and slim, with long, pale blond hair and light gray eyes that are a touch unsettling. He's dressed in a rich sapphire jacket, with a golden pocket watch chain hanging from the breast pocket.

Like the maids we saw earlier, he was in the foyer when I begged Lord Ambrose to let me stay.

The man steps directly in the middle of the hallway, blocking our path.

"Hello, Ian," Regina says briskly, nudging me to the side so we may pass the man.

"I have yet to officially meet the young woman," he says as he subtly blocks our way once more. He smiles at me, but it's a calculating look. "What, exactly, is your relationship to Brahm?"

"Lord Ambrose," Regina corrects sharply. "And there is no relationship. For the time being, Alice simply works in the manor."

The man laughs, stepping forward as if he means to take my chin. "If Brahm has no attachment to her, I would be glad to take her in."

As if appearing out of thin air, Lord Ambrose steps around me from behind, putting himself between the man and me. "I do not like to share, Ian. I believe you know that."

I stare at the back of the marquis's deep red jacket, my heart beating like I was just cornered by a predator. Lord Ambrose is close enough I could touch him, his broad shoulders blocking the disconcerting Faerie from view.

"I'm well aware." Ian laughs. "But if you get bored of

her, I'll take her off your hands. And I must wonder, if you're so eager to protect her, why not tether her and claim her for yourself?"

"She won't be in West Faerie that long," the marquis says.

"Interesting," the man muses from the other side of Lord Ambrose. "Does your mother know you intend to return an illanté to the wild?"

"I don't see why this is any of my mother's business," the marquis replies stonily.

"She might disagree."

"The girl requested work," Lord Ambrose says in his deep, cultured voice. It's controlled and measured, curt and heavy with nobility. "It's a business transaction and nothing more."

"Brahm," Regina says, interrupting the conversation. "Perhaps it would be best if Alice and I excused ourselves?"

"Yes," Lord Ambrose replies. "Take her away."

The housekeeper firmly grabs my arm and all but drags me down the hall.

"If you don't wish to make her your illanté, why don't you set her brother free and be done with it?" the man asks from behind us, the words sounding like a subtle taunt.

"I have no desire to show mercy on her brother," Lord Ambrose answers.

Ian replies, but we're now too far away for me to hear what he says.

"Who was that?" I whisper urgently.

"Count Ian Treald," Regina says. "One of Lord

Ambrose's mother's loyal spies. She likes to keep tabs on her children, but she prefers to send her minions instead of coming herself."

I'm dying to learn who this woman is, but I hold my tongue.

Instead, I ask, "What's an illanté?"

Regina glances at me, frowning as we walk. "In the ancient Faerie language, it means 'obligation.' Hundreds of years ago, it became fashionable for the Fae of high standing to embrace humans with hardships, essentially making them their wards. Though the act seemed benevolent on the outside, most did it because they felt they were superior and decided it was their duty to care for lesser beings. Throughout the years, the illanté agreement became even more twisted. Now illantés are treated as pets, the Fae doing with them as they please. Some dote on their illantés, coddling them like pampered lapdogs. Others…are not so fortunate."

This is what the bandit was speaking of—this is what he warned me about.

"You said it's an agreement—like a bargain," I say. "Don't both parties have to give their consent? Why would a human wish to enter such a contract?"

Regina looks uncomfortable with the subject, but she keeps talking. "The magic does require agreement on both sides, but the situation is rarely just. Some humans agree with a blade to their throat; others are simply deceived. Many comply to keep loved ones safe."

I nod, uncomfortable.

Regina looks over, giving me a small smile. "But it's nothing you need to worry about, not while you're under

Lord Ambrose's protection. If he wanted to tether you to him, he would have done it already."

I'm not sure that makes me feel all that much better.

"You called the marquis by his given name," I say. "Are you and he close?"

"Brahm is my cousin."

"Have you lived here long?"

"Five years," she says, her tone becoming abrupt. "Now enough chatter. The dressmaker is waiting."

4

BRAHM

I barely have a leg over the top of the stone balcony railing when Alice opens the door that leads into her room and comes out to meet me, saying, "You must tell me your name. All day long, I've thought of you as 'the bandit,' and to be honest, it's quite tedious."

"You've thought of me all day, Alice?"

Her eyes go wide, and I smile at her discomfort.

"That's not what I meant," she insists, ushering me into her room. "I was merely hungry, and you promised food. Perhaps I am no better than a stray cat, but I'm quite fond of people who promise me meals."

"Was I supposed to bring food?" I ask, intrigued by her strange mood.

She whips back, hand on her stomach dramatically, looking like she's going to perish from hunger. "You didn't forget—you wouldn't." She narrows her eyes into slits. "You *couldn't*."

Instead of a meal, I produce a small vial that was entirely too much trouble to procure. I had just returned from Corrinmead when I found Alice and Regina in the hall with Ian.

"What's that?" she asks.

"Let's call it an antidote." I take her hand and press the precious vial into her palm. "Place one drop on your tongue before you eat, and the effects of the Fae food should go unnoticed."

"Truly?" she asks, looking properly impressed. She studies the small glass container, turning it in her hand. It glows faintly in the candlelit room. "So, it's bottled magic?"

"Something like that," I say with a smile. "And it's not easy to obtain—do not misplace, break, or misuse it."

She turns her eyes on me. "Where did you find it?"

"I have my ways."

"Shall we test it?" She nods her head toward a tray that lies abandoned on a table by the fire. A kitchen maid must have brought it this evening. "I'll feel better if you are with me the first time I use it, just in case there are ill effects."

I jerk my head toward the table, telling her to be my guest.

She pauses after opening the stopper, shooting me a look. "You realize this requires me to put a lot of trust in you, don't you?"

I lean against the wall, enjoying this far too much. "If I had nefarious intentions, I had plenty of opportunities to act upon them before now."

She frowns, pressing her lips to the side as she thinks. "I suppose that's true."

Before she takes a drop from the stopper, she turns

back to me, eyeing me so intently, I almost squirm under her gaze.

"What's your name?" she finally asks.

"Why does it matter?"

"How can I possibly trust someone who won't even give me his name?"

I push away from the wall, stalking toward her, careful to keep my head tilted away from the candles. "How can you eat if you do not take the concoction?"

"Fine." She smiles, looking mischievous. "Instead, show me your face."

"I'm leaving." I turn to go. "Take it or don't—starve or let yourself become a puppet of the Fae. The choice is yours."

"Wait!" she cries softly, chasing after me. "Don't go. I won't ask again, I swear. Eat with me—there is plenty."

I look back, worried by how tempted I am by Alice's offer. It wouldn't be a hardship to share a cozy meal by the fire, just the two of us, no titles getting in the way.

"It's not safe for me to linger," I remind her.

Her face falls. "Oh, yes."

"Be cautious while you are here. This time, listen to my warning when I tell you not to make bargains or agreements."

She follows me to the door like a puppy. "Why does it sound like you don't plan to return?"

I step into the night, refusing to indulge in the desire to look at her once more. "I don't."

"I won't see you again?" she demands, sounding aghast.

"I'm not any safer than Lord Ambrose," I tell her. "You would be wise to stay away from me as well."

I swing over the railing, catching the lattice that's attached to the wall between Alice's balcony and mine. Knowing she will watch me until I'm out of sight, I resist the urge to leap to my side and be done with it.

Visiting her like this is inconvenient, but I cannot reveal my secret to her. Knowledge is dangerous—especially this kind of knowledge.

So I drop to the ground and slip into the cover of the forest, using my magic to blend in with the shadows. Once I'm concealed, I turn back, watching Alice in the night.

Sure enough, she stands by the balcony like a ghost maiden in a tale, staring into the woods as the light breeze tugs her long, silken hair. After several minutes, she hugs herself as if cold and then returns to her room, closing the door behind her.

I reach out with the magic that connects me to the natural world and turn the lock she forgot to set, keeping her as safe as she can be in the borderlands of Faerie.

It's only when I'm back in my bedchamber that I realize I forgot to warn her about tomorrow's full moon.

"ARE you telling me you refuse to explain tonight's dangers to Alice?" I demand, knowing that arguing with Regina will do me no good. Once she's made up her mind, it's as good as set.

"I didn't say that," my cousin responds calmly. "I merely suggested you tell her yourself."

I lower my voice even though we're alone in my quarters. "You know I cannot. I've had too many conversations with her while masked."

"I've been meaning to ask you about that. Out of all the humans you've found in the woods, why did you bring her here? You've never been prone to returning with strays."

Uncomfortable with the question, I look down. "She was determined to speak with me."

"That may be, but you didn't have to take her in," she says.

"Do not act like you didn't have a part in her staying."

Regina laughs under her breath. "We both know how often you listen to me. It must have been something else."

I pause, not eager to voice my thoughts aloud. "Does Alice seem...familiar to you?"

Regina's face softens. "I knew that was why you gave in to her pleas."

I look up sharply. "Then why did you make me admit it?"

"It's good for you to be honest with yourself occasionally. After all, you are the only person you can truly lie to."

I roll my eyes, sitting back in my chair. After a moment, I ask, "Is it her? Is it possible?"

She sighs. "I very much doubt it."

"But her name..."

"Is common," Regina points out. Her eyes soften. "I think, perhaps, we would like it to be her, and therefore we're seeing connections that do not exist."

"Drake would know."

"He was so young," she argues. "If he does remember, looking upon this Alice might be painful. He might resent her."

I shake my head. "He's still obsessed with roses. If he regretted his decision, he would have purged the girl from his memory."

"I took Alice to the conservatory yesterday," Regina admits, looking slightly haunted as she gives me an apologetic look. "I was curious."

I lean forward. "And?"

"She lit up," Regina says.

We fall into silence, *wondering*.

"It doesn't matter," I finally say, rising. "Either way, my mother must not discover her. She'd punish Alice for even resembling the girl we knew—and if not that, certainly the kindness I was foolish enough to show her."

"Your mother is cruel," Regina says bitterly, murmuring words that no one else would dare voice, even in privacy. Her hands clasp over the black satin of her skirt, and her eyes become distant.

Regina's bouts of melancholy are common—they have been since she married her childhood love young and then lost her husband to court politics not even a year later. He made the mistake of disagreeing with my mother, and he was executed for treason.

It was the final straw—I couldn't bear to even look at my mother, much less remain at court. I left for my paternal family's estate, donning Father's title and attempting to abandon the royal one I was born with. I rescued my broken cousin from Mother's wicked clutches. She and I have remained here ever since, living as peacefully as people can when ruled by an evil, malicious queen.

It's been five years, but Regina still mourns. I somewhat doubt she will ever shed her black clothing.

"What will we do about Ian?" Regina asks.

I clutch my head in my hands. "I don't know."

"If you don't claim Alice as your illanté, he can take her despite your command to stay away—you know the rules."

Any human who wanders into Faerie is free game. They are protected for one day only, while they conduct business, but if they remain overnight...

"If I make her my illanté, she can never return home."

"If you don't, she is untethered property."

"She's not *property*," I snarl under my breath.

"I believe that, but you know I'm right. Too long, our people have amused themselves at the humans' expense. She will be enslaved, caged, tortured...perhaps *worse*. If you keep her, you must bind her to your side."

"I don't want to *keep* her." I stand abruptly, sending my chair backward, the legs scratching against the wooden floor. "I want her to go home."

"Where are you going?" Regina asks, rising with me.

"To speak with Alice."

"As whom?"

I glance out the window, knowing I only have one option. The evening sunlight filters into the forest, too light for me to bend the shadows to my will.

I'll have to visit her as Lord Ambrose and hope she doesn't recognize me.

5

ALICE

I forgot to ask the bandit about Lord Ambrose's mother.

The thought of never seeing him again makes me feel rather listless, but I try not to dwell on it as I tend the plants in the conservatory. Today, I have been instructed to remove all fading, yellow, or misshapen leaves from each and every plant.

I work quietly, glad to have been given a chore that keeps me away from the others. The marquis appears to be a solitary man. He doesn't entertain many high-titled Fae, thank goodness, but even his staff looks down on me —and they likely would even if my family name was still in good standing. It's because I'm a human in Faerie, lingering where I don't belong, still wearing my torn gown since the others won't be ready for a week.

Pausing next to a pale yellow rose, I breathe in its sweet fragrance, letting it soothe my frayed nerves as it reminds me of happier times in Grandmother's garden.

I nearly jump when a man says behind me, "You seem content with your position."

The bandit.

I whirl around, a broad smile spreading over my face, delighted at the prospect of seeing him in the light…

And then I freeze.

Lord Ambrose stands behind me, hands clasped behind his back, looking rather put out. His deep brown eyes roam the glassed room with an air of distaste. His short hair is perfectly groomed, swept away from his forehead in a crisp style that's not unlike the human fashion that's becoming popular in the cities.

He's so handsome, he's hard to look at. His shoulders are broad, not slender as I always imagined the Fae to be, and his waist is trim. He wears a tailored jacket in rich, deep green, paired with an amber brocade waistcoat. The colors bring out the warm, golden tone of his skin. Though exquisitely masculine, he's too beautiful, and that alone makes him look a touch otherworldly.

I let out a peep of surprise, and fear paralyzes my limbs.

The marquis turns his dark eyes on me, narrowing them slightly. "Well?"

"Well?" I repeat stupidly.

"Are you content with the position Regina has chosen for you?"

"Oh, yes," I say in a rush. "I like it here."

He studies me solemnly for several seconds, and then he nods toward my hand. "I see my reputation has preceded me. Do you intend to stab me?"

I look down and realize I'm holding the garden shears like a weapon.

"No." I quickly set them on the ledge of the raised pond. As I straighten, I spot dirt on my bodice. Flustered, I quickly brush it away. "Forgive me. I wasn't expecting anyone."

He doesn't answer.

"Do you wish for solitude?" I ask, already edging toward the door. "I can leave…"

"I've come to pay you for your service." He carries a velvet bag in his hand.

My eyes latch onto it, noting the way the contents bulge against the fabric.

"I don't understand." I raise my eyes to his. "I've only worked two days."

As if Lord Ambrose doesn't want to hold my gaze, he glances around the conservatory once more, looking bored. "Everything seems to be in order here. You did a fine job—our arrangement is complete. Take the money and return to Kellington."

"And my brother?"

Lord Ambrose's expression tightens, and he finally looks back. "There is nothing I can do for your brother."

"You will not show Gustin mercy, yet you would give me a small fortune for a day and a half of work?" I say skeptically.

The marquis's expression hardens. "I find your presence uncomfortable. Take the money and go back to your side of the bridge, where you belong. Never again will you be presented with such a generous offer."

The words sting. Lord Ambrose finds me *uncomfort-*

able? What have I done to earn his distaste? I've barely seen him.

"I cannot accept your charity," I say primly. "I will work until I may purchase supplies, and then I will paint your portrait, as I promised."

"Do not let pride blind you," he says sharply.

I stand taller, disregarding the bandit's warning. "Give me my brother instead, and I will go."

"Your brother bound himself to Faerie," Lord Ambrose says impatiently. "He made a wager he could not afford, and now he's paying in years."

"Count Treald asked why you wouldn't release him," I say, stepping forward. "I heard him! Doesn't that mean it's in your power to forgive Gustin's debt?"

"Ian also wants to claim you as a pet—he cares nothing for you or your brother. He would crush you in the palm of his hand, and then he would move on to the next amusement. He was taunting me, not showing you mercy."

I stare at him, breathing hard. "Give me the money once I've earned it."

"Why are you so determined to stay?" he demands.

"Why are you so determined to get rid of me? Is it that miserable to have a human in your midst? Am I *that* repulsive?"

I hold my breath when his hand tightens on the bag.

Perhaps I should accept his offer and flee, but what about Gustin? I can't just leave him in Faerie.

"Fine," I say when he doesn't answer. "Give me the gold. I will go to the debtor's prison and pay for Gustin's freedom myself."

"You will do no such thing," the marquis says curtly, and his eyes flash with warning.

"Why do you care?" I exclaim, frustrated.

His jaw hardens, making the slight cleft in his chin more prominent. "Is your life worth his?"

"What?"

"That's the only exchange the jailer will offer you—no amount of gold will buy your brother back. I am the only one with the power to release him, and I cannot do it."

"Cannot? Or won't?"

He pins me with his dark eyes. "Won't."

I think about it, coming to a decision. I nod to myself, determined.

"What is it?" he asks, sounding like he wishes he hadn't instigated the conversation.

"I simply have to change your mind, and I cannot do that if I take the gold and run away. I will stay, tending the plants and eventually painting your portrait, working diligently until I can win your admiration, hoping your heart will eventually soften toward my plea."

"Alice," he says, sounding genuinely exasperated now. "Go *home*."

His change of tone catches my attention, and I quirk my head to the side as I study him. My eyes land on the subtle points of his ears.

"Not yet," I say slowly.

Letting out a frustrated growl, he narrows his eyes. "Have it your way, but be warned—the full moon is tonight. The creatures of Faerie become wild—including the ones in my own household. I will not be here to ensure your safety. Lock the door to your room, and do not answer it for anyone."

He turns to leave, but I call to him, "And my balcony door? Should I lock it, too?"

Lord Ambrose stops abruptly and turns back, giving me a look I cannot read. "Every door, every window."

"When will you return?"

"Tomorrow afternoon."

"Have a good trip."

"Not likely," he mutters, and then he leaves the conservatory.

I sit on the edge of the fountain, thinking very hard about Lord Ambrose.

Deciding my head is playing foolish tricks on me, I brush aside my rogue thoughts. I then pick up my shears and return to my chores.

I LOCK ALL my doors and windows, as Lord Ambrose commanded, but I wait for the bandit's knock.

I fall asleep at the tea table, roused in the middle of the night by a wail that comes from somewhere on the grounds.

Unnerved but curious, I walk to the balcony door and peek out the window. Below, in the middle of the grass near the forest's edge, a large fire glows. I recognize several members of Lord Ambrose's staff, along with many Faeries I've never seen before. There are at least twenty of them gathered. Many laugh loudly, and another shrieks, though it's obvious no one is in peril. They're most likely drunk on the Faerie wine they pass between them.

One couple is twined around each other, kissing like they fear the world is going to end. I frown at them, unsettled at the public display, never having seen something like it in my life.

One of the maids sees me at the window, and she grins and nudges her elbow into her friend's side.

"Come down, human!" the second girl yells with a sharp giggle, holding up a bottle that glows green in the firelight. "Join us!"

Most laugh, but someone appears to shush her, and the two maids reluctantly turn from the window.

I let the curtain drop, wishing I hadn't let curiosity get the best of me. What are they doing out there? The marquis said it's a full moon. What does that symbolize in Faerie?

Disconcerted, I go to bed, hoping morning will come quickly.

It does not.

The night drags on until dawn finally chases Lord Ambrose's staff to their beds.

Regina doesn't wake me as she has the last two days, so I stay in my room, unsure if the marquis is back yet and not daring to venture into the halls alone after last night's display.

The day passes. Dusk falls on the forest, and still, no one has come for me. No meal is delivered; no one tells me I must tend to the plants.

Soon, night blankets the sky. The moon is hidden behind clouds tonight, and the landscape is dark. There are no fires or gatherings.

All is eerily still.

I pace back and forth before I decide to do something that could be remarkably foolish. Before I can change my mind, I step outside and study the distance between Lord Ambrose's balcony and mine. It's not far, not really. If it can hold the bandit's weight, surely it can hold mine.

Nodding to myself, determined, I pull up my skirts and loop them over my arm. I swing a leg over the side of the balcony, telling myself I will not look down.

I find a foothold, pressing down to test it before I reach for the lattice with my left hand. The rough wooden slats dig into my palm, making me worry about splinters. But I don't have gloves to fetch, and I've already come too far to change my mind now.

Holding tight, I transfer my weight to the lattice, thankful the ivy that grows up the wall doesn't have thorns. Slowly, moving like a crab on a net, I make my way across the short distance. It doesn't take long, but it feels like I've been up here for ages.

Finally, I reach Lord Ambrose's balcony. I grab hold of the stone railing, holding on for dear life as I attempt to swing my leg over. But I'm not quite high enough. Somehow, I went down a little on the way across.

My arms begin to tremble as I hang here. What was I thinking? I'm not an adventuress, brave and full of spirit.

I'm a painter accustomed to afternoon tea and leisurely walks through the park.

"Surely you didn't come all this way to give up now?" a man asks from the balcony.

I yelp, nearly losing my grip on the lattice.

Before I fall, the bandit wraps his gloved hands around my waist. He then pulls me up and over the balcony rail as if I weigh no more than a ragdoll and sets me on my feet.

Shaking, I loop an arm around the man's waist and hold tight.

"You startled me," I say, smacking his chest with the flat of my palm.

"I'm sorry." He clears his throat, trying not to laugh.

I rest my forehead against his fitted leather jacket. "You almost made me fall."

"I don't think I should take all the blame for that," he says, attempting—but failing—to nudge me back. "In fact, I think I am the reason you didn't tumble three stories to your death."

Shivering at the thought, I hold onto him tighter, waiting for my pulse to return to its normal pace. "I'm very grateful for your existence."

"You and few others," he says with a quiet laugh.

After one more deep breath, I finally compose myself and step back, staring up at his shadowed face. "What are you doing here?"

"I could ask you the same thing." His tone is lighter than I've ever heard it, making me think he's still amused by the predicament he found me in.

"Lord Ambrose told me to stay in my room until he returned, but I didn't know if he was back, and I was too spooked by last night's events to go into the hall. I just wanted to knock on the door to see if he was in."

"So, you decided to scale the lattice?" he asks incredulously.

"You did it first!" I exclaim, and then I lower my voice. "And we should be careful. Lord Ambrose might hear us."

The bandit jerks his head toward the room. "He's not in."

I turn toward the dark windows, deciding he's likely right.

"Truly, why are you here?" I ask again. "Were you stealing something from the marquis?"

In the woods, he said he wasn't a thief, but I find that very hard to believe. Who else dresses in black and masks their face?

"What happened last night?" he says instead of answering.

I shrug, feeling foolish. "Nothing really. Lord Ambrose's staff was having a gathering of some sort. They tried to get me to come down, but I went to bed."

"Did they?" he asks stonily, again making me question something that I shouldn't be questioning.

But his voice.

I mean, *their* voices...

And he and the marquis are both so tall, with such broad shoulders.

"You are human, aren't you?" I ask suddenly.

Looking startled, the bandit takes a step back. "Why would you question it?"

"Let me see your ears."

"My *ears?*"

I set my hands on my hips. "I know you're desperate to conceal your identity, but surely you don't think I can recognize you by your ears alone?"

Shaking his head, the bandit sweeps his hat aside.

With the moon behind the thick clouds, it's too dark to make out his exact hair color, which is a shame. But it's dark, like Lord Ambrose's.

"I can't see anything," I complain with a huff.

"Just remember, this was your idea." Suddenly, the bandit loops an arm around my waist and tugs me against him, closer than we were even a moment ago.

I draw in a sharp breath as he runs his free hand down my bare arm. When he finds my hand, he raises it to his head, guiding my fingers across the *rounded* top of his ear.

"You're human," I breathe.

"Did you think I was one of the Fae?" he asks, still holding me close.

"To be honest, I thought you might be..." I laugh to myself, too embarrassed to admit it. "Never mind. You can let go of me now."

"And if I don't want to?" he asks lightly, making my stomach flutter.

I suddenly remember what he said when we first met —that the only things he's ever stolen are hearts, and if I'm not careful, he'd be tempted to steal mine. Desperate for a distraction from this strange world I've found myself in, just for a moment, I imagine what it would be like to be wooed by this man.

But I can't think these sorts of thoughts about a masked bandit who refuses to give me his name.

I reluctantly pull away from him. When he doesn't resist, I decide he is only playing anyway.

With a sigh, I look across the expanse between Lord Ambrose's balcony and mine. "How am I going to get back?"

The bandit opens the marquis's door. "Come on."

I latch onto his arm, tugging him back. "You mustn't!"

"Why mustn't I?"

"What if we're caught?"

"I told you—Lord Ambrose is not in."

I hold firm. "But what if he comes back?"

"He won't," he says confidently. "Trust me. Have I misled you yet?"

Slowly, I drop my arm. "Fine...but be quiet."

The bandit presses a finger to his lips, promising to stay shushed. He then motions for me to follow him.

I stop short in the marquis's bedchamber, looking around.

"What is it?" the bandit asks, sounding a little unsettled.

"The marquis's sister has personal touches everywhere, and she doesn't even live in the manor. But this room..." I shrug. "It feels empty."

The bandit looks around. "So?"

"It's sort of sad, isn't it?"

"Why is it sad?" he demands.

"It just seems...lonely."

He crosses back, taking my hand to keep me moving. "It doesn't matter whether Lord Ambrose is lonely or not, and you certainly shouldn't trouble yourself with such things."

Moments later, we stand outside my room in the hall.

"It's locked." I press my hand to my forehead, realizing this was all for naught.

The bandit gives me a strange look as he produces a key and slides it into the lock.

"Where did you get *that?*" I hiss as he opens the door.

"Lord Ambrose's room," he says without apology, dragging me inside and locking the door behind us.

"Why do you have it?"

"It doesn't seem like something that should be lying around while the marquis is away."

I hold out my hand. "Give it to me."

Laughing as if that idea is ludicrous, he drops it down the front of his jacket.

"What are you doing?" I demand. "Why should you keep it?"

Not as careful to keep his face in the shadows now, the bandit stalks across the room. He wears a smile that steals my breath. When he's very near, I take a step back. He continues forward, stopping only when my shoulders bump into the door.

I gulp as I look up at him, wishing he'd remove the mask.

"For occasions exactly like this," he says darkly, lowering his face close to mine.

My voice is too high as I ask, "And what, exactly, is the occasion?"

He's going to kiss me.

"For when you lock yourself out of your room," he teases near my ear. He then pulls back, walking toward the fireplace.

"Tell me your name," I demand, feeling lightheaded... and maybe a little disappointed.

He takes a seat on the chaise longue and crosses his arms. "Why do you want it so desperately?"

"I just...do."

He watches me intently. "I'll make a deal with you, Alice. If you let me take you back to your people, and you swear not to tell a soul, I will give you my name."

"You're very persistent."

"The same could be said about you," he points out.

With a sigh, I sit in the chair across from him. "Lord Ambrose doesn't want me here either. He said I am 'uncomfortable.'"

The bandit smirks. "That bothers you?"

"Of course it bothers me!" I exclaim. "Who would want to be called that? He might as well have said I am a hideous creature—an unpleasant human."

He laughs as if enjoying the conversation. "I do not believe that is what he meant."

"What else could it mean?"

"Maybe 'uncomfortable' is another way of saying you are a *nuisance.*"

I wrinkle my nose, not liking that much better.

"You don't like being disliked, do you? A pretty girl like you must be adored at home." He watches me closely. "You have dozens of friends, don't you? Suitors as far as the eye can see as well?"

"I had both of those." My mood darkens. "But they disappeared just as quickly as my fortune."

The bandit is quiet for several seconds before he asks, "Are you truly here for your brother...or are you running away?"

The words are a sharp dagger to my pride. Instead of answering, I hide my pain and latch onto the least important detail of the conversation. "So...you think I'm pretty?"

He looks taken aback, almost as if he's wondering how to deny it. "Does it matter what I think?" he finally says.

"A little," I admit.

The bandit stands, slowly closing the distance between us before he pulls me to my feet. "Very well, I do think you're pretty. In fact, Alice, you are the most beautiful *nuisance* I've ever met."

I laugh, oddly warmed by the words.

"I need to go," he says, his tone turning solemn. "I've already stayed too long."

"When will I see you again?"

I refuse to believe this will be the last time.

"I can't keep visiting you. You know that, don't you?"

Slowly, I nod.

"Eventually, no matter how careful we are, we will be caught."

"What would happen to you?" I ask. "What are your crimes?"

"I patrol the main thoroughfare in the evenings, looking for human stragglers who are not where they belong."

"Like me," I say softly, suddenly not feeling quite so special.

"Like you," he agrees. "Though you are the first human I've met who was determined to travel deeper into Faerie after dark. The rest are happy to let me escort them to the bridge."

"You think I'm foolish?"

He laughs under his breath. "I know you're foolish."

"Wait a moment." I study the edge of his soft black mask, wishing I were brave enough to pull it from his face. "Surely escorting people to the bridge isn't a crime?"

"The Fae don't like it when I steal their playthings— the queen is especially irritated that I dare to meddle in the affairs of her subjects."

"The queen?" I repeat, trying to remember all I've heard about her.

She's said to be stunningly beautiful, with a voice like the tinkling of silver bells. But her affection is toxic, and she never keeps a husband for more than a year. She's like a perpetual widow spider, remarrying as soon as each mourning period is over.

How much is rumor, I don't know.

"Yes, Queen Marison." He pauses for emphasis. "Lord Ambrose's mother."

The revelation is startling, and I stare at the bandit for several seconds before I can respond. "But that would make Lord Ambrose..."

"Brahm Ambrose Severin, Prince of West Faerie, eldest son of Her Majesty and her first husband, Lord Kallin Ambrose."

"What's he doing in Rose Briar Woods?" I ask, aghast.

"Some say he grew tired of court politics and retired to the peace of the forest. Others claim he and his dear mother had a falling out, and she banished him to the borderland."

"What do you think happened?"

"It doesn't matter what I think. The only thing I need to know is that I am at odds with the marquis. It's his duty to punish the humans when they overstep their boundaries, and it's mine to keep them safe from the Fae's manipulations. You understand why our relationship cannot be an amicable one?"

"Where did his title come from?"

"It was his father's."

"Wait," I say. "If Lord Ambrose is the eldest son, does that mean he will be king?"

"In West Faerie, the throne passes to daughters."

"Only in West Faerie?" I ask. "The other Fae courts don't follow the same rule?"

"As far as I know."

As I process the new information, I study the bandit. The light plays with my eyes, making it impossible to see him well, but I memorize all the details I can—his dark hair peeking out from under the brim of his hat and his equally dark eyes under the mask. Clean-shaven skin, expensive leather, well-tailored jacket.

"You're not a bandit," I finally say.

"I told you I wasn't."

"You're…"

"Yes?"

Is it my imagination, or does he look a touch nervous?

"Well, you're rather heroic, aren't you?"

He swallows, his throat visibly moving. "I think that might be an exaggeration."

"Not to all the people you've saved." I meet his shadowed eyes. "Not to me."

We're closer now, drawn together as if connected by an ever-shortening cord.

"You've never let me thank you for saving me that night," I whisper.

His voice is rough as he says, "It's not necessary."

"Surely you can at least accept a small token?" My eyes move to his lips, which are perfectly visible in the candle-light. "A kiss for a hero? Isn't that the way the stories go?"

"Alice," he says, his voice strained.

I press a chaste kiss to his mouth, our lips meeting for only a few brief seconds before I pull back. Just for a moment, his eyes flicker into focus, but then he tilts his head slightly, and the shadows obscure them once more.

"Thank you for saving me," I whisper, moving forward again.

It's just another soft kiss—lingering, one-sided, and slightly disappointing. But the bandit doesn't move away, nor does he nudge me back.

And then…his lips subtly move against mine, and my heart skips a beat. His hand finds my side, his fingertips grazing my waist, and I move in closer.

Suddenly, he jerks back. Half a second later, a knock sounds at the door.

"Alice," Regina calls from the hallway. "Are you still awake?"

When I turn to tell the masked man to hide, I find he's already gone. The balcony door shuts behind him, and his shadow disappears over the rail.

6

BRAHM

When I finally make it back to my quarters, I sink into an armchair and bury my face in my hands.

Tonight shouldn't have happened. I had no intention of meeting with Alice again, but then I found her hanging from the lattice. What else could I do but help her? And she looked so relieved to see me—she held on to me so tightly after I pulled her onto the balcony.

Also, I believe she suspects my identity, though that is no surprise considering how much time I've been spending with her.

So far, I've hidden myself with my magic, obscuring my features with tricks of light, making my ears appear human. But if I keep visiting her, it will only be a matter of time before even that will fail. Familiarity can see through illusion.

Maybe I could tell her.

Immediately, I dismiss the thought. It would put Alice in danger. If my mother were to get her hands on her, heaven forbid, ignorance would be the girl's only defense.

Our queen can sense a human lie as keenly as a hunting hound can track a scent. If she believed Alice was an accomplice to my crimes...

Shuddering, I slam a door on that trail of thought. No, I can't see her again. Tonight was the last.

I must put an end to it before this goes any further.

A WEEK PASSES, and then another. True to my vow, I haven't visited Alice again—not in the shadows and not as myself.

I sit, tapping the end of a quill to a blank piece of parchment, consumed in my thoughts as Regina rattles off household details I couldn't care less about.

"She's going to make herself ill," Regina says, finally catching my attention.

I look over, frowning. "Who is?"

"Have you listened to a word I've said?" she demands.

"More than one." I smirk at my cousin. "At least five, maybe even as many as ten."

"And I thought you cared about the girl."

I sit straighter. "Alice? What's wrong with her?"

Regina raises her eyebrows, taking note of my reaction. "She picks at her food. She does her work, but she looks pale and listless. I don't think she's been sleeping. She must be homesick."

"Homesick?"

My cousin gives me a dry look. "It's a condition that afflicts those who are actually happy in their homes before they leave them."

"I wonder what that must be like."

I joke because Regina expects it, but my mind is on Alice. Surely her listlessness isn't due to my absence. She didn't know the masked man that well.

"She asked me a strange question, though," Regina says as she glances over her shoulder to ensure the door is closed. "She wanted to know if the Highwayman had been caught. She said she heard the maids talking about him, and it made her nervous."

I frown. No matter what the maids said, Alice knows I am no threat. "Why would she ask you that?"

"I think she was searching for information. Perhaps she's worried you were apprehended?" Regina whispers. "Have you seen her recently?"

I slowly shake my head. "Not for weeks."

"She's attached to you," Regina scolds. "What did you do?"

"I didn't do anything," I hedge, remembering the kiss. Alice initiated that, though. "I saved her in the woods. I visited her a few times after that. I brought her the concoction I bought in Corrinmead."

"Why don't you just claim her as your illanté and be done with it? I had Wallen look into her family as you asked. Except for her brother, she truly has no one to return to. Would it be so wrong to keep her? Make her your ward; let the tether protect her." When I begin to protest, Regina cuts me off. "And you're fond of her—don't bother trying to find a way to deny it. She reminds you of our Alice."

I *can't* deny it, and that is worrisome. I feel the lie tugging at me no matter how I try to twist the words.

"Maybe you should get to know her as Lord Ambrose?" Regina suggests. "See if she likes your true self as much as the one you created?"

What if she doesn't?

"It's just an idea." Regina rises. "But believe me, the girl is lonely. If you're what's brought on this sadness, know there is a chance she will go looking for you in the night if you don't do *something*."

"You think she would?" I ask, uneasy.

Regina shrugs as she stands to leave my quarters.

I sit in silence for several minutes, thinking too hard.

Maybe I'll visit Alice in the conservatory, gauge her mood myself. Surely there is no harm in that.

"Good afternoon, Your Highness," Edalessa says as I pass her in the hall, smiling at me coquettishly.

I merely nod toward the maid and keep walking. It irritates me when the staff members use my royal title, but I refuse to tangle myself in a conversation with the maid. She's too persistent for my liking, too calculating and driven—too much like my mother.

"Is there anything you require?" she asks, undeterred by my dismissal. "Are you going to your study? Shall I fetch tea and refreshments?"

"No, thank you," I say curtly.

"Company then?" she asks, sidling up close.

I stop short. "Edalessa."

"Yes?" she asks eagerly.

"You seem bored. Should I inform Regina you require more daily tasks?"

Her eyes flash. "No, my lord."

"Very well." I motion her down the hall, in the opposite direction I'm walking.

"Should you change your mind…" she says flirtatiously.

"I know where to find you," I deadpan.

She's the illegitimate niece of Lord Vamber, the gruff keeper of the northern territories, and I accepted her into my household as a personal favor to him. Even though I am no longer at court, I prefer to keep my alliances strong.

I'm not sure she's worth the trouble, however. Edalessa has been like a harpy ever since she arrived, eager to dig her talons into me at the first sign of weakness. She would like nothing more than to elevate her position and become lady of the house.

Thankful to have shaken her, I walk into the conservatory. As always, I'm mildly surprised to find it's so humid. I look for Alice, certain she must be here somewhere.

Drake is the only one besides Alice who frequents the room, and the vast space is nearly silent except for the fountain that bubbles in the center. It's where I found Alice before, but she's not here now.

I walk the stone paths that meander through the planted beds and shelves of potted plants, trying to ignore the sheer number of roses, worrying about my brother's obsession.

Drake was the closest to young Alice, only a few years older than she. They were playmates, nearly inseparable. She was an illanté who became beloved to the royal family, treasured. Cherished.

No one knows where she came from. According to the traders, she wandered into West Faerie near the eastern border of our family's lands, near the mountainous human territory of Fallon. Only a toddler, old enough to say simple, short sentences that were half-nonsense, she was captured and given to Mother as a gift. With her large honey eyes and teak-colored hair, she was the loveliest human child anyone had ever seen.

She said her name was Alice. She repeated it constantly, clutching hold of even Mother's stone heart.

She lived with us for five years, not quite a sister—but never a pet.

Father loved her as much as the rest of us, treating her like a true child. He wanted to adopt her into the family—give her our name, make her belong.

Mother refused, saying a human would never sully her line.

"Lord Ambrose?" Alice says from behind me.

Startled, I turn, my mind still in the past.

The girl who reminds me so much of the Alice I knew looks at me in question, so familiar it haunts me. Her hair and eyes are wrong, but the resemblance is uncanny.

And her name.

There must be some connection—there must.

No longer in her tattered dress, Alice wears a full brown gown, topped with a white, sleeveless overdress. It laces at her waist, making her look like a milkmaid from a human child's picture book. The top half of her blonde hair is held up with a ribbon, and the length of it falls down her back.

She's entirely too lovely. My chest suddenly aches, remembering the way she kissed me.

Not me, I remind myself. The masked man—a hero in her eyes. *Human.*

Would Alice have given that same kiss to a Fae prince, eldest son of the bloodthirsty queen of West Faerie?

"Do you need something?" she prods when I don't answer, her eyes betraying how wary she is of my true identity.

Her expression answers my question.

"No," I say, turning to leave. "Please, excuse me."

I walk swiftly toward the doors, tugging at my cravat.

"Are the roses always in bloom?" she calls to me, making me pause on the stone path.

Slowly, I turn back. "I'm sorry?"

She jerks her head toward one of the bushes. "I've been here for weeks, and as soon as one bloom fades, it's replaced with another."

I look at the rose, frowning. "I imagine they are charmed."

Looking thoughtful, Alice leans down to fill a tiny, tin watering can from a spigot in the fountain.

"You imagine?" She turns her eyes on me, her expression cooler than it is when I'm wearing the mask. "They're your flowers. I thought you would know."

Feeling as if she's scolding me, I nod toward the watering can. "That doesn't seem terribly efficient."

"How else do you expect me to water your plants?"

Before I can answer, she disappears down the winding path, leaving me standing here like a fool. I find myself following her, hurrying to catch up. Though the conservatory is large, it's not so vast that it's difficult to find her.

She slowly pours water into an earthen pot holding a young spruce. It only takes a few seconds, and then she turns back toward the fountain to repeat the process.

"So, this is the chore Regina gave you," I say skeptically, wondering if someone else had this tedious task before her. But a Faerie wouldn't need to resort to such a simplistic process.

Alice doesn't even spare me a glance. "I trim the plants a bit here and there as well."

I watch her work. She doesn't protest my presence, but I can tell I make her uncomfortable. When I can take no more, I catch her arm and pull her to me. Not close—I leave space between us. Still, Alice's crystalline eyes go wide, and fear dilates her pupils.

"It's all right," I say quietly.

I expect her to dart back when I release her, but she stands her ground.

Raising one hand, I create an invisible shield above us. With the other, I draw moisture in the room into clouds inside the high ceiling. Fog swirls around us, warm and wet. The first raindrops fall on the stones near us, followed by more on the leaves of the hothouse plants.

Alice gasps, marveling at the magic as it showers the room in a gentle rain. It patters against my small overhead ward, streaming over the edges and falling to the ground around us. The smell of a forest storm, rich with earth and life, envelops us.

After a moment, Alice turns back to me. Her breath

comes too quickly. She's as scared as she is in awe. "How?" she asks softly.

"I am Fae," I say. "The elements bend to my will."

"Can you all do that?"

I nod slowly. "Most."

Alice glances down at the watering can and then laughs. "Why is this even in here?"

I find myself smiling as I shake my head. "I don't know."

"I doubt you came to water the plants for me." She studies me. "Why are you here?"

I pause before I answer. Why *am* I here? What did I hope to accomplish with the meeting? "I don't know that either."

Her frown becomes thoughtful. "Please don't ask me to go home again. I haven't even worked off these dresses yet."

"Short of physically removing you from the grounds, I honestly don't know how to persuade you to leave."

Her lips twitch with a suppressed smile.

"May I ask you about your childhood?" I ask before I can think better of it.

Surprised, Alice cocks her head to the side as she looks up at me. "Why?"

"If we are going to coexist peacefully, it seems we should make an effort to be cordial and get to know one another."

"All right," she says slowly, clearly suspicious there is more to the question than I'm letting on. "I was born in Kellington. My parents died in a carriage accident when I was nine. My maternal grandmother already lived with us, so she became our guardian. She passed away shortly after Gustin came of age, and then I became his burden. There isn't much more to tell."

And though I don't have my mother's talent at reading human lies, I notice the way her eyes dart from mine—she's reluctant to divulge the entire truth.

"What about before your parents died?"

She shakes her head, looking away. "I don't remember much."

My intuition pricks, and it becomes hard to breathe.

"Have you ever been in Faerie before?" I demand.

Alice turns her eyes back, no longer hiding from me. Her brow creases as she shakes her head.

"No." She leans moderately closer as she gives me a self-deprecating look. "Everyone knows only the foolish venture past the bridge."

I laugh in response, but the air catches in my throat because I don't sense a lie this time. As far as Alice knows, she's telling the truth.

Yet I believe this is the girl—I feel it.

But how is it possible? As far as anyone knows, our Alice is *dead.*

7

ALICE

The marquis watches me with the strangest expression. He looks like I've flummoxed him.

It's been a strange meeting, even disregarding the sudden downpour. Though Lord Ambrose claims he wants to get to know me—that we should be cordial—his expression is shielded.

He seems leery of me, unsure and hesitant. It's as if he's here against his better judgment. But why?

Even after he lowers his hand, rain continues to fall around us, making my job obsolete.

I stare at the rain-drenched flowers as the shower begins to let up. With a sigh, I say, "Now what am I going to do with my afternoon?"

"Whatever you'd like," he answers, perhaps thinking he's doing me a favor.

"While the sentiment is appreciated, I'm not sure there's much for me to do here, my lord."

"Brahm." His eyes meet mine, and they hold. Lowering

his voice marginally, he says again, "Please, call me Brahm."

"Brahm," I say slowly.

He nods.

"All right…" I frown. "If we are now on a first-name basis, then perhaps you will permit a question?"

He looks unsure, but he nods once more.

"The last time I spoke with you, you were gruff and abrupt. Why are you being nice now?"

"I've come to terms with the fact I cannot get rid of you." He softens the words with a weak smile. "So, we might as well make the best of it."

"If you free my brother, I will leave," I can't help but point out.

Slightly amused, he says, "I'm not that benevolent."

Not yet anyway, but I cannot help but feel that my goal to win him over might not be so impossible.

As if bracing himself for something unpleasant, he clasps his hands behind his back and says, "You haven't left the manor in several weeks. I imagine you are growing restless. Shall we go into Kellington and see a show?"

"You would take your garden maid on an outing?" I say skeptically.

"You are not a garden maid, Alice. You are the daughter of Lord Gravely, born of noble blood. I am merely humoring you by allowing you to tend the plants. We are equals."

"But…I am human," I remind him. Never mind the fact that he is actually a royal, though he doesn't bring that up.

Brahm almost smiles. "I haven't forgotten."

I study him, remembering the bandit's warnings. After a moment, I set my hands on my hips. "I know what this is."

"What is it?" Brahm asks, his brow furrowing.

"You're going to trick me into following you across the bridge, and then you're going to leave me."

"While that is certainly a tempting idea, I have no intention of it."

"How can I possibly trust you when you're desperate to oust me from your house?"

"Because lies do not come easily to the Fae of West Faerie—our magic does not allow it. Surely you've heard that?" His dark eyes earnestly meet mine. "I will bring you back, safe and sound, at the end of the night. You have my word."

I look for a loophole, a way he could be twisting his words. But it doesn't matter. I won't go with him. What if the bandit were to finally visit and find me gone? Worse, what if he were to see me together with Lord Ambrose?

Though I now realize it's honestly not safe for him to return.

He was right—the Fae know of his existence. They call him the Highwayman, and his moniker graces a good portion of the estate gossip. The men whisper of his treachery. The women say he'd be an exciting paramour if he could be tamed.

The thought gives me chills.

Part of me hopes he's not foolish enough to visit. The other part knows I will wait by my balcony just as I have every night for the last two weeks, just in case.

"Not tonight," I say to the marquis. "But thank you for the offer."

Disappointment passes over Brahm's face, maybe resignation as well. "Perhaps a different day."

He then looks up, and the remaining clouds disperse. He steps away from me, no longer needing to shelter me from the storm. "Have a pleasant afternoon."

I nod silently, watching him leave the conservatory, feeling unsettled by the conversation.

ANOTHER WEEK PASSES, and there is still no sign of the masked man.

I worry; I pace. I nearly make myself sick.

He said he couldn't keep coming—I *know* why he couldn't keep coming—but that doesn't soothe my rampant worries.

Maybe he met someone else in the woods and moved on.

Perhaps I should as well.

I glance toward the wall that separates my room from the marquis's.

Lord Ambrose hasn't asked me on another outing, nor has he come to speak with me again. He seems to be keeping his distance. When he passes me in the halls, I get a respectful nod, and that is all.

I haven't become friendly with the marquis's staff either. It would be challenging to forge a relationship with them, considering they don't want me here, and I don't trust them.

Regina is pleasant, but she's rarely around.

I've become my only source of company, and I'm not all that interesting. Maybe it's because I'm a human in Faerie, and it's inevitable, but I feel like I'm going mad.

Irritated with myself, I decide I've had enough. I'm obviously waiting for a man who doesn't intend to return.

I stalk into the hall, turn left, and stop in front of a door I've only been through once.

I rap on it loudly, crossing my arms as I wait for the marquis to answer. I wait...and I wait.

Finally deciding he's either not in, or he has no intention of answering, I turn to leave.

And then the door opens.

When I look back, I nearly lose my nerve. Lord Ambrose stands inside his room, his shirt partially open. His hair is mussed. He wears no waistcoat or jacket.

My mouth goes dry, and I realize I'm staring at him like a fool.

"Miss Alice?" he asks, perhaps wondering why I'm outside his room at this hour.

In a rush, I say, "I know it's late, and I know you're likely going to think I'm insane, but I need a little fresh air—right now."

His eyebrows fly up, and though he does, in fact, look at me like I'm insane, a smile edges across his face. "Right now?"

"Now."

Slowly, he nods, glancing down at his open shirt. "May I dress first?"

84

My cheeks heat, but I nod curtly. "I will wait for you in my room. Knock when you're ready."

"Where are we going?" he asks.

"Anywhere," I say. "Just...away."

I disappear inside my room, resting my head on the door when I'm alone, wondering what's wrong with me.

A few minutes later, there is a knock.

Bracing myself, I open the door. A girlish part of me swoons at the idea of Lord Ambrose calling on me—even if I commanded it.

None of my suitors were as handsome as he. Obviously, none of them were Fae, either. But the marquis is not a suitor, nor do I want him to be.

I just need someone to talk to. And right now, he is my best option.

He offers his arm. "Shall we?"

Grateful, I take it. We walk down the hall, neither of us speaking. It's not awkward, however. It feels as if we are waiting until we can breathe outside the confines of the manor before we begin the conversation.

"Would you like to walk?" he asks when we leave the house and begin down the steps. "Or should I rouse a groom to prepare the carriage?"

I glance toward the dark forest. "Is it safe?"

"No one will bother you while you are with me."

"Not even goblins?" I ask, trying to joke. The question comes out timid.

His arm stiffens slightly. "Not even goblins. We won't find any inside the estate grounds anyway—they cannot cross the fence."

Though I'm nervous, I nod.

"Am I correct in assuming that your reluctance means your time in Rose Briar Woods has not been pleasant?" he asks.

"Your estate is lovely," I answer automatically.

"There is far more to Faerie than my estate. And much of it is beautiful."

"And deadly," I say under my breath.

The marquis tugs me to a stop, turning me so I have no choice but to face him. "You're safe with me, Alice."

"And if I were to leave your side?"

A true smile flickers across his face, transforming him. "I wouldn't advise it."

He's like a different man when he smiles—still just as handsome, but far more approachable.

"Carry on, my lord. I will stay by your side."

"My name is Brahm," he reminds me solemnly, his voice heartbreakingly familiar. "Brahm."

For a moment, my heart stutters. I study him in the night, questioning what I know cannot be true.

I can make out his ears in the lantern's glow—they're noticeably pointed. I know if I were to trace them with my fingers, I would feel the difference. They are not human ears, but those which belong to the Fae—not as prominently pointed as the northern elves', but certainly not rounded at the top.

And yet, I cannot shake the strange suspicion that I've met this man in the shadows before—that I've waited for him every night for three weeks straight.

"Brahm," I repeat, knowing my thoughts are nonsensical.

The marquis nods, his dark eyes on mine.

"Are we going to walk?" I ask weakly.

As if shaking himself, he moves with a start, leading me into the woods.

Creatures watch us from the brambles. I can see their glowing eyes from the corner of my vision, but every time I turn, they're gone.

"What are they?" I finally ask, uneasy.

Brahm smiles. "Faunaweavers. They're shy."

"But they exist? I'm not losing my mind?"

He chuckles. "They exist. If you're patient, and you stop trying to find them, they'll come out."

"Are they...unnerving?"

He flashes me a questioning look. "Define unnerving."

"Terrifying? Grotesque?"

He laughs again. "I've never heard them described that way, no."

We walk, eventually finding ourselves surrounded by the roses that grow wild in the wood, so different from the ones I tend in the conservatory. Raspberries grow amongst them here as well, their fruit hanging red on the canes, now ripe.

I gesture toward the berries. "I suppose if I eat one, I'll lose my mind?"

"How have you been avoiding the effects of our food thus far?"

I glance at him, unable to shake these strange suspicions. "A concoction."

He doesn't so much as flinch. "A smart thing to keep close in Faerie."

"Yes..."

"Do you have it with you?"

"I don't."

He raises a dark eyebrow. "Do you trust me?"

"Not particularly."

Humor lights his eyes. "Then I don't suggest you eat one."

We continue, and I begin to wish I had worn boots the day I came into the woods. Tiny rocks and sticks jab into my slippers, making it uncomfortable to walk. I'm about to suggest we turn around when a wooden bench appears right in the path. It's simply there, waiting to be sat upon.

"I swear that wasn't there a moment ago," I say.

"You must have wished for it."

"I did?" I say dumbly.

Brahm nods. "The woods are a strange place. They take pity on those they favor."

"And they...favor me?"

"They must, or you wouldn't be alive." He gestures for me to sit. "Even though it was well after dark, you arrived at my estate when most humans who wander Faerie after dusk disappear forever."

I want to argue that it was thanks to the Highwayman, but I hold my tongue.

Not sure I'm comfortable with benches appearing out of thin air, I sit slowly, expecting it to wink into nothing and send me crashing to the ground.

"Let's test my theory," Brahm says casually, crossing his arms as he stands in front of me. "Wish for something."

"Something like what?"

He smiles. "Anything."

For a moment, my thoughts flicker to the bandit. Immediately, I dismiss them, irritated with myself.

"A little more light would be nice," I say.

Suddenly, the surrounding woods flicker to life as dozens of floating fairy lights illuminate the space. I let out a startled squeal, nearly darting under the bench.

"You spook very easily," Brahm says, grinning for the first time since I've known him.

"It's not natural," I argue.

"Not the natural you're familiar with," he corrects.

"I'm not sure I can get used to it."

"Does that mean you're ready to return to Kellington?" he teases.

"Not yet."

Shaking his head, he sits next to me. The bench isn't large, and we're very close. His shoulders brush against mine, but he doesn't seem to mind.

Unable to help myself, I say with only a mild bite in my voice, "Do you find me less uncomfortable now?"

Brahm turns his head to look at me. "No."

"Is it because I'm human?"

The edges of his eyes crinkle slightly. "No."

"Because I'm difficult?"

"You *are* difficult," he says. "But no."

"Then why?"

He thinks about it for a few seconds. "Because you remind me of someone, and I worry if you remain here, your fate could be the same as hers."

"What happened to her?" I ask, suddenly not feeling so comfortable alone in the woods.

Brahm's expression becomes pained, and he shakes his head. "I thought I knew, but now I'm not so sure."

"Was she someone you cared about?"

"Yes."

"Family?" I ask.

"Not exactly, but she was something like that."

"I lost a sister when I was young," I admit, looking at the lights as they flicker in the trees. "It's not something you forget."

"A sister?"

"That's right."

He mulls it over, perplexed. "What happened to her?"

"She vanished while we were on holiday. There one moment, gone the next."

"How old was she?" Brahm asks slowly, looking as if he's thinking very hard. "Where did it happen?"

I don't like to think about Eleanor's disappearance. It was the event that destroyed our family. After she went missing, my parents spent their last years obsessed with finding her. People claimed she must have been stolen by the Fae. How else could she disappear without a trace? And everyone knows that people stolen by the Fae never return.

Still, Father and Mother searched for her tirelessly, leaving Gustin and me with Grandmother as they scoured the Fallon border. They died during one of their trips, killed in a rockslide that took out the road they were traveling upon.

I don't think I've ever quite forgiven them, to be honest.

Brahm leans back, perhaps reading my dark expression. "Never mind."

"It's late," I say. "We should go back."

He nods, offering his hand as he stands.

As soon as I rise, the bench disappears. I step closer to Brahm, not liking it one bit.

"Alice," he says suddenly, his tone off. "I'm sorry I brought up the subject. I can tell it's painful—we needn't speak of it again."

I nod, taking his arm.

The walk back to the manor doesn't take long. When we reach my room door, Brahm turns to me, clasping his hands behind his back. "Why were you so desperate to leave tonight? You never said."

"I just needed some air," I answer. "Thank you for walking with me."

Brahm nods, wishing me goodnight as I slip into my room.

8

BRAHM

Wallen stands before me, silently frowning. "You want me to find information about Alice's sister?"

I nod, shuffling papers on my desk. "That's right. A child who disappeared when she was very young."

Regina shifts next to me, uncomfortable. "Do you think…"

I look over. "I believe it's possible."

But mostly, I want assurance that I'm wrong. Because if I'm right, then my family has committed a wicked crime against Alice's family—something she is not likely to forgive.

"The chances are so slim," Regina says quietly. "You're aware of that, aren't you?"

"I need to know."

"I will look into it," my valet says, bowing before he leaves.

"Tell no one," I instruct, though I know he won't. He and Regina are the two people in my life I trust explicitly.

My brother and Sabine come in at a close second, though sometimes I'm unsure exactly where my sister's allegiances lie.

Wallen slips out the door, shutting it silently behind him.

Regina turns to me, looking uncomfortable. "Sisters don't often share the same name."

"I'm counting on it. I just need to be certain."

"Brahm," she says gently. "I think you need to free Alice's brother and send them home. Pretend this never happened."

"Lord Ambrose does not show mercy," I remind her. "That's why I created the Highwayman."

And Alice's brother does not deserve mercy—something I believe even more strongly now that I know his sister.

"You're stumbling in too deep with this girl. Her presence alone is dredging up things best left buried."

I choose not to answer.

"Do you have any idea what your mother would do if she found out you're taken with a human?"

I jerk my head up, dropping the papers on my desk. "Excuse me?"

"This isn't about our Alice anymore. This is about *this* Alice. The feelings you have for her aren't brotherly as I originally thought."

"She's human," I say, trying not to remember the kiss.

"Tell me I'm wrong," Regina demands. "Bluntly say your interest isn't romantic in nature. Tell me you aren't attracted to her as a woman."

I struggle, fighting my magic before I finally give up. Defeated, I admit, "I can't."

"Then you are walking a dangerous path."

I know she's not wrong.

In Faerie, it's acceptable to take a human as a pet, even to go as far as to keep them as casual lovers and shower them with riches.

It's not allowed, however, to court a human. It's certainly not allowed to give them our name and let them mother children.

In Faerie, humans are for entertainment and sport—both of which I find abhorrent.

If I let myself develop feelings for Alice, as Regina knows, I would begin to want more than I'm allowed—and that puts Alice in even more danger.

But I cannot think of that now. For the time being, all that matters is learning more about her sister.

IT'S BEEN A LONG EVENING, partially because I slept little last night, but mostly because a barghest found an elderly peddler before I did.

I discovered the man's horse, sans rider, grazing in a soft patch of grass near the entrance of the bridge.

After walking the road, I found blood in the dirt, along with the signs of something being dragged into the woods.

I finally found the unfortunate man in a small cavern about three miles from the bridge, unconscious but alive. The others before him were not so lucky.

Unfortunately, the beast didn't sense my authority soon enough. The nightmare canine lunged at me when I entered his den, grazing the side of my neck with a sharp tooth before he pulled back. He then retreated, whimpering in the corner like a cowering puppy.

I managed to carry the man back to his horse, hoist his still-unconscious self over the saddle, and then send him to the other side of the bridge where his people will hopefully find him—all while bleeding like the nightmare dog tried to decapitate me.

My magic will heal the injury after a few hours of decent sleep, but I feel like I'm dead on my feet now.

Because of it, I'm not careful enough to remember there is a girl in the room next to mine who might be out on her balcony, looking for me.

"Bandit!" Alice whispers urgently when I'm close.

I look up sharply, startled by her quiet voice in the dead of night. With dread, I realize she's likely spotted the blood. It would be impossible not to—I'm covered from neck to boots.

She leans over her balcony railing, loose hair blowing in the slight breeze, dressed in a white nightgown Regina must have had made for her.

"Can you climb?" she asks urgently.

Realizing I have no choice but to follow this through even though all I want is my bed, I climb the lattice up to Alice's balcony.

She panics when she sees the trails of blood and the gash on my neck. "What happened?"

I stumble forward, growing lightheaded as my magic draws from my energy stores in an attempt to knit the wound. Alice grabs hold of my shoulders, too small to support me if I were to fall.

"I'll clean it," she says. "And I'll find a way to bandage it. Come inside."

"I'm fine," I protest, tempted to tell her the truth so I can go to bed and be done with it. But she looks up at me, her pretty blue eyes filled with anxiety, making me less eager to leave.

"Sit," she commands, leading me to the chaise longue. Then, changing her mind, she directs me toward the bed. "No, lie down."

"I'll get blood on—"

"The coverlet will come clean," she insists. "I'll scrub it myself."

Knowing Sabine won't be pleased if she learns I bled all over her bed, I fumble with my leather jacket's buckles. Alice pushes my hands away, taking over the task herself. Once the jacket is out of the way, she begins to remove my blood-stained shirt.

"Can you lean over a little?" she asks as she pulls it up.

I do as she requests, and what little blood is left in my body rushes hot as her cool, soft hands brush over my bare skin.

I draw in a hissing breath when she presses a hand to my shoulder to leverage herself high enough to slip the shirt over my head. She murmurs apologies, misunderstanding my reaction, worrying she's hurting me.

Even I wince when I look down. Blood seeped under the collar of my shirt, saturating large sections of the fabric and leaving my entire torso smeared in red.

Now that I'm dressed only in trousers, Alice coaxes me onto the bed. It's softer than mine, with dozens of down-stuffed pillows.

My eyelids grow heavy as Alice fusses about the room, and I barely remember to pull the sides of my mask over the top of my ears before I drift. Hopefully, it's enough. I don't have the energy for illusion tonight.

I wake when the bed shifts next to my shoulder. I crack my eyes open and find Alice hovering close to my face, wet cloth in hand.

"This will probably sting," she warns as she dabs the cloth to my neck.

Though I brace myself, the toxin from the barghest's saliva makes the area especially tender. I fist my hands, pretending it doesn't hurt. When Alice gets to a particularly tender spot, I arch my back slightly, cursing the Faerie beast to oblivion and back.

"I'm sorry," Alice murmurs, "but you must stay still."

She pushes her hand firmly to my chest, holding me in place as she cleans the wound. I focus on the feel of her palm against my skin, thankful when she's finished.

I draw in a deep breath, wishing she hadn't witnessed that.

"I don't have a bandage," she says, "but this will do for tonight."

I recognize the square of cloth as a handkerchief Sabine embroidered. Alice must have found it in a drawer. Before I can stop her, she wraps it around my neck.

"Tomorrow, go into Kellington and see Thomas at the

apothecary shop on the corner of Wellington and Main. He's a retired army doctor and an old friend of my father's. Tell him I sent you, and he'll stitch your wound without asking questions. For now, this should stop the bleeding."

"Alice," I say raggedly, setting my hand on hers. "I need to tell you—"

"You don't have to explain why you disappeared for three weeks and then showed up in this state. I'm not going to demand an explanation."

"That's not..." I gulp, unable to finish the sentence.

Now that Alice is finished with the urgent task of bandaging my wound, she begins to clean blood from less vital parts of my body.

She runs the cloth over my shoulders, rinsing it in the warm water as needed. She moves to my chest, and then to my abdomen.

My breath comes quicker, and the pain in my neck dulls to a low ache that's easy to ignore.

Alice stills when my muscles clench under her hands. Slowly, her eyes move to my face. Though I wear the mask, I feel revealed.

"Am I making you uncomfortable?" she asks quietly.

"Not uncomfortable," I manage, pushing myself up on my elbows. "But you should stop."

Her eyes dart down to my stomach before she looks back up. "I'm almost finished."

"I'm not so close to death's door that I'm not affected by your hands on me, Alice." I try to say it lightly, but my voice is rough, betraying the truth of my words.

She lowers her gaze, dabbing again at my stained skin. "You think that it's not distracting for me as well? But you're covered in blood, and I'm not going to leave you like this. If I can control myself, I expect you should be able to do the same."

9

ALICE

The bandit falls silent, and I work quietly, a little embarrassed by my honesty.

"I missed you." I stare at his stomach as I remove the last of the drying blood. "I kept thinking you were going to return. Kept hoping. I thought...well, I thought we were becoming friends. You didn't even say goodbye."

"Alice..."

"Will you answer one question?"

He nods slowly, wincing as he raises his hand to the makeshift bandage.

"I understand why you didn't visit me...but did you want to?" I hold my breath, preparing myself for disappointment.

He stares at me, looking torn.

"Is it that difficult to answer?" I look at my blood-stained hands. "There are only two possible responses: yes or no?"

"Yes," he says, the word sounding like it was dragged right from his lungs. Like it was painful.

I meet his eyes, feeling my heart squeeze.

He sits up, which puts our faces very close. "Yes," he says again, and this time it doesn't sound like it's ripping him apart. "I've thought of you every day, Alice."

My heart pinches, making me worry I'm growing too attached to this man of secrets.

I move my eyes to the bandage. I panicked when I saw him walking toward the manor, worried he had to be close to death in that state.

But the wound, though ghastly, is nowhere as severe as I feared when he showed up covered in blood. Once I cleaned the area, I found the gash to be manageable enough, though he will need it stitched in the morning. At least it's wrapped now.

I stand, and the bandit lowers his legs over the side of the bed.

"Don't move too quickly," I warn, gathering my supplies, trying not to think of the way the water has been stained deep pink. "You've lost a lot of blood."

He watches me as I walk to the basin and wash my hands. How am I going to explain this mess to Regina in the morning?

As soon as the thought crosses my mind, I glance back at the masked man, wondering if I'll have to.

It's Brahm on my bed. I *know* it—I'd have to be a fool not to recognize him.

But why has the marquis created this secret identity? And how do I explain his ears? They're hidden under the mask now, but his deep brown hair is mussed just as Brahm's was when I knocked on his door the night we walked into the forest—as if the marquis had been wearing a hat only moments before.

Once my hands are clean, I walk back to him. "How are you feeling? Feverish at all?"

Before I place my palm against his forehead, the bandit gently catches my hand and pulls me to him. It's a languid movement, and yet it speaks volumes.

Like lovers, we're close. His legs brush mine. Unsure what to do with my free hand, I clench it into a fist behind my back, sternly telling myself I will not explore his bare skin with my fingers, no matter how tempted I might be.

He brings the inside of my wrist to his lips. "Thank you for tending me, Alice."

The gesture makes me flush, the warmth beginning in my cheeks and then traveling down my neck.

When I realize he means to rise, I press down on his shoulders, making him remain seated. "You're leaving?"

He studies me in the candlelight. "We both know I can't stay."

"But you can't go, not like this. Sleep for a while. I'll wake you when you must leave."

Smiling as he rubs his thumb over my knuckles, he drops his voice and says, "How will I sleep with you hovering over me?"

"I won't hover." My lips twitch as I try not to smile. "I'll pull up a chair."

"I'm not going to chase you out of your bed, Alice— not even for a few hours."

"Have it your way," I say stubbornly, crawling onto the bed and sitting primly on the other side with my back against the headboard. Sternly, I point to the pillow beside me. "Sleep."

The masked man twists around to face me, looking like he knows he should protest. Exhaustion, however, wins.

"Fine," he says with a heavy sigh. "But only for a few minutes."

"I'll wake you after a bit," I promise.

He shifts until his head is atop the pillow and his back faces me.

When I run my hand over his shoulder, he flinches. But his muscles soften as I slowly stroke down his arm, back up, and then repeat the movement.

Minutes later, his breathing becomes deep and even.

I look at the bandit's still figure—his long legs, slightly bent, his broad shoulders and tapered back. He's truly beautiful.

If he were mine—if this were our room—I would lean down and press a kiss to his back, wrap an arm over his waist, and then snuggle in close.

Perhaps he'd stir, rolling over and taking me into his arms, kissing me long and slow before we both drifted to sleep. I wouldn't have to wake him; he wouldn't have to leave.

These are fanciful thoughts considering he won't even share his identity with me. Why does he trust me enough to sleep in my presence, but he won't take off the mask?

I could do it now, while he's unconscious and so close, but I won't violate his trust like that.

He'll show me when he's ready.

I wake with a jolt, realizing I fell asleep. The sky is lightening with early dawn, and birds chatter outside the window.

I roll over in the bed, preparing to urgently rouse the masked man.

But he's gone.

Coming to my senses, I realize he must have woken on his own and left. The bloodied jacket, shirt, and cloth are missing as well, and there are no stains on the coverlet.

There's no sign of his visit whatsoever, making me wonder if I dreamed the whole thing.

But I'm still atop the covers, and I'm now blanketed by a quilt. The thought of the bandit draping it over me while I slept warms me more than the blanket itself, and I close my eyes and snuggle into the pillow, preparing to sleep for a while longer.

When I do rise, I realize that we parted without a goodbye yet again.

How long will it be before I see him this time?

10

BRAHM

I knock on Alice's door after finding the conservatory empty. She's careful, heeding the warning I gave her as the bandit, never wandering the manor alone. She must be in.

Sure enough, Alice opens the door, her eyes betraying that she's still cautious of me, even after the brief time we've spent together.

"Is there something I can do for you, Lord Ambr—" She corrects herself when I raise my eyebrows. "Brahm?"

As she says my name, her eyes dart down the hall as though she doesn't want someone to overhear.

I extend a small velvet purse. "The staff gets paid today. Regina was going to bring your wages, but I wanted to give them to you personally."

Alice shakes her head, stepping back so she doesn't have to take the money. "I haven't paid off the dresses yet."

"Consider the dresses a gift."

"I couldn't," she protests. "I'm here to right a wrong, not become an imposition."

I reach for her hand and press the small pouch into it, refusing to let her have her way this time. "Tomorrow, I have business in Kellington. If you accompany me, we will buy your new supplies. From this point forward, you are no longer a member of my staff, but a visiting artist, here as my guest."

Alice continues to stare at me, looking unsure...and something else. It's unnerving.

Trying to hide my discomfort, I say, "Also, I am here to request that you join me for dinner."

She steps forward, her eyes moving to my neck.

"Your cravat is askew." She steps very close as her hands find the material. "I'll fix it for you."

I freeze, realizing what she's looking for—acknowledging that now, without a doubt—Alice suspects.

She goes very still, seeming puzzled. Pulling the material aside, she runs her finger along my neck.

"Miss Alice?" I ask stiffly. "Is something the matter?"

But I know what's causing her distress. The wound is gone, healed completely overnight. As I expected, there is no sign of it today. But apparently, Alice doesn't know that is a gift of the Fae.

She steps back, eyes slightly narrowed, studying me like I'm a riddle.

I offer my arm, trying not to smirk at my good fortune. Though it wasn't planned, this will buy me time. "If you are finished fussing with my clothing, shall we go to dinner?"

Alice shakes her head, raising her eyes from my neck

to my face. "As generous as the offer is, I must decline. I have nothing suitable to wear."

My eyes drop to her garden gown. This one is ivory linen, laced with an overdress in light beige. It's plain, but that cannot hide how lovely she is, and I doubt she is unaware of that. "What's wrong with what you're wearing now?"

Alice gives me a droll look. "You're a man of nobility, always impeccably dressed. Don't pretend you don't know."

I smile despite myself. "I will be your only dining partner, Alice. Who will care?"

"I care." She turns, dismissing me. "But thank you for the offer."

"You will go with me to Kellington tomorrow, won't you? Or do you require a special gown for an outing into the city?"

"I'll make do tomorrow." She looks back, smirking at me in a way that makes my collar feel a little too tight. "But thank you for asking."

I DINE ALONE, reading a book by the light of the overhead crystal chandelier. Though the manor is far less opulent than the castle I grew up in, it's too much for me.

For the first time in my life, I wonder what it would be like if it were filled with the noise of a family. It's been too long since I've been in a woman's company, and Alice's presence is a little too comfortable.

I woke just before dawn and found she had fallen

asleep next to me. She slumped against the headboard with a pillow clutched in her arms. Her long, blonde hair was falling from its ribbon.

She looked like a porcelain doll, too perfect and fragile.

Without realizing it, I'd rolled toward her sometime in the night. My mask slid down while I was sleeping and was around my neck when I awoke. If Alice had stirred before me...

But she didn't.

I wanted to pull her into my arms and go back to sleep, but I forced myself out of the bed.

Regina's right. I'm in too deep, have started to feel things for Alice that go beyond mild affection. I need to forgive Gustin's debt and send the two of them back to their home, where they belong. We'll purchase Alice's supplies tomorrow, and I will let her paint me.

Let her think she traded her family's fortune back for a portrait. I will deal with the repercussions once she's gone.

"I'm sorry to interrupt," Wallen says from the doorway. "But may we speak?"

I nod my valet inside, and he shuts the door behind him.

After setting the book on the table next to my plate, I turn toward him. "You're back already?"

"The information you were seeking was not difficult to find," he says, looking troubled.

"Alice had a sister who disappeared?"

He nods. "Her name was Eleanor. She went missing while the family was on holiday in Fallon."

Growing cold, I lean forward. "How old was she?"

"A few months shy of three years." He watches me carefully, his gray eyes full of regret. "Lord and Lady Gravely looked tirelessly for the girl. A few years after she disappeared, they were caught in a landslide while searching. That's how they died."

My stomach plummets. "Did you get her description?"

My valet stares at me, his expression sympathetic. "I found a portrait. It was with the family's things in the auction house. It had been set aside."

I swallow, finding it hard to breathe. "Did you bring it with you?"

"I did."

Slowly, I stand, setting my napkin next to the plate. "I want to see it."

"Of course. I've taken it to your quarters."

We say nothing else as we walk down the hall. Regina steps from a parlor, smiling when she sees us. Almost immediately, her expression becomes distressed. "What's the matter?"

I loop my arm through my cousin's, tugging her so she'll follow. "Wallen has found a portrait of Alice's family."

"Is her sister in it?" Regina asks, and the color drains from her face.

"She is," Wallen answers.

It can't be her—our girl was named Alice, not Eleanor. But the location, the age...

The three of us enter my sitting room, and Wallen closes the door behind us. In the center of the room, a covered portrait rests on an easel, waiting to be revealed.

I walk across the space, hesitating once my hand clasps the white cover. Steeling myself, I pull it away.

Regina lets out a soft, heartbroken cry.

Alice, *our* Alice, sits upon her mother's lap. She wasn't much older than a baby when this was painted, a year and a half at the most. She has chin-length, dark brown hair and a red satin bow atop her curls. Her amber eyes are as bright as her young grin, and she's surrounded by a family that quietly smiles for the artist.

Her older sister holds her hand. At three or four, the girl is just as lovely as she is now, with pale blonde hair and piercing blue eyes that match her mother's.

Regina cries softly, clutching my arm. "It's her."

I turn away, choking back emotion that doesn't usually plague me.

"Her name was Eleanor," I say to Regina, tilting my head back to stare at the ceiling, willing my weakness to leave me.

"Why did she say it was Alice?" Regina asks, tears streaming down her cheeks.

"She was young," Wallen answers. He's older than Regina and me by almost two decades and was Father's valet before he started attending me. "It was difficult to understand her. She was probably asking for her sister."

I was eight when Eleanor came to us. I remember... but not as well as Wallen.

Well enough, however, to know that this is her.

Why did it have to be her?

Regina chokes on a sob, turning from us, and dark memories flood the room. Though Eleanor was never truly ours, we loved her.

And none of us will be able to forgive Mother for what she did.

"Do something with the portrait, Wallen." I clear my throat. "I cannot keep it in here."

"Would you have me destroy it, Your Highness?"

"No," I say immediately, the idea unthinkable. "But store it somewhere we don't have to look at it. Somewhere my mother won't find it."

"Or Drake," Regina says softly.

Drake.

"Yes," I reply.

Wallen covers the portrait and steps into the hall, leaving me with Regina.

"Brahm," she cries, hugging herself.

"I know," I murmur gently, wrapping my arm around her shoulder.

"They looked so much alike," she says. "Do you think...do you think Ali—*Eleanor* would have grown up to look like Alice?"

My face tries to crumple, but I fight it. "Don't do this to yourself."

Regina nods and steps back, her eyes already red from crying.

"It's getting late," I say gently. "Go to bed."

"Are you all right?" she asks, dabbing her face.

"I'm not."

She blinks quickly. "If you need me..."

"I know."

I wait until she's gone before I sink into a chair and let my head hang. Alice's parents died because they were searching for her sister. Her life has been turbulent because of us.

If we had tried to locate Eleanor's family when she was first brought to us instead of treating her like a puppy, perhaps the tragedy could have been avoided. Eleanor might have lived a normal life. She and Alice would likely be with their parents tonight, content and happy, maybe chattering about a ball they would attend come the weekend.

Untouched by Faerie and its cruel ways.

Before I can think about my decision, I stand and pull off my jacket, quickly dressing in my black garb. A few minutes later, wearing my mask and a bandage I do not require, I stand outside Alice's balcony door.

11

ALICE

The knock at the balcony door is so unexpected, I slosh tea onto my hand.

Quickly, I set the cup in its saucer and wipe up the mess before hurrying toward the door. I peek through the curtain, *hoping*.

The bandit waits in the dark, his wide-brimmed hat clutched in his hands.

I throw open the door.

"Two nights in a row?" I whisper with a grin. "What have I done to earn such a thing?"

He steps inside, softly shutting the door behind him. He's so tall, I feel dwarfed next to him.

Exactly as tall as Brahm.

My eyes fall on the bandage at his throat, and my thoughts churn with confusion. I was so sure...

"How's your neck?" I ask.

When he doesn't answer, I grow worried. Stepping closer to inspect the injury, I ask, "Did you go to the apothecary?"

"My neck is fine," he finally says, taking my hand in his before I can fuss over the bandage.

"Then why do you look like you're in pain?" I whisper.

"I am." He looks down at our clasped hands. "But not from a physical affliction."

"All right… Then why are you here?" Quickly, I add, "Not that you aren't welcome."

He interlaces his fingers with mine. "I just wanted to see you."

"Something happened."

After several heavy seconds, he nods.

"But you can't tell me what it was?"

"I don't think it would be wise."

I hate that he's keeping so much from me, but I don't know what to do about it. Maybe the best thing I can do is show him he can trust me.

"I have tea." I tug him toward the small table. "Have a cup."

But instead of letting me lead him, he steps up behind me, wraps his arm around my shoulders, and tucks me close. His cheek presses against mine, and the soft satin of his mask brushes against my temple.

"I'll leave if you ask me to," he murmurs.

"Why would I do that when I've been waiting for you for weeks?" I say, working hard to keep my voice steady so he won't know how deliciously flustered I am. "And this time, you're not even covered in blood."

He laughs softly near my ear. The sad sound of it tugs at my heart.

"How was your day?" he asks. "You're working in the conservatory, is that right?"

"My day was fine, and I was relieved of my position this evening." I angle my head to look at him. "Lord Ambrose said I am now a guest."

"He must be fond of you," the bandit says quietly.

"Do you think?"

He watches me with a steady gaze. "How couldn't he be?"

"He's taking me into Kellington tomorrow to purchase new supplies."

"You could stay, you know. Remain in Kellington, resume your normal life."

"Do you think the marquis will give me that option?" I ask.

The bandit's eyes are solemn behind his mask. "Most likely."

"So, is this our goodbye? Is that why you're here?"

"You can't have a life in Faerie," he says, turning me so I face him and then dropping his arms. "Too many humans think it's possible, but you must believe me when I say it's not. Each day marches you closer to peril. Your life expectancy is far too short here."

"What about you?"

"Me?"

"You're a human in Faerie, aren't you?" I press.

But is he? Is he really?

"I don't know where I belong anymore."

"Neither do I." I let my fingers brush against his. "But there is one reason to remain here, and no reason to stay in Kellington. Arithmetic was never my strongest subject, but even I know the answer to that problem."

"Your brother isn't worth the risk."

"I wasn't speaking about Gustin."

Incredulously, he asks, "You would linger in Faerie because of me?"

"I think you need me," I say.

"*I* need *you*?"

Instead of answering with words, I set my hand on his cheek and let my thumb edge over his black, silken mask.

I expect him to shy away, but his hand moves to my side.

"You're lonely," I say quietly. "I recognize the symptoms. I've battled them most of my life."

His grip tightens on my waist as though the statement cuts him to the core. "Were you unhappy as a child, Alice?"

I shake my head. "No, but when I was young, my parents were often gone. To be honest, things didn't change all that much when they died. My grandmother tried, and I had a kind governess, but I was alone much of the time. And Gustin…well, my brother and I were never close. When he was old enough, he began drinking and gambling, spending most of his time in the clubs. I rarely saw him."

The bandit's frown deepens.

"Don't misunderstand," I say quickly. "I know what a blessed life I led. I never wanted for anything; I never went hungry. I'm not ungrateful for all I had. Even Gustin, vacant though he was, gave me a generous allowance, letting me have whatever I wanted, buying me expensive gowns and all the art supplies I could ever want. I was well cared for."

"When did you begin painting?" he asks.

"I don't remember exactly. It seems I always had a brush in my hand when I was little. When I was ten, Grandmother brought in a tutor to help me hone my gift. I completed my first commissioned portrait when I was sixteen. A friend of my grandmother's asked me to paint her dog. Apparently, I did an adequate job. A month after the first portrait was complete, she commissioned me to paint her *with* the dog."

He smiles a little. "And you've done other commissions since then?"

I nod, torn between humility and wanting to impress him. "I have." I grin. "Even some without pets."

Suddenly, he stands straighter as if something has occurred to him. "What did you do with your earnings?"

My mood sours a little. "I happily, and naively, gave everything to Gustin. It was my contribution to our family's estate."

And now it's gone.

I had no idea my brother would gamble with our home. I still feel the sting of betrayal, though I've tried to ignore it.

Perhaps I should wash my hands of my brother altogether, let him reap what he's sown. But I've lost too many family members to sacrifice the last to the Fae.

"Your money wasn't his to gamble," the bandit says, growing excited. "Tell Lord Ambrose."

"What difference will it make?"

"All the difference in the world," he says urgently, grasping my arms. "Alice, you must tell him."

And despite all the evidence to the contrary, I can't

help but think Lord Ambrose knows...because I'm speaking with him now.

"Will it free Gustin?" I ask.

Immediately, the bandit releases my arms. Sounding frustrated, he shakes his head. "No."

"Then what's the point?"

"The point is Gustin gambled with assets that didn't fully belong to him—it breaks the agreement. It allows Lord Ambrose to give you back your home and life without any repercussions."

"It *gives* him the opportunity? You're saying he doesn't have it right now?"

"He's not as free as you believe. The queen watches him, waiting for the slightest sign of defiance."

I arch a brow. "For being the marquis's arch-nemesis, you certainly know him well."

"It's always wise to know your enemies."

"What will happen to Gustin?"

"No more than what he deserves," he says darkly.

"You said the queen watches Lord Ambrose. What would she do if she thought he was acting out of kindness and not because I found a loophole in the agreement?"

"She'd execute him," he says without reservation.

"Execute?" I demand, dropping my voice to a horrified whisper. "But you said he is her son."

"Without remorse, she has killed five husbands, her sister, her niece's husband, and so many more. Whatever you may have heard about her in the human-occupied lands is a mere shadow of her wicked heart. She is truly the most wretched woman alive. Even the rulers of the other Fae courts refuse to have dealings with her. West Faerie is a dark place because she is its queen."

Suddenly, staying here doesn't seem so wise.

"Do you understand now?" he asks. "That's why you must return to Kellington. Tell Lord Ambrose what you told me."

I set my hands on my hips, nodding to the wall that separates Brahm's quarters and mine. "Should I tell him now?"

Surprise flashes across the visible parts of the bandit's face, and then he slowly nods. "If you wish."

"Do you think he's in?" I prod.

"There's only one way to find out."

I eye him with suspicion, wondering how fast he can hop across the balconies and change.

I suppose I will test him.

Without another word, I turn on my heel and walk swiftly into the hall.

I knock on the marquis's door, wondering how long it will take Brahm to answer.

"Alice," Regina says softly from down the hall. "Did you need something?"

I frown when I realize her eyes are red and her face is pale. It looks like she's been crying. What happened tonight? What is Brahm hiding from me?

Carefully, I say, "I was hoping to speak with Lord Ambrose."

Grief passes over her face for a split second before she composes herself. "Tonight isn't a good night."

I glance toward the door. "But...he's in?"

"I was just with him."

Stumped, I step away slowly. "I'll speak with him tomorrow."

"I think that would be for the best. Would you like tea? I can have a pot brought up to you."

"I have some, thank you."

She continues walking, glancing at my face before she quickly looks away. "Have a good evening, Alice."

I watch her disappear down the hall, feeling flummoxed.

When I open the door to my room, I find the bandit sitting on the chaise longue, staring at the ever-burning candles in the fireplace. "You weren't gone long," he says. "Did you speak to him?"

"No," I say slowly.

I fully expected to find my room empty. I'm not sure what to make of his presence.

He drums his fingers on his leg. "Tomorrow will be soon enough."

I study his handsome lines and muscular build. The only thing soft about him is his lips.

Lips I've kissed.

Lips I want to kiss again.

I stand in front of him. "Even if Lord Ambrose gives me back my family's estate, I will still ask to paint him."

The bandit looks up sharply. "Why would you delay returning home?"

"I wouldn't feel right leaving without offering something in return."

The bandit rises, his movements betraying his frustration. "Alice, you owe Lord Ambrose nothing. This was never your wager—it was between your brother and him.

The fact that you've been affected doesn't make you a party to the crime."

"I feel responsible for Gustin's actions," I argue. "He's my brother."

"Gustin is—was—your guardian. It's not the other way around. He is a grown man who had too much to drink and made a foolish decision in the heat of the moment."

"How do you know he'd been drinking too much?" I ask.

The bandit looks startled. After a moment, he hedges, "Don't all habitual gamblers drink while they are playing?"

"I wouldn't know."

I can only imagine what goes on in the places Gustin patronized.

The bandit says, "It's getting late, and I interrupted your sleep last night. I'll let you rest."

"I slept well," I say boldly. "Better than I have since I left home."

He pauses, looking back.

"Stay a little longer," I whisper.

Glancing toward the window, he says reluctantly, "I can't, Alice. It's already past dark, and I haven't done my rounds."

"Do you do them every night?"

Slowly, he nods. "Most."

"You're a good man. You know that, don't you?"

He smiles as he slips through the balcony door. "Goodnight, Alice."

I follow him out, wishing he would stay. He sits on the rail and swings a leg over the side, about to climb down.

"Wait," I say before he goes.

He looks over, and the moonlight catches on his face as he turns.

"For protection." I lean forward and place a quick kiss to his cheek.

"For protection?" he asks, sounding bemused.

It's an old tradition, usually implemented by grandmothers. Sadly, there is no actual magic in it or my parents wouldn't be dead.

"It's just an old wives' tale," I explain, feeling a little ridiculous. "A kiss on the cheek for protection and luck. Haven't you ever heard it?"

He shakes his head as he crooks his finger, telling me to come close. My breath catches as I do as he asks.

The bandit takes my chin in his fingers and brushes his lips over my cheek. "For protection and luck," he whispers. "Sleep well, Alice."

He then swings from the balcony and onto the lattice, once more disappearing into the night.

I go inside, feeling dazed. When I reach my bed, I sit and let my fingers drift over my cheek.

It wasn't a real kiss, but it was something.

12

ALICE

I look at my reflection in the mirror, angling my head to the side, wishing I had something else to wear. Of the gowns Regina ordered, this pale gray is the nicest. It has a full skirt, a fitted bodice, and a low neckline that doesn't make me look like a garden maid—or like I'm five years old. But it's still very plain.

Turning to the side, I press my hand to my stomach, biting my lip as I study my reflection, wondering if I will see anyone I know today. It's possible.

In fact, it's likely.

What will my old acquaintances think when they see me dressed like this? It doesn't matter really, and I know it's a vain thought. But I'm self-conscious nevertheless.

Since we're going into the city, I wear my hair up, held into place with a black satin ribbon that falls almost to my shoulders. I have no jewelry, no brooches or other adornments.

Why didn't I keep Grandmother's ring with me? Why did I pack it?

Now it's gone, lost to the goblins. Everything else was boxed up and taken to the auction house.

It's amazing that a person's life can change so drastically in such a short period of time. It's a lesson you'd think I'd have learned by now, but it seems tragic things have a habit of catching me unaware.

A knock sounds at my door, making my pulse jump. That will be Brahm.

But when I answer the door, I find the marquis's valet instead. Standing in a tailed jacket and tall hat, he bows his head. "I will be driving you and Lord Ambrose into Kellington today, miss. Is there anything you require for a more comfortable outing? It will be cold once we cross the bridge, so I've packed a blanket, and I believe Regina has requested the cook send you with a basket of light refreshments."

I study him, momentarily caught off-guard by the offer. "That sounds fine. As long as we make it there and back without issue, I will be content."

He smiles, and his eyes linger on my face in the strangest way—as if maybe it hurts to look at me. "I expect Lord Ambrose will be ready shortly."

I nod, smiling though I'm a bit baffled by his concern. As he turns to leave, Brahm's door opens.

The marquis pulls on his jacket as he steps out, pausing in the hall when he spots us. A quiet smile crosses his face, and he gives me a greeting nod that touches raw places in my heart. "Are you ready, Miss Alice?"

"I believe so."

Wallen excuses himself, saying he'll go ahead and make sure the horses have been prepared.

I am left alone with Brahm. With his eyes never leaving my face, the marquis offers his arm. His dark brown hair is perfectly combed, and there's not a wrinkle or speck of lint upon his clothing. Everything about him proclaims power and nobility.

My gaze moves to the steel dagger at his side. It's Fae-crafted, with the hilt wrapped in leather to protect the wielder from the metal.

"Do you expect trouble?" I ask when he catches me looking at it.

Brahm lets out a soft snort. "I always expect trouble."

"Perhaps if I adopted your mindset, I wouldn't be surprised by it so often."

His arm stiffens under my fingers. Looking straight ahead, he says, "While you are with me, I won't let trouble touch you."

"Yes, but you have a bad habit of trying to send me away."

Quietly amused, Brahm looks over, and our eyes meet. It's a gaze I'm beginning to know well, one that even a mask cannot hide.

I want to ask him why he insists on hiding himself from me—ask him if he thinks I'm so unobservant that I can't tell that he and the bandit are the same man.

It's not because he doesn't play his parts well—he does. Brahm is controlled and reserved. His tone is usually indifferent, and it's always careful and cultured.

The bandit, however, is dashing. He's familiar and comfortable. And I suspect he's *real*.

I believe the bandit is Brahm's true identity. The only

way he found freedom to be himself was under a mask, and it hurts my heart just thinking about it.

What would it be like to have a mother who would execute you for the slightest misstep? To have a life so caged, you must create a different persona simply to survive?

We reach the carriage, and Wallen opens the door.

"Thank you," I murmur to Brahm as he offers his hand to steady me while I step inside.

I twist my hands in my lap once I'm seated, suddenly anxious. The walls of the carriage feel as if they're closing in on me, and I draw in a shaky breath.

"Alice?" Brahm says as he sits across from me. "Are you all right?"

"I haven't been in a carriage since…"

It's not as if the incident will happen twice, and besides, I have Brahm with me now. But the memory of waking in the abandoned carriage comes back with perfect clarity, and the nearby smell of wild roses doesn't help.

"Did you ever find my coachman and his horses?" I ask Brahm. "Regina said she'd mention it to you."

He shakes his head, looking apologetic. "I did not."

"It was still daytime when he disappeared," I say quietly. "I always understood Faerie is safe until dark."

"Humans are not to be touched on the roads during the daylight hours. But it's apparent something disregarded the law."

"Then…why was I unharmed?"

"As I said before, the forest must favor you. It protected you, Alice."

"Do even the creatures obey the queen?" I ask, unnerved by this strange kingdom.

"Only the sentient ones. But the rest can sense the royal family's magic, and their will can be made to bend if confronted."

"Are there many sentient creatures?" I ask quietly, disturbed at the thought. "More than just the goblins?"

Brahm suddenly laughs, and then he chokes his mirth back at my horrified look. "Yes, Alice. There are many."

"Are all of them wicked?" I whisper.

He slowly shakes his head. "No, but those that are have thrived under the current rule. The others keep to themselves."

Unsure how to respond, I stare at my lap.

"You're safe with me," he says yet again, his eyes falling on my white knuckles. "Nothing can touch you while you're in my care."

"Nothing but your mother," I point out.

Though he doesn't look surprised, he studies me. "You know."

I nod, wondering if it's a good time to tell him what else I know.

"Luckily, my mother wants very little to do with me," he says. "She requests my attendance at her moonlit masquerades once a month, and that is plenty for us both. As long as I do not ignore her summons, she rarely visits."

Rarely.

The word feels ominous, but I nod as if relieved.

Deciding it's time to change the subject, Brahm crosses his arms. "Where shall we eat? It's my first time going into Kellington with someone who knows the city well."

"You've never had a human woman on your arm before?" I say skeptically.

Brahm meets my gaze, smiling with his eyes alone. "Never willingly. There have been several I've been forced to shake off."

Trying not to smirk, I turn toward the window. "You must forgive them. Your people have quite the reputation after all."

Brahm leans forward slightly. "Do we? And what might that reputation be?"

As if he doesn't know.

I boldly meet his eyes. "People say Fae men are wickedly romantic. Others claim your kisses are intoxicating. I can't imagine there's a human girl alive who hasn't passed a Fae man on the street and didn't wonder what it would be like to have him woo her."

He cocks his head to the side. "Even you, Alice?"

I shrug as a smile toys at my face, refusing to answer.

"I'm afraid it's nothing but a rumor," Brahm says with a dismissive wave. "There are as many unromantic Fae men as there are human ones, and there is nothing about our magic that would have that effect. But I find the thought flattering nevertheless."

"Perhaps it's because you're all so handsome. It would be a shame to have a face like yours and not be at least a little romantic."

"You think I'm handsome?" Brahm asks, his amusement finally shining through his facade.

"How could I not? But don't worry—you're safe from my advances. I fancy someone else."

His forehead creases. "Someone else?"

"I met him before I came to your estate," I admit, observing him carefully.

"Who is this man?"

"Just a…human."

"Why didn't you go to him instead of coming to me when your brother lost your home?" Brahm demands.

I almost smile. "It's complicated, but I don't think he wants me. Even when we're close, I feel like he's pushing me away."

Brahm stares at me. His eyes narrow, and he opens his mouth even though it seems he's been struck mute.

"I wish he would trust me." I lean forward. "He would learn that I'm painfully loyal to those I care about."

Slowly, Brahm nods. "Perhaps he has his reasons."

"Perhaps." I sit back. "And I will respect that."

"You will?" he asks, startled.

"I don't want to." I wrinkle my nose. "But I will."

After another heavy moment, Brahm laughs as if uncomfortable and rubs the back of his neck. "We've gotten off subject. You never told me where you would like to eat."

THE TEAHOUSE IS slow early in the afternoon, as I knew it would be—that's why I picked it. If I was the subject of gossip before, just imagine how people's tongues will wag when they see me dining with the man who locked up my brother.

Even I wonder if I'm being disloyal to my family in some way, but I'm not allowing it to bother me too much. I have too many legitimate concerns to give that much thought.

I recognize the hostess immediately. Callie's eyes widen when I step inside with Brahm, and she hurries forward to greet us. We are casual friends, though she works too often to be close—another reason I chose this establishment. She's the youngest daughter of a local businessman, sweet and rational, and I know she's not likely to spread rumors.

"Alice!" she exclaims.

Her eyes flutter to Brahm before she gives me a very subtle questioning look.

"Everyone says you disappeared. We thought you went to stay with family after..." Her expression softens. "I'm so glad to see you."

"Hello, Callie." I glance around and find other curious eyes watching us. I don't recognize any of the patrons, but that doesn't necessarily mean they don't recognize me. "Brahm, this is my childhood friend, Callie. Callie, I'd like to introduce you to Lord Ambrose."

Her face goes slack. Apparently, she knew he was a Faerie, but she didn't realize *which* Faerie.

Brahm inclines his head toward her. "Pleased to make your acquaintance."

Visibly shaking herself out of her stupor, she drops into a curtsy. "Glad to meet you as well. Shall I seat you in the main room, or would you prefer something private?"

"Private, please," I say immediately. It's another reason I chose the teahouse.

"Of course."

As we follow Callie through the room, Brahm leans close and whispers, "Embarrassed to be seen with me, Alice?"

I turn to him, ready to defend myself, but I stop short when I see the unexpected humor shining in his eyes. Instead of answering, I nudge his shoulder, wordlessly telling him to behave.

We walk past a grizzled, older man roughly the size of a bear who's dining with a petite woman who I assume is his wife. He watches us, narrowing his eyes at Brahm with a fruit danish halfway to his mouth.

The next table holds three young women, all dressed for a day on the town. They, too, watch Brahm, but their eyes are hungry, and they look seconds from leaning their heads together and giggling like young girls.

Thankfully, I recognize no one.

"Here we are," Callie says as she escorts us into a small room with a large picture window that looks out on the bustling street. Gentle, lazy snow falls on people as they go about their business. They carry packages and parcels and hurry to and from waiting buggies and carriages.

I've been at Brahm's estate for almost a month now. In just a few more weeks, it will be Year's End. For the first time ever, I won't have any family to spend the holiday with.

Nor will I be home. I'll be in Rose Briar Woods, where it's eternally late spring, right on the cusp of summer. And I doubt the Fae celebrate human holidays anyway.

"You're thinking very hard about something," Brahm says as he surveys the menu Callie gave us before she left.

"I went ice skating with Gustin last year about this time." I watch the people as they pass by outside the window, feeling a painful tug at my heart. "Grandmother passed away that summer. It was the first holiday season we spent alone."

If I can't secure Gustin's freedom, it might be our *only* holiday.

Brahm sets the menu down, clasping his hands on top as he gives me his full attention.

"Afterward, we came here and had hot chocolate and the yule log Callie's mother makes. It's delicious." I turn to him, working up a smile. "It was a good day. One of the very few good memories I have with Gustin."

"I've heard of ice skating," Brahm says, "but I've never seen it."

"The pond in the middle of Danson Park is shallow, and it freezes over early in the year. About this time, they clear it and set up stands where you can rent blades that attach to your boots. Local businesses construct booths and sell spiced wine, squares of chocolate nut fudge, and candied apples."

A sob builds in my throat, taking me completely unaware. I choke it back, looking away.

"Are you all right?" Brahm asks gently.

"I'm sorry." I laugh as I blink furiously. "I don't know what's gotten into me."

He pulls a handkerchief from his pocket and offers it to me. "According to Regina, it's called homesickness."

I dab the cloth to my eyes. "I didn't realize what it would be like to come back and not feel as if I belong."

"This is your home, Alice. Of course you belong."

"I have nowhere to go, no one to even spend the holiday with."

"Alice." Brahm watches me carefully. "When a human barters with a Faerie—when he makes a bargain or a wager—magic binds the agreement. It becomes a vow that's very difficult to break. However, if you can think of any reason why Gustin's wager was unjust, *please tell me*. Let me give you back your home."

Brahm might as well pull the mask from his pocket and proclaim he's my bandit. Why is he being so transparent?

But I told him I would play along, and I will. Even if it's terribly frustrating.

With a sigh, I say, "Though Gustin was my father's heir, and he carries the title and the inheritance, I contributed to the estate with money I made from the portraits I painted over the last few years. The money my brother gambled did not solely belong to him, and I did not agree to the wager."

I give him a pointed look, asking him if he's happy. It's not like he doesn't already know. Why must we go through all these ridiculous steps?

A satisfied smile tugs at Brahm's lips. He looks down at the menu once more, furrowing his brow as he contemplates the options. "Do you have a record of payments you received? I'm assuming you deposited the funds into your family's account at one of the local banks."

Slowly, my stomach sinks. "I gave Gustin the money."

Brahm looks up sharply. "All of it?"

I flounder. "He's...he's my brother. I didn't believe we needed a *paper trail.*"

Brahm brings his fingers to his temples, groaning. "Alice."

"I was paid, though. You can ask anyone who sat for me."

"But you cannot prove you contributed to the estate."

"You don't believe me?" I ask, growing offended.

"Of course I believe you," he snaps, and then he draws in a breath, silently apologizing with an extended hand. "It will be enough. And for now, let's just enjoy the afternoon. What are you going to order?"

"Let's get an assortment of the tea sandwiches. I'm rather hungry." I pause. "And since it's the holidays, let's order peppermint tea."

"Is there a season for peppermint tea?" he asks, smiling to himself.

"It tastes better now. You'll just have to take my word for it."

Callie returns, and Brahm gives her our order.

"I'll be back shortly," she promises, giving me a look that says she's dying to ask me what I'm doing here with Lord Ambrose.

When she's gone, I set my hands in my lap. "You said you have business here today. Where are we going after we eat?"

"The auction house."

"Oh." My stomach flips, and I look down. Lacing my

fingers together, I say, "The auction is in a few days, isn't it?"

"I've decided to cancel it."

Slowly, I pull my eyes to his. "Why would you do that?"

He drums the tips of his fingers on the table. "It's possible the next owner would prefer to have the home furnished."

"Why are you doing this for me?" I whisper. "You had to settle with the bank when you learned about the lien on the property. You're going to lose a small fortune."

He leans forward. "It won't come for free."

I swallow, wishing I had tea for my suddenly dry mouth.

"I expect a very detailed portrait, miss artist."

My heart warms, and a tiny knot unfurls in my stomach. And as easy as that, this attraction I've felt since I first met the bandit in the woods—this fascination—blooms into affection. I like Brahm, both sides of him.

And I like him here, with me in Kellington.

Very much.

———

THE SKATERS TWIRL on the ice, some graceful and others fortunate to stay on their feet. Brahm snorts under his breath when a young man lets out an awkward squeal and falls on his tail-end.

We watch people through the carriage window, but I wish we could join them. My dress, however, is not warm enough for winter.

"Is it very sad living in eternal spring?" I ask Brahm, sitting back in the seat. "Do you ever wish you experienced all the seasons in Faerie?"

"I've never put much thought into it to be honest." He smiles, shaking his head before he sits back as well. "But I'm beginning to see its appeal."

I glance at the packages of supplies next to me in the seat. "You've already done so much for me, but I have a request."

"All right."

"Will you bring me into Kellington for the holiday? We can walk through the streets and look at the tree when they light it in the main square. I want to see it." I pause. "With you."

"Alice…" Brahm says, his face darkening with regret.

"It's my first year without family around me. I'd like to spend it with a friend. We are friends, aren't we, Brahm?"

Looking torn, he slowly nods. "We are."

"So, you'll do it?"

"I will."

I smile, looking down.

"I have a request as well. I would like you to complete the portrait by the last day of the month. I don't want you to begin the new year in Faerie."

"You're always so eager to get rid of me." Though I tease, my stomach gives an unpleasant tug.

"Will you try?" he urges.

"All right." I gather my courage. "Will you visit me after I go home?"

"I don't know if that's a good idea."

"Will you do it anyway?"

His dark eyes churn with emotion. "If I can."

Wrinkling my nose, I shake my head. "I don't like that answer. But I'll accept it."

Brahm glances out the window once more. "Are you ready to return?"

After I say I am, Brahm informs Wallen, and the carriage begins down the cobblestone roads, heading toward the river.

"Is the bridge in West Faerie? Or in Valsta?" I ask Brahm as the snow quickly fades. We cross the bridge and end up in spring once more.

He makes a thoughtful noise. "I don't believe it's in either. Perhaps you could say it's neutral territory."

"Strange."

When we arrive at the manor, Brahm excuses Wallen and helps me with my supplies himself. Gathering the packages in our arms, we head inside, laughing as we try to balance everything.

"Isn't this domestic?" a man says when we step into the foyer, startling me so badly I nearly drop my parcels.

Ian leans against the wall, focusing on us a little too intently.

"I see you're visiting again," Brahm says tonelessly.

"Your mother has sent your invitation to her monthly masquerade."

"I don't know why she bothers. It's not as if I'm unaware of the moon's cycles."

"Yes, well." Ian's eyes slide to me, and he smiles. "She's always so concerned about you—she likes it when I keep her informed of your affairs."

"How very motherly of her," Brahm says wryly, nodding me along.

"I see you haven't made the girl your pet yet, but... you're so very cozy, aren't you?"

Brahm's eyes flash.

"The offer still stands." Ian pushes himself off the wall and walks past me, pausing entirely too close to my shoulder. "I'd be happy to take her in. I'm quite good with pets—always careful to feed them regular meals, train them well." He smirks at me. "And keep them entertained."

Putting himself between the count and me, Brahm says, "Get off my property, Ian."

"You're always so sensitive, Your Highness," the man says with a low chuckle. "I'll send your regards to your mother."

I watch him until he steps out the door, shuddering once he's gone.

Suddenly sober, Brahm says, "Let's get these to your room."

"Is your mother going to be angry?" I ask quietly.

"I haven't done anything wrong," he says, his voice heavy. "Ian just likes to stir up trouble. But don't worry—he's gone now."

I try to put the confrontation behind me, but I'm uneasy long after we part for the evening.

13

BRAHM

"I thought you were a painter," I say as I stand near the light of a window in a seldomly used sitting room, already growing bored. It's the third time we've met this week. "Don't painters *paint?*"

Alice laughs as she sketches me. "There are steps, my lord. I like to thoroughly study my subjects before I begin."

A smirk tugs at my lips as a roguish retort comes to mind, but I decide to hold my tongue.

Though standing for the portrait is tedious, watching Alice is not. I'm not sure what I expected, but it wasn't this.

She's pulled up a large velvet armchair and planted herself in it, drawing her legs under her dress and resting her sketchpad in her lap. Her hair falls over her shoulders as she works, and she continually shoves it behind her ears. There are supplies scattered on the ground around her. She looks like a young girl pretending to be an artist.

Every few seconds, she looks up, studying me before she returns her attention to the charcoal in her fingers.

"When must you leave for your mother's masquerade?" she asks, frowning at her work.

"The day after tomorrow."

"And you'll be back the following day?"

"The next morning," I promise.

"Auvenridge must not be far from here."

"It only takes me a few hours on horseback, but it's double that by carriage," I say, dreading it more than usual. I'm positive Ian said something to Mother about Alice, and I'm not sure how much trouble I will have to manage.

Thankfully, he was not a loyal lapdog when he was young, and he never met Eleanor. He has no reason to believe Alice is anything more than a human girl I have business with—which is unusual, certainly, but not forbidden.

"How will you return so quickly?" Alice asks, setting the sketch aside.

Glad she's finished, I stretch my neck and cross the room to meet her. "I'll ride back as soon as the masquerade is over."

"At night?"

"I'm not human, Alice," I say lightly. "I have little to fear from the residents of Faerie."

She looks like she wants to argue, likely remembering the night I came to her covered in blood, but she keeps the thought to herself.

"Let me see," I say, nodding toward the sketchbook.

"They're just sketches," she says, handing it to me,

looking a little self-conscious. "They're rough, so don't expect a masterpiece."

I pause as I flip through the pages, studying a dozen images of myself. She's captured my expressions, sketched my frame from different angles. It's like looking into a mirror.

It's no wonder she found me out so quickly. Is it possible to hide one's identity from an artist?

"I'm afraid you're trying to flatter me with these," I say, a little uncomfortable as I return the sketchbook to her.

"Hardly. Of all my subjects, you are easily the most handsome."

The thought of her painting someone else feels too intimate. I don't like the idea of her studying another man this carefully, watching him closely enough to learn his secrets.

"Perhaps that is an exaggeration," I say.

"You're like a work of art—your eyes, your nose, your..."

She lets the words trail off, laughing to herself nervously.

"My what?" I ask, intrigued by the way her cheeks turn pink.

She shakes her head. "Look at the mess I made. I always spread out so much while I'm working."

I catch her waist—something I've never had the nerve to do without the mask.

Alice's eyes widen, and she goes still.

"My what?" I repeat quietly.

Her eyes drop to my lips, answering my question.

My pulse quickens, and time seems to still. I find myself leaning down, tempted. So tempted...

"Brahm!" Regina cries urgently, and the sitting room door flies open with her entrance. Fear is etched into her face, and it grows when Alice and I fly apart.

"What is it?" I demand, knowing my cousin is not easily ruffled.

"Your mother," she breathes before she turns to Alice, looking as if trying to find a place to hide her.

Cold panic rises in my chest. "What about her?"

"She's *here.*"

I stare at Regina for a full second, processing her words before I leap into action. "Hide Alice in my room. Is Sabine here as well?"

"She is," Regina says. "And Drake."

"Go to Alice's room and remove all of her belongings —Sabine will notice if anything is amiss, so be thorough."

"But your mother knows I'm staying here," Alice says, her eyes a little too wide. "Ian's surely told her."

"She doesn't need to know you're staying outside the servants' quarters."

Alice nervously fists her hands at her sides before she nods.

"Are they in the front sitting room?" I ask Regina.

"They are. I said you'd join them for tea."

"That's fine. Go now—take the back stairwell."

I leave, striding through the halls, ignoring the way my heart beats like a violent drum in my chest.

When I walk into the room, I find things to be as they always are. Sabine and Mother quietly bicker, and Drake stands near the window and stares at the courtyard beyond. Ian hovers behind my mother, resting his hand on the back of her chair. Perhaps he is vying for the honor of being her sixth husband. I, for one, would heartily support their marriage. It would be a tidy way to be rid of him.

A radiant smile spreads across Sabine's face when she spots me. "Brahm!"

Drake looks over, saying nothing.

I offer my sister a small smile, and then I turn my eyes on Mother. "What are you doing here?"

The queen of West Faerie arches a dark eyebrow. "Do I need an invitation to visit my son? Must I send a messenger ahead to ask permission to call on him?"

"I hope the visit is a brief one considering you haven't given my staff a chance to prepare rooms for you."

"We'll stay where we always do," Mother says. "I know how rarely you have guests, so what could the problem be?"

I stare at her, my magic revolting every time I try to come up with a retort that's laced with even the faintest lie.

"Good," she says triumphantly, her bright green eyes flashing. "I'm glad that's settled."

"Your masquerade is in two days," I say tonelessly. "It would be a shame to cancel it."

She laughs, sweeping off the chair, her full, bronze skirt flowing with her as she walks across the room to meet me. "I do not plan to cancel it."

"You traveled all this way to leave in the morning?" I ask.

She looks around the room, smiling to herself. "I

always forget how quaint your father's estate is. But it will do."

A sense of foreboding travels my spine. "It will do for what?"

"I intend to hold the ball here." She runs her finger over a side table, inspecting it for dust. Though there is none, she wrinkles her nose as if there was. "I've already informed my court."

"I have no suitable place in which to hold your masquerade," I say coldly. "There's no ballroom here—you know that."

Mother waves toward the window. "We'll hold it outside. Doesn't that sound lovely? It will be a garden party of sorts." Slowly, she turns her feline gaze on me. "Is that a problem?"

"Do what you will," I bite out.

She looks past me like she's searching for something. "I must say, I'm quite disappointed. Ian says you have a new pet. I was so hoping you'd introduce us, and yet she seems to be absent."

"Strange," Ian says lazily. "They seemed so close when I was here a few days ago."

"I can only assume you're referring to the visiting artist, who is here to paint my portrait," I say, ignoring the count. "She is nothing more and nothing less."

Mother acts surprised. "You commissioned a portrait for yourself? I never realized my son is so vain."

I could point out that she has no less than ten portraits of herself hanging in the castle, plus a statue in the garden, but it would play right into her hand. She wants to keep me talking, hoping I will eventually slip.

"Where is she now?" Mother asks when I don't respond.

I begin to tell her that I don't know where Alice is, but my magic practically strangles me—because I do know. She's in my quarters.

"Why should I concern myself with the whereabouts of a human girl?" I say instead, giving her a look of disdain.

"Indeed," Mother says smugly. "Well, nevertheless, I expect her to attend the masquerade tomorrow." She turns to Ian. "It will be such a treat for a human girl, don't you think?"

"A great treat," he agrees.

"Alas, she will not be joining us," I say.

Alice can't attend a Fae gathering—not when she's untethered. Who knows who might stake a claim before the night is over?

"She wishes to spend the holiday week in Kellington," I continue, grateful when my magic lets me speak the words. It must be true.

"How quaint. But surely she can cancel her plans?" Mother asks. "It's not every day a human girl gets to attend a Faerie masquerade."

"We will see."

Mother narrows her eyes. "At the very least, fetch her for tea now. I want to meet her."

A ball of lead forms in my stomach, and I give her a respectful nod before I turn from the room. I rack my brain, searching for plausible excuses without having to lie.

When I open the door, I find Regina.

"Mother wants Alice to join us for tea," I say heavily. "I don't know what to do."

"She's not here."

"Where is she?" I demand.

Regina sets her jaw and shakes her head. "I can't tell you, not right now."

"What do you mean—" The air rushes from my lungs when I realize what she's done. "Thank you," I breathe. "Regina, you're brilliant."

"I know the way your mother works," she says icily, her eyes flashing with memory.

"Keep her safe," I say.

She wrings her hands at her waist. "What are you going to do?"

I open my mouth to answer, and then I shake my head. "I can't tell you."

"Oh." She nods quickly. "Of course. Hurry back—if you're gone too long, Aunt Marison will come looking for you."

Sick with relief, but still on edge because Alice is here somewhere, I hasten back to the sitting room.

Mother's eyes move to the empty space behind me when I enter. "Where is the girl?" she demands.

"I have no idea," I snap. "I do not intend to wander the estate searching for her. Are we going to have tea or not?"

Drake turns from the window, giving me a suspicious look. I ignore him, focusing on my sister instead. "Your dress is lovely, Sabine."

She preens, brushing her golden hair behind her shoulder. "Do you like it? It's a human creation—came all the way from Albright." Her eyes sparkle. "Mother detests it."

"Your fascination with the vermin is growing old," Mother says, once again turning her ire on my sister, where it usually rests.

When Mother isn't looking, Sabine flashes me a genuine smile, and I nod my thanks. No one is capable of distracting the queen like her own daughter.

14

ALICE

As Regina instructed, I sit in the fresh straw, trying to stay as still and quiet as possible in the closed stall. It's difficult when the hay makes my nose itch, and I've been holding back a sneeze for what feels like hours. It's uncomfortable sitting for so long, and no matter how I stretch my legs, I ache to stand up.

Regina didn't know how long I'd have to hide here. It could be all night for all I know. Will the Faerie beasts find me in the stable? Twilight is already darkening the building. The horses are quiet as they eat their nightly rations, with only an occasional knicker and the shifting of large bodies.

Surely there is some sort of protective charm warding the stable. How else would the horses stay safe at night? Or do the Faerie creatures only prey on stray humans?

I draw my legs to my chin, looping my arms underneath my knees and skirts as I wait.

A sound makes my ears prick. I go still, holding my breath, not daring to move a muscle.

There it is again—a soft thump against the ground, like a muffled footstep.

I break into a cold sweat, imagining all the things that might have found me. How many are in the queen's entourage? For all I know, the grounds could be prowling with Fae men who would be all too delighted to find a human girl cowering in the straw.

"Alice," a soft voice calls, so familiar I almost burst into tears. "Where are you?"

My response catches in my throat. What if it's a trick?

The owner of the voice pauses just beyond the stall door, directly above where I hide. "Alice?"

I need to say something—it's Brahm. I'm sure of it.

"Where did she go?" he mutters, sounding so much like himself I decide I have no choice but to take the risk.

"I'm here," I whisper, my voice barely audible.

The shuffling continues, and the stall door I'm leaning against suddenly opens, nearly sending me backward.

Brahm sighs, kneeling next to me in his full bandit garb. "Are you all right?"

Gulping, I nod.

"Come on," he says, taking my hand. "I need to get you out of here."

"Where are we going?" I ask.

"Across the bridge. It's the only place a queen of Faerie cannot touch you."

Holding tightly to Brahm's hand, I hurry through the grounds after him, staying in the shadows, hiding behind trees when he instructs it. We cut through the woods, avoiding the road. Things scamper around us, and golden eyes watch from the bracken.

A shrill squeal nearly paralyzes me, but Brahm urges me to keep moving.

"Not much longer," he promises. "We're close now."

It feels like it must be midnight before we arrive at the bridge. The nearly full moon crests the forest just as we reach it, sending its eerie glow across the landscape. Just beyond, Kellington flickers with merry firelight. I can just make out a candlelit Year's End tree in the window of a distant farmhouse.

For the first time since we fled, we must walk into the open. I tremble as Brahm assures me it will be all right, feeling as if there is no way my shaking legs will carry me across the bridge.

"We'll go together," he says, squeezing my hand.

"Do you think we were followed?" I ask.

"I don't believe so."

I take a deep breath, and then I nod. "Let's go."

Cautiously, we step onto the road. Nothing leaps at us; there is no sudden yell.

I feel like a deer in a hunter's range as we run across the bridge. Brahm blends into the night in his black clothing, but my gown is pale, and the moonlight practically glows on it.

The warm air turns cold when we're halfway across, and the bridge is suddenly slick with ice. I nearly fall as we run, but Brahm loops his arm around my waist to keep me upright.

As soon as we're across, he pulls me into the winter forest on the other side, holding me around the waist as we both gasp for breath.

The knee-high snowdrift is freezing against my legs, but I'm too preoccupied with our success to care.

I shiver against Brahm, and he rubs his hands up and down my arms. "It's too cold to linger. We need to keep going."

"To where?"

He pushes a wayward strand of hair behind my ear. "I'm taking you home."

My heart gives a leap, and my eyes sting.

We wade through the snow and return to the road, which is thankfully easier to travel. I'm shivering by the time we make it to my parents' estate, desperately grateful it's not far from the border.

We pass through the gates and walk by the fountain, past the formal gardens and the dormant rosebushes. I pause in the courtyard, hugging myself as I stare at the dark manor.

"I've never seen it so…"

Empty.

Brahm produces a key, and we step inside the foyer.

The smell of lemon oil hits me like a tidal wave, bringing back too many memories. Even the sound of the door closing behind us is familiar.

But this darkness…is different. It's new and sad and so lonely it makes the hair on the back of my neck stand on end.

"There used to be a lamp on the entry table," I tell Brahm, fumbling in the dark. "I'm not sure if they left it."

Suddenly, there is light. I turn, so startled, I let out a small yip.

Though he looks like the bandit, and has pretended to

be human up to this point, a small ball of golden fire burns in Brahm's gloved hand, casting bright light in the room. I stare at the magic for several moments, and then I turn away, relieved to see that the lamp and the table it sits upon have been left.

Avoiding my eyes, Brahm lights the wick just as easily as he lit the air. He then turns toward me, lamp in hand, and the silence becomes heavy.

"There's a fireplace in the parlor," I say. "Can you light a fire in there as well?"

Appearing relieved I don't mention the magic, he follows me through the halls and up the stairs. I shiver as we walk into the room, beginning to feel as if I'll never be warm again. My toes are numb, and the tips of my fingers sting like I burned them.

A small stack of firewood remains in the log rack near the hearth.

As Brahm arranges wood in the fireplace, I look around the room. It's been stripped bare. The furniture hasn't been returned from the auction house, and only a few odds and ends remain. The settee, all the chairs, the piano, the end tables, and Mother's secretary desk, which Father gave her when they were married, are all gone.

Thankfully, the window seat remains since it's built into the house and impossible to remove. Hopefully, the men Brahm hired to move the furniture didn't think to check the cubby underneath. I open the padded lid, relieved to find the quilts within.

I pull out several heavy ones, each made by my grandmother in this very room during the long hours of winter. I wrap one around my shoulders and place another on the floor in front of the fireplace like a picnic blanket. Shivering so much my teeth feel like they're chattering, I sit down, huddling under my blanket, and wait for Brahm to finish.

He stands once the flames take and then walks to the window, closing the drapes to block out the chill coming in through the glass.

"Better?" he asks when he's finished, setting the lamp on the floor near the blanket.

I see my bandit in full light for the first time, and it almost makes me smile. I'm not sure how I ever questioned his identity.

Nodding, I turn toward the door. "It's so quiet."

"Wallen hired people to maintain the property, but I don't believe there's anyone who stays the night."

I try to smile. "I suppose we'll find out soon."

He laughs under his breath, taking off his hat and shoving a hand through his thick hair.

"We had a full staff when I lived here," I say absently. "Even when Gustin stayed out all night, I was never alone."

After a moment, Brahm sits next to me on the floor. He looks as if he doesn't know what to say.

"What time do you think they'll arrive in the morning?" I ask. "When do I need to leave so they won't find me?"

"Tomorrow is the beginning of the holiday week," he says. "I believe Wallen gave the caretakers the time off."

A sad thought strikes me. Slowly, I turn to look into the corner.

"What is it?" he asks.

"That's where the tree goes," I whisper. "It's been there every year for as long as I can remember. When I was a child, I thought it was the prettiest thing, all lit with candles. I'd make hard ginger cookies with the cook, and we'd string them from the boughs. Grandmother played the piano in the evenings until arthritis in her fingers made it impossible. After that, I took over."

"You play?" he asks, following my gaze to the empty corner where the piano used to sit.

I rub my hands together. "I do. But even if the piano were still here, my fingers would be too cold to play for you."

Brahm scoots closer. He removes his gloves and then takes my hands. He clasps them between his larger ones and brings them to his mouth. He blows hot air that must be laced with magic because it feels like I just slipped into a warm bath. Every inch of me goes warm, and I lean forward, blissfully content.

"If you can do that, why didn't you do it earlier?" I laugh.

When I look up, I realize our faces are only inches apart. Brahm still has my hands, and his thumb rubs over my skin.

"I'm glad you're safe," he says, his voice deep with emotion. "I'm truly sorry."

"What will happen when you go back?"

"I don't know," he says honestly.

I tighten my hands over his. "Then stay here. Don't return."

His gaze moves over my face, and he drops his voice. "You have no idea how tempted I am by that offer."

He lowers my hands, setting me free...but he doesn't shift away. He gives me the choice to stay close or move back. Slowly, he lifts his hand to my face, caressing my cheek before he slides his fingers under my hair to cup the back of my neck.

My heart leaps, and fear mingles with desire.

Brahm gives me several seconds to protest our nearness. When I don't, he touches his lips to mine.

It's a feather-soft kiss, so gentle I feel as if I might cry. I lean into him as he kisses me again, placing my hands on his shoulders, drowning in sensation.

His mouth is warm and tender, the kiss sweet and telling. It's not about passion—it's a wordless confession.

I care for you.

It's like sunrise chasing away night, leaving me standing in the light of warm morning. Even when it's over, I bask in its glow.

Brahm leans in once more to finish with a last, brief kiss.

We then study each other, chests rising and falling in tandem, marveling in the quiet newness. I feel like a butterfly, emerging into the world on new wings.

I raise my hand to the edge of his silken mask. "May I?"

"Say my name," he says hoarsely, his fingers gently moving against the back of my neck.

"Brahm," I whisper. "Lord Ambrose. Marquis of Rose Briar Woods. Fae prince of West Faerie. My friend, and the man who has stolen my heart—just as he warned he would when we first met."

I hold my breath as he loops a thumb under the edge

of the mask and pulls it from his face, stripping himself bare.

Brahm stares back at me with his familiar, dark brown eyes, the two most important men in my life merging into one.

"Your ears." Choked up, I reach for them and run my fingers over the subtle points. "And the wound on your neck. How?"

"Magic."

I kiss him even as I cry, so grateful he decided to share his secret with me. He holds me close, pulling me into an embrace and smoothing his hands over my hair.

"Why did you create the Highwayman?" I ask, wrapping my arms around his middle.

Brahm returns my embrace like he's afraid someone will steal me away. "Behind the mask, I can do things I otherwise cannot. Protect those I cannot protect."

"But *why*? Why do you care about humans?"

Except for the rapid beating of his heart, he's perfectly still. He adjusts his hold on me, clutching me even closer. "Because a young human girl came into my family many years ago."

"The girl you mentioned before?" I whisper.

Slowly, he pulls away, shaking his head when I try to tug him back.

Brushing his knuckle over my cheek, he says quietly, "I need to tell you about her. We called her Alice, but you knew her as *Eleanor*."

15

ALICE

I listen to Brahm's story in complete silence. Maybe it's due to the evening's events, but I feel numb.

Or maybe incredulous.

Yes, we believed Eleanor wandered into Faerie, or thought perhaps she'd been kidnapped by the Fae and stolen across the boundary, but it seems the chance of her ending up with Brahm's family is too unlikely. West Faerie is a large territory.

"I don't understand," I say when he finishes. "If Eleanor is dead, why did you think I might be her?"

"No one knows for certain what happened to her. Mother decided to execute her, but she disappeared. Later that day, Mother learned my brother stole her out of Auvenridge. Her guards apprehended Drake near the eastern border, but they never found Eleanor. Since there is no way a human child could survive in Faerie alone, it's always been assumed she died."

Brahm watches me, looking as if he's waiting for me to lose my composure. But I don't know how I feel. I don't remember Eleanor well. Over time, her existence was reduced to a name. She was the reason my parents were so often gone, the reason they died. I was five when she disappeared, not old enough to understand their anguish. I just knew they were rarely home. When I was older, it felt as if they were chasing a ghost. She didn't seem real.

But one thing was certain in my young mind—they must have loved her the most. Why else would they abandon us for all those years?

Now that I'm older, I understand. But the shadow of my young resentment remains.

"How do you know this girl was Eleanor?" I ask. "You were young as well—your memory must not be much better than mine."

"Eleanor didn't leave us until she was eight. Drake was ten, and I was fourteen. Though I've spent the last ten years trying to forget, I remember her."

I frown as an uncomfortable thought hits me. If Brahm is right, and this girl was my sister, he spent more time with her than I did—more than my parents, who feverishly searched for her.

"You said your family loved her—that she was far more than a pet. What happened to make your mother hate her to the point of wanting her dead?"

"Mother loved Eleanor as much as she is capable of loving anything, which is very little. When my father announced he wanted to give her his name and make her a true part of the family, Mother decided we were too attached and that Eleanor needed to go."

"What did she do to your brother when she found out he tried to help Eleanor escape?"

Brahm doesn't answer right away, but his face contorts with emotion. After a long few seconds, he says, "She executed our father."

I gasp, unable to even imagine it. "To punish your brother, she killed your father?"

His face hardens. "She said it was Father's fault her child betrayed her, that he put the ridiculous notion that humans could be our equals into Drake's head. She declared it was treason and that he planned it to undermine her authority." His eyes flash with memory. "As punishment for his crime, she made Drake watch."

I stare at him, horrified, unable to imagine what kind of monster this woman must be.

"He was the first in her endless string of executions. The next was her younger sister, Regina's mother, who told her she'd gone mad. That was only a day later.

"It's gotten to the point that anyone who so much as looks at her the wrong way is accused of treason and murdered. West Faerie is awash in blood, and there's no one who will dare put a stop to it."

"That's why you donned the mask—to save those you can, just as your brother did."

"I wear the mask because I'm too gutless to confront my mother," Brahm says bitterly. "I have too many I care about—Regina and Wallen, Drake and Sabine. I cannot imagine what she might do to them if I were to openly oppose her."

Softly, I ask, "How did Drake and Eleanor escape?"

"Eleanor was only tethered until Mother decided to end the agreement."

"Tethered?"

"It's part of the illanté bargain. Eleanor couldn't go much further than the castle grounds. The boundary was a garden where she and Drake used to play."

"Are all tethers a certain length?"

"No, it depends on how far the owner will let their illanté travel. Once a human is tethered, they are moderately safe to go about Faerie. Many become messengers and stewards, attending to their Fae's business."

"What keeps them safe?"

"It's forbidden to lay your hands on someone's illanté, and the binding magic protects them."

I wrinkle my brow. "Why didn't you make me an illanté as soon as I came to you? Wouldn't that have been safer?"

Brahm's expression darkens. "The illanté agreement is binding for life—the human's life. The only way I could release you would be to decide I wanted to kill you. Drake used the small window after Mother made her decision to steal Eleanor away—he found a loophole in the magic. But I could never release you, Alice. I'd never wish for your death. If I had given you my protection and made you my illanté, you could never have returned home. That's why it was so dangerous for you to come into Faerie. That's why I tried so hard to dissuade you from staying."

I store away everything he tells me, saving it to mull over later.

"I need to go," Brahm says reluctantly, pulling his hand from mine. "Will you be all right?"

Though the thought of staying in the empty house isn't pleasant, I'm glad to be somewhere familiar.

"It's better than sleeping in your stable," I point out.

A frown darkens Brahm's face.

"When will you return?" I ask as we rise.

"Not until my mother goes back to Auvenridge. After that, I'll have Regina pack your things, and I'll bring them to you."

I grasp his arm. "My things? But I haven't even started the portrait."

Brahm's forehead creases with confusion. "You can't come back into Faerie. Surely you understand the danger now."

"But...you're in Faerie," I say softly.

He slides his fingers into my hair, gently stroking my cheek with his thumb. "It's late. Now is not the time to discuss this. You need to get some sleep."

I grasp his wrist, keeping him from stepping away. "Promise me I'll see you again."

"This would be a poor final goodbye."

"That's not a promise."

Brahm's expression softens. "I will do everything in my power to return soon."

"Everything in your power?" I demand.

I think of his mother and her reputation for murdering subjects who disobey her.

"Are you in danger?"

"I'm always in danger," he answers. "I've lived the last five years of my life defying my queen's wishes."

"Brahm."

"Every minute I linger here, my chance of detection increases," he reminds me. "I need to go."

I unhand him immediately, nodding even as my breathing becomes stilted and panicky. "Be careful," I say softly.

I carry the lamp as we walk to the door, trying to ignore the jumping shadows it creates on the walls.

When we reach the entry, I resist the urge to cling to Brahm and beg him to stay. Instead, I stand on my tiptoes and press a light kiss to his cheek. Softly, I say, "For protection and luck."

He takes my hand, holding it like he, too, is reluctant to part. I think he's going to kiss me again, but he merely copies the gesture, brushing his lips over my cheek, very near the crease of my mouth. "Promise you won't go back into Faerie?"

"As long as you return for Year's End, I won't come looking for you."

"Alice," he says urgently, "If something were to happen to me, you'd be vulnerable. For my sanity, I need to know that you'll heed my warning this time."

Even though I hate it, the worry in his eyes bothers me too much to refuse.

"I won't go into Faerie without you," I say. "But don't forget your promise to return."

Brahm nods solemnly, and then he unwraps my fingers from his. We stand near the doorway, studying each other for several seconds before he steps into the night, leaving me utterly alone in this big, silent house that suddenly feels like a stranger.

16

BRAHM

A knock sounds at my outer chamber door only minutes after I return. Ignoring it, I quickly undress, kicking off my boots. I then stash the clothing in a dark corner of my armoire.

The knock sounds again, this time with an air of impatience.

Relaxing when I recognize that particular brand of irritation, I take my time dressing. When I swing open the door, I grin at Sabine. "I see you're as impatient as ever."

My sister stands in the hall, tapping her fingers on her crossed arms. "Took you long enough," she says, pushing past me.

"Please, come in," I tease, closing the door behind us.

"Of all nights, why did you decide to go out as the Highwayman *tonight?*" she demands. "What if you'd been caught?"

"Does it look like I was out?" I say, motioning to my nighttime attire.

Sabine points a finger at me and narrows her eyes.

"Don't try that with me—I saw you slinking across the yard. What if Mother had caught you?"

"And that's why you get the room on this side of the manor when you visit."

She huffs out a breath, shaking her head. "What did you do with the girl?"

"What girl?"

"Brahm!"

I laugh to myself, enjoying riling my younger sister more than I should. One day, she'll inherit the crown and be my queen—but today is not that day.

"She's in Kellington."

"Mother is furious."

"I'm not sure what I've done wrong."

"You know how she feels about humans, and now you've let an untethered girl into your household."

"I don't remember that being strictly forbidden. Though it's certainly a risk for them, every once in a while, untethered humans stay in Faerie for an extended time on business. What's the name of that group of humans you're so taken with?" I pause, trying to remember. "The traveling theater troupe?"

"That's different," Sabine argues. "They came as a goodwill gesture to celebrate my sixteenth birthday—as honored guests."

"And Alice came to paint my portrait to try to win my favor so I'd release her brother."

Sabine's expression sharpens. "What's her name?"

I realize my misstep, and I press my mouth into a thin line, assessing her.

Sabine and Eleanor were never great friends. The

164

truth is, Sabine was jealous of the attention Eleanor received, though she'd never admit it. We haven't talked about it, but I believe she still resents the girl for what Mother did to Father, though that was in no way Eleanor's fault.

"It's not her," I say simply.

"Well, of course it's not," Sabine replies. "That Alice is dead."

I narrow my eyes. "Must you be so callous? What if Drake had heard you?"

"Do you see him?" she asks bluntly, spreading her arms wide. "And it's been over ten years, Brahm. She was just a human."

"Sabine."

She raises her hand. "I don't want one of your lectures. I know how you feel about them, and I've never given you any trouble over it. I've protected your secret, and I always will. But don't expect my heart to bleed for them the way yours does."

"I don't understand you." I sit in a chair, waving for her to take a seat as well. "You, more than anyone, are fascinated with human culture, and yet you have no compassion."

"Compassion is overrated." She softens her words with a smile. "Humans are interesting, yes. But they're still just humans. Whoever this girl is, she's certainly not worth dying for."

"I don't think I've ever met someone as apathetic as you, Sabine. You are not cruel, and yet you will so quickly turn a blind eye if it suits you."

Her expression hardens, and she leans forward,

clasping the arms of her chair. "I will always—*always*—choose you first. You're simply going to have to live with that. If it comes down to it, I will gladly let Mother take out her madness on this girl as long as she doesn't direct it at *you.*"

I sit back with a sigh. It's hard to argue with that sort of loyalty, disturbing though it might be. But that's why Sabine is dangerous—that's why I don't trust her quite as much as I would like.

"Alice isn't coming back to Faerie," I finally say. "Let's put this behind us."

Suddenly, Sabine's brave mask slips, and she looks shaken with relief. "You swear?"

"I will do everything in my power to keep her out."

"And you won't go into the woods again while Mother is visiting?"

I hesitate before I agree. "I won't—but you must promise to get her back to Auvenridge as quickly as possible. I'll go out of my mind if she stays for long."

She nods quickly. "I will, I swear."

I study my sister, and familiar guilt nips at my conscience. "How are you faring?"

"Oh, you know." Sabine lets out a long sigh. "It's the same as always. I'm sure Mother will marry again soon, and I'll have a temporary break from her continual nagging."

My lips twist with morbid humor. "One, maybe two months."

Sabine grins. "One or two blissful months, and then I'll get to wear black again. You know how well it suits my complexion."

"How is Drake?"

She shrugs, suddenly avoiding my eyes. "Who knows? He walks through his days like a wraith."

As if killing our father wasn't punishment enough, Mother commanded that all were forbidden to speak to Drake after the incident, lacing her decree with magic so it could not be disregarded.

Sabine and I rebelled when we three were alone, finding ways around the magic as much as possible. But even with that, the punishment was too much for his young mind. In just a few years, he withdrew into himself, shutting others out entirely. He now haunts the family like a ghost—always there, but always silent.

"Do you remember the rose garden you planted for him and Alice all those years ago?" Sabine asks. "Behind the hedge, where they liked to play?"

"Yes," I say, startled she said the name. She usually avoids it.

"Mother discovered it recently." Sabine studies the skirt of her gown, running her hand over the silken material. "She withered the roses, and then she burned the entire garden."

A lump forms in my throat.

Sabine's eyes become misty. "Drake watched it smolder, and then he walked away."

"He knew she'd find it eventually," I say. "Why else would he bring cuttings with him every time you visited?"

"How many are in your greenhouse now?" she asks.

"Several hundred."

"It's a strange obsession."

"What else does he have?" I ask gently.

She shakes her head, threading her fingers together.

"I'm sorry," I say quietly.

Sabine glances up, looking unusually vulnerable. "What for?"

"You are the bravest out of us—I ran away. Drake withdrew. You've stood strong, dealing with Mother practically singlehandedly."

We both fall silent for several seconds as distant memories come too close.

Though Sabine seems callous, she's had to grow a thick skin. The fact that she can care about anything at this point is a miracle.

"I'm glad you took Regina away all those years ago," she says quietly. "I've never blamed you for leaving. What Mother did..." She blinks quickly, looking away. "Don't give her a reason to hurt you, too, Brahm. I would never forgive you."

Slowly, I nod.

Standing abruptly, Sabine dabs at her eyes and then gives me a smile. "It's late, and you look like death. I'll let you get some sleep."

I walk her to her door in the hall, making sure she gets in all right, and then I wander, knowing I have too much on my mind to find sleep just yet.

No conscious decision leads me to the conservatory, but that's where I end up. Now that the sun has set, the room is cool and damp. No lamps glow from within, but the almost full moon shines through the glass wall, making it easy to spot the dark shadow near the pond.

I walk down the path, wrestling with the magic that

tries to bind my mouth. It's as strong now as it was ten years ago.

It's easier when Sabine is with us—she and I can talk to Drake through each other, including information we want him to hear. But when I'm alone with my brother, it's impossible, even when I try to reason with the magic that I'm just talking to myself.

With a sigh, I give up and clasp my brother's shoulder. He turns to me, nodding once before he looks back at the roses.

It's frustrating that he could talk if he chose—he could tell me what's bothering him, and I could listen.

But he won't. Perhaps it's too hard to have a conversation with someone who can never answer.

It's a miserable existence.

Maybe if he'd left Faerie and gone to a human kingdom, he could have had a normal life. They aren't bound to obey like we are. But Mother tethered him like an illanté.

Feeling as if I'm intruding, with no way to speak what's on my mind, I bow my head and then turn toward the door. Drake doesn't try to stop me. He simply stands in the moonlight, living a wraith's life, just as Sabine said.

17

ALICE

The night is one of the worst I've spent in the house. It feels like my parents and grandmother died all over again. The quilt does little to soften the hard wooden floors, and the manor makes all kinds of noises that seem louder when you're alone.

Even though I got up several times in the night to add wood to the fire, when I wake in the morning, the coals are gray, and the room is frigid.

I sit up, wrapping the quilt around me, and draw my knees to my chin as I stare at the cold hearth.

It's only a week until Year's End. When I set off into the Rose Briar Woods, I imagined Gustin would be free long before now. I also didn't think I'd be spending the holiday in this house.

Though it's cold and lonely, the morning light chases away some of the sadness. I'm home—a place I never imagined I'd set foot in again. It's empty, but it's comforting all the same.

A knock sounds at the front door, echoing through the estate. I jump, and my pulse races at the thought of someone catching me and believing I don't belong here.

Immediately, I imagine the humiliation of being dragged onto the snowy streets, maybe even taken to the constable and accused of squatting.

I push myself to my feet and peek past the curtains.

Several wagons are parked out front, each pulled by a pair of chestnut draft horses. Their loads are covered with canvas tarps, and several men mill around, looking toward the entry as if waiting.

What could they be here for?

The man at the door finally steps into view, and my fear subsides.

Running my hand over my unruly hair, knowing I must look frightful, I work the heavy locks and crack the door open.

"Wallen?" I ask, still wrapped in the heavy quilt.

The Fae man turns, bowing when he sees me, not looking the slightest bit surprised to find me here. "Good morning, Miss Gravely. We've just been to the auction house. Lord Ambrose has asked me to oversee the furniture's delivery."

My eyes move to the wagons, and my heart leaps when I realize what's under those heavy covers.

"Come in," I say quickly, throwing the door open. "Forgive my appearance, I…"

Unsure how to finish the sentence, since I can't admit I ran away from the queen of West Faerie last night, I let the words trail off.

As I watch the men carry settees, sideboards, chairs, tables, and more into the house, a public coach pulls into the circular drive.

A man and woman exit, both bundled in heavy cloaks. The man is tall, with a somber look about him. He speaks with the coachman, presumably about the trunks on the luggage rack.

The woman has soft, rounded features, with bright pink cheeks and graying hair that used to be a fiery orange shade of red. When she spots me, she lets out a muffled cry and runs across the snowy entry. The baskets and bundles she carries swing and bobble as she trots, and I laugh even as hot tears stream down my chilled cheeks.

"Mrs. Fletcher!" I cry, clutching the quilt as I meet her.

"Alice!" She pulls me into a tight embrace, accidentally cuffing me in the head with one of her packages. "Where have you been? You vanished. No one knew where you were or when you were going to return—if you were going to return at all. We were all terrified the Fae—"

She cuts off abruptly, sending a suspicious look in Wallen's direction.

He speaks with one of the auction house men in front of a wagon. I'm not sure whether he heard Mrs. Fletcher or not, but either way, he doesn't seem to be paying attention.

She drops her voice to a whisper. "We were afraid they'd kidnapped you, that perhaps Gustin somehow roped you into servitude."

"I was in Faerie, but I went freely." When my family's

housekeeper's eyes widen with horror, I quickly assure her, "I'm all right. And I'm so glad to see you, but what are you and Mr. Fletcher doing here?"

"We received a message from a courier a few days ago, asking us to return to our posts. I'm not sure how Lord Ambrose found us. We'd been staying with my sister in Foxglen, but then Shirley asked us to spend the holiday with her family, so we traveled to Farhaven."

"How is your daughter?"

Mrs. Fletcher beams. "Oh, she's just fine. Had another baby boy last spring, you know—he's going to be a wild one, he is. I can already tell."

"You didn't have to rush back before Year's End," I say, realizing how close we are to the holiday. "You and Mr. Fletcher always spend the week with Shirley and her husband."

Mrs. Fletcher waves her hand. "Nonsense. I needed to come back and make sure the news was true. Imagine you returning to the house, Miss Alice. You must have worked some magic to make that come to pass."

She gives me a pointed look, silently informing me we will be having a long chat later.

"I'll tell you everything," I promise, shivering when a cool gust of wind blows snow in our direction. "But let's go inside first."

Mrs. Fletcher frowns as if finally taking a good look at me. "Good heavens, you must be freezing! Inside with you. Go along."

She lets out a small gasp when she sees the accumulating pile of furniture in the entry.

"I'm surprised he didn't try to sell the drapes," she mutters under her breath, her eyes narrowing to slits. "Nasty wretch of a—"

"Lord Ambrose let me return to the house," I point out gently. "And he gave me room and board this last month, asking for nothing in return."

"Why did you go to him?" she asks, looking like I've ripped out her heart. "Mr. Fletcher and I talked—we were going to take you with us. I would have had you married by now, but you disappeared."

"I'm sorry for worrying you," I say with a catch in my throat, not realizing how much she cared. It eases some of the sadness that's nestled itself in my heart, the one that's buried so deeply, I don't even realize it's there most of the time.

Mrs. Fletcher's eyes soften, and she scrunches her face. "Now don't you go and start crying again, or I'll start too, and the men will come in and find a blubbering mess, and everyone will be uncomfortable."

I suppress a laugh, nodding toward her parcels. "I don't suppose you have food in one of those?"

Her mouth falls open. "How long have you been here alone, *starving to death?*"

"Just a night."

She bustles toward the kitchen, muttering about wretched Fae men. When we walk through the swinging doors, we both stop short.

The kitchen has been stripped clean.

"Oh," she says with a soft exhale. "Have you ever seen a more depressing sight?"

"They're bringing everything back," I try to say brightly, but the truth is she's right. The kitchen was once the liveliest room in the house.

Mrs. Yaley always kept hard candies in a cut-glass jar on the counter, different types for different seasons. There would be peppermints now, each wrapped in tiny squares of white paper and twisted at the ends.

There was always bread in the oven, and I can't remember a time when there wasn't a cake under a dome on the glass stand.

But mostly, I miss Mrs. Yaley.

"I don't think Nancy is going to come back," Mrs. Fletcher says as if reading my mind. "She found a little cottage near her son by the coast. The weather is more temperate there—you know how she complained about the cold."

I try to smile. "I'm glad she found somewhere nice."

"I'm not a terrible cook." Mrs. Fletcher gives my arm a nudge. "We'll make do until after the holidays, and then we'll find someone proper."

I smile. "You should probably speak to Lord Ambrose before you begin making too many plans. The house is his property, even though he's been kind enough to let me return."

She gives me a sideways look. "I'm not sure I care for the way you say that man's name."

Laughing softly, I motion again to her packages. "Am I going to have to snoop through them myself?"

Making a tsking noise, she sets her things on the workbench and produces half a dozen scones. "I bought them at a bakery in Bailen. I remember pumpkin has always been your favorite."

I gratefully accept one and breathe in the aroma, savoring it slowly. "You have no idea how lovely it is to eat without worrying if the food is laced with Faerie magic."

Mrs. Fletcher's approving smile becomes a scowl. "What were you doing in West Faerie, Alice?"

I pick at tiny pieces of the scone, eating it slowly. "I had hoped to bargain for Gustin's freedom—a portrait in exchange for his release."

"I don't see your good-for-nothing brother, so I assume you were not successful."

"I was attacked by goblins on the way to Lord Ambrose's estate. They destroyed my painting supplies, so when I arrived at the marquis's house, I was destitute, without a way to even earn my keep.

"Lord Ambrose agreed to take me in and let me work to buy new supplies. He never said he'd free my brother, but we had an arrangement of sorts."

"What kind of arrangement?" she asks darkly.

Laughing, I wave away her concern. "Not the kind you're worried about. It was all very right and proper."

"I still don't like it." Then her face softens. "But I'm glad you're home."

"He's been nothing but kind to me," I assure her. "Wallen and the housekeeper as well."

"And the rest of his staff?"

I wrinkle my nose. "Let's not talk about them."

Mrs. Fletcher laughs, shaking her head as if it's all too

ridiculous to contemplate, and then she nudges the scones my way. "Go on, have another. It sounds like you've been starving this whole time. You can tell me more as you eat."

I don't mention the loophole Brahm discovered in Gustin's wager, or that my heart has gotten far more involved than is safe. I don't tell her about the queen, or the fact Lord Ambrose is actually the eldest prince of West Faerie. But even with omitting all that, Mrs. Fletcher's scowl becomes darker as I continue my story.

Deciding it's best to change the subject, I direct the conversation back to her grandchildren, where it stays until Wallen clears his throat in the doorway.

"The wagons are unloaded, Miss Gravely," Brahm's valet says solemnly, his expression cooler than it was when he drove Brahm and me into Kellington. Perhaps he's uncomfortable on this side of the bridge. "We'll return shortly with another load. The transfer will take the better part of the day. I hope you don't mind."

"Of course not," I say quickly. "I'm so grateful."

With a grim smile and a nod, he leaves the room.

Mrs. Fletcher produces a rag from her bundles, and she begins bustling about the kitchen, dusting the workbenches as if desperate for something to do. "So, tell me, when will I meet this Lord Ambrose? Surely he'll want to introduce himself to his staff."

"I'm not sure." I grow worried as I think about Brahm returning home last night. "It might not be until after Year's End."

I look out the window, toward the back of the estate.

In the distance, past fields and small groves of dormant trees, the thick, tall conifers of Rose Briar Woods rise toward the gray sky.

Never has the river that separates our world and theirs felt so vast.

ALICE

I wake on the morning of Year's End with Brahm's promise heavy on my mind. But I know he won't be able to spend the day with me if his mother is still staying with him.

I convinced Mrs. Fletcher to visit her husband's sister for the holiday, feeling guilty that she and Mr. Fletcher would be away from family out of pity for me. But now I'm not so sure about my goodwill gesture.

I wander the manor as the sleepy sun slowly creeps over the horizon, feeling a bit like an untethered ship floating wherever the waves take me.

Soon, the sun shines on the newly fallen snow, catching the tiny crystalline flakes and making them sparkle. A storm came through last night, leaving a thick blanket on the frozen ground.

The sound of harness bells catches my attention, and I stand by a front window and watch a sleigh pass on the distant street at the end of the lane. The merry sound cuts through the hushed silence, dredging up memories of holidays long past.

If the furniture hadn't been returned earlier in the week, the men would have to wait until all this melted. It could be days, or it could be weeks—it's impossible to know this time of year.

Despite the trouble he caused, I think of Gustin. Does he even know what day it is? What must it be like in a debtor's prison in Faerie?

Does he miss me at all?

I shake away the thoughts, knowing it will do me no good to dwell on them today.

Continuing my aimless tour of the house, I end up in the doorway of the upstairs sitting room. The furniture has been returned, including Grandmother's piano.

But there is still no tree in the corner. Mr. Fletcher said the cut trees in the main square had been picked over, and all that was left were scraggly, browning things that were only suitable for kindling.

Last year, Gustin and I took a wagon to a heavily wooded area in nearby Calsaund and cut our own, but I certainly didn't feel that ambitious on my own. Nor do I have a wagon at my disposal.

The room fills me with memories, most of them too painful to face alone, so I continue down the hall.

I end up in the kitchen, loitering near the heavy cast iron stove.

When Grandmother was alive, she always sent the staff home to be with their families for the holiday, and she'd bake yule cakes for breakfast, just as her mother taught her. It was a family recipe, passed down from generation to generation. I'm not terribly gifted when it comes to baking, or cooking for that matter, so I didn't attempt it last Year's End.

This year, however, I feel the need for family tradition. Maybe baking the festive tea cakes will make me feel as if I'm not so alone.

As I try to remember the recipe, I find Grandmother's old apron on a hook in the pantry, just where it belongs. It must have been overlooked in the initial sweep of the house, first ignored and then forgotten.

Seeing it there, hanging by itself, steals my breath.

Suddenly overwhelmed, I clutch it in my hands and sink to the wooden floor, crossing my legs under my skirts. I wrap the apron around my hand, trying to swallow back the emotion building in my chest.

I'm not sure how long I remain on the kitchen floor, and when the door opens, it scares me half to death.

"Alice?" a male voice calls from the entry.

"Brahm?" I stumble to my feet, nearly tripping over my skirts as I rise.

My breath catches when I find him in the doorway, looking every inch a prince of Faerie in a fine jacket and waistcoat. My eyes move to the festive sprig of holly pinned to his handkerchief pocket—a very human tradition.

My throat tightens.

"You're here." I blink quickly, chasing away tears that try to spill onto my cheeks.

Brahm crosses the room, concerned. "Why were you on the floor?" He gently tugs the apron from my hands. "And what's this?"

I give him an airy smile. "That? Oh, just an old apron."

Slowly, he meets my eyes and quirks a questioning eyebrow, seeing through my lie.

"My grandmother's apron," I admit, turning quickly. "Forgive me. I'm feeling emotional today."

Brahm steps up behind me. He carefully places the crumpled apron on the workbench and then sets his hands on my shoulders. "I have something to show you."

"Something?" I ask, dabbing away the lingering moister with my knuckle.

"A surprise."

I look over my shoulder, intrigued by his tone. "Is it safe for you to be here?"

"My mother left with my sister and brother this morning," he says. "And I believe I promised you we'd spend the day together. Did you forget?"

I shake my head.

"Good." He laces his fingers through mine and then leads me out of the kitchen.

"Where are we going?" I ask, my eyes focusing on our clasped hands. The connection chases away the last of my sadness.

Brahm is here, just as he promised.

We pause outside the sitting room, and he turns to me. The corners of his eyes crinkle as he smiles. "Cover your eyes."

"What?" I ask with a laugh, startled by this light side of him.

He steps close and lowers his voice. "It's a surprise."

Butterflies flutter in my stomach, and I slowly close my eyes, holding a hand over them to prove I cannot see.

Brahm guides me inside the room, holding onto my shoulders as he stands behind me.

"Okay," he says near my ear, the words tickling my skin. "Open."

Slowly, I flutter my eyes, unsure what to expect.

It's a tree, but it's not lit with candles. Hundreds of shifting, ethereal fairy lights twinkle from the boughs. Instead of glass balls, short red roses in tiny glass jars hang from the limbs. Their velvet petals sparkle as if dusted with powdered mica.

"It's...beautiful," I breathe, though the word feels insufficient. I've never seen anything like this in my life.

"Do you like it?" Brahm asks, unsure.

I turn to face him, laughing. "Of course I like it. It's amazing."

"I didn't have time to shop for...whatever the bobbles you put on these things are called."

"It's perfect," I insist.

"I've brought gifts, too," he says softly. "Regina bought you a cloak, and she packed the rest of your things. I have a few packages for you as well."

"You've done enough for me already." I look at the tree, overwhelmed by the sweet gesture. "And I have nothing for you."

Brahm shrugs, nodding toward the two packages by the side table near the tree. "One is a selfish gift, more for me than you anyway."

My curiosity piqued, I cross the room and pick up the larger of the two packages. "May I?"

"Not yet. Open the other first."

I set the package down and turn toward the small

tubular case that's bound in brown leather. I expect to find paintbrushes, or something of the like, but the gift holds a rolled piece of parchment.

It's yellowed with age, and the paper is thick. My heart beats too quickly as I slide the paper out. "Brahm."

"The house is now in your name," he says, standing with his hands behind his back. "It belongs to you."

A lump forms in my throat. "But all that money you paid the bank…"

"Was worth it."

I blink quickly, wondering if my heart can handle so many emotions in such a short time. Carefully, I slide the precious document into the case and then clutch it to my chest. "Words don't seem sufficient, but Brahm—I'm so grateful."

"Now you may open the other." He sits on the settee and motions for me to join him.

Carefully, I set the package on my lap and untie the cheery red satin ribbon. When I pull back the brown paper, it reveals a wooden box. It's wide and only a few inches tall, about the size of a large legal document.

"Open it," Brahm coaxes.

I smile at him, wondering what could be in such a flat package. When I pull away the lid, I find my reflection staring back at me.

Carefully, I pull out the rectangular mirror, running my finger over the silver edging. It's Fae crafted, intricate and rare. Brahm has included a stand as well. The highly polished hickory is shaped like two identical flourished Ls, and they're hinged on the long side. When opened, the stand will cradle the mirror, allowing it to rest on a table or vanity.

"It's beautiful," I say quietly.

"I want to commission you for a painting, and I hoped it would be useful."

Intrigued, I turn to him.

"Instead of painting me, I want you to paint a self-portrait." His smile flickers. "So I can remember you."

Immediately, I set the mirror back into the box. "Remember me?"

"You can't come back into Faerie, Alice," he says gently. "We already discussed this."

"But..." I shake my head, not liking the direction of the conversation. "I promised I wouldn't go back without you—not that I wouldn't return at all."

He reaches for my hand as he studies me. "Do this for me, and I will free your brother."

"That's not fair," I whisper. "You can't ask me to choose between him and you."

Brahm leans forward, speaking volumes with his dark brown eyes. He brushes my hair back, looking as if he's struggling as well. "I'm not asking you to choose, Alice. This isn't up for negotiation."

I pull away, setting the box aside as I stand. As I try to put my thoughts in order, I walk to the window. This can't be a goodbye, not today of all days.

Hugging myself, I stare at the snow, wondering how it could suddenly seem so much colder in here than it does out there.

Brahm steps up behind me. "I let this go too far—I

began to care for you in ways that aren't allowed. I cannot let myself love you, Alice. And I cannot let you love me."

In my reflection, a lone tear spills down my cheek. In all my recent daydreams, we were together. We somehow found a way to end his mother's tyrannical rule, and we were happy.

But that's all they were—dreams.

I knew in my heart that Brahm and I couldn't live that life. Who's ever heard of a Fae man marrying a human woman? It's absurd.

Slowly, I turn to look at him. "Then make me your illanté. I've lost too many people. I don't want to lose you as well. I'll live with you as an obligation if you let me, a friend only. And if I love you in silence, that's my choice —not yours."

"No." The word is a whisper, voiced like a caress. "I will not allow you to forfeit your future for me."

"Shouldn't I have the right to choose?"

"I want you to get married and have a family," he continues. "Spend holidays in this room with a real Year's End tree. Your past was so turbulent, Alice, and much of that has been my family's fault. I want you to have the best life possible. And that life isn't as my illanté, and it's certainly not in Faerie."

I stare at him. "So, this is it? Our last day then?"

Solemnly, he nods.

In a flat tone, wishing we could start the morning over and avoid the conversation, I ask, "How will I deliver the portrait to you?"

"Wallen will fetch it in a month, and then he will see to Gustin's release."

"Fine," I say, "I don't want to speak of it anymore. If our time is short, let's enjoy what we have left and put the rest out of mind."

Brahm's expression eases with relief. He takes both of my hands and nods. "It's my first Year's End. Let's celebrate it properly."

19

BRAHM

Every time I look at Alice, I remember the flash of fire in Sabine's eyes when she vowed to protect me at the cost of anyone and everyone. This must end—it shouldn't have started.

I should have sent Alice away in the very beginning, escorted her to the bridge and never looked back. She would have found someone to take her in—someone suitable, a man who could have given her a future.

It's difficult to believe we met only a little over a month ago. If I could turn back the hands of time... But, alas, that is not one of our gifts. No one needs that kind of power—we already possess too much.

Alice and I stand side by side, watching men climb wooden ladders to light the candles on the large tree they've brought into the square. There are hundreds of people around us, all bundled up in heavy cloaks, scarves, and hats, happily braving the cold for the sake of tradition.

We have traditions in Faerie as well, but they're different. They're based on revelry, and this is not. Year's End is about family, community, and honest, heartfelt thanksgiving.

Around me, the humans are grateful for the year they were given, and they rejoice in the possibilities of the next.

Nearby, a man lifts his young son onto his shoulders to give him a better view of the candle lighting. The boy laughs, and the mother looks at the pair with an expression that makes me wish, for the first time in my existence, that I was human.

I glance at Alice, feeling more conflicted than I've ever been. Could I walk away from my life in Faerie and stay? Could we live here, together, away from the wicked queen, away from the memories and the scars? Would Alice truly want me?

Immediately, I dismiss the idea. Though Alice is safe from my mother's manipulations and wrath here in human territory, I am not. I am a citizen of Faerie. It's my lineage and my life. I have a duty to it, to my family, and to the people I save each night in the woods.

Knowing we must part soon, hating that night has already stolen the day, I savor this last gift of time.

But too soon, the lighting is over. The crowds begin to part. Many people cast me curious looks as they return to their homes with their loved ones. They know what I am, and some may even recognize me as Lord Ambrose.

"What comes next?" I ask Alice, crossing my arms to keep from reaching for her in the crowd.

"There is nothing else," she says quietly.

We linger until the square is nearly empty. Soon, I imagine they'll begin to snuff out the candles—a sad thought. But it would be a fire hazard to leave them burning all night.

Wallen waits with the horses and the sleigh I asked him to purchase for Alice's use. The new coachman will take his post tomorrow, and the majority of the staff will arrive as well.

My valet has been strangely quiet the last few days, but we've all been on edge thanks to my mother's unexpected visit. Hopefully things will return to normal now that she's gone home.

"I'll meet you back at the Gravely estate," Wallen says as he hands me the reins and then mounts his waiting horse.

I offer my hand to Alice. She steps into the sleigh, and the hem of her new heavy white cloak brushes against the frame, sending snow falling to the ground. I slide next to her and pull the blanket over our laps.

"Are you warm enough?" I ask, my voice stiff.

She nods as she runs her hand over the thick woolen blanket.

At my silent command, the horses plod forward. The sleigh cuts through the snow, the bells chiming in the icy air. Clouds blanket the night sky, and before we arrive, snow begins to fall.

Alice interrupts the silence suddenly, making me think she's been holding her tongue the entire ride and finally found the courage to speak. Staring ahead, she says, "I stood next to you tonight, pretending we belonged together. Wishing you were the human bandit you pretended to be."

"Alice…"

"I decided it was cruel of you to make me believe you were someone you are not—someone I could care for. But I'm glad I got to know you outside the shadows. Just as glad as I am that I got to know you inside the shadows. I can't regret the time we spent together, both with you as the bandit and Lord Ambrose, even if I hate that you're pushing me away now."

An apology seems too weak, too trite, so I stay silent.

"I wanted to save you…somehow." She laughs a little. "You wouldn't believe the thoughts I've had in the last few days. Solitude isn't my friend."

"Save me?" I ask thickly as we glide to a stop in front of the manor.

"Right the wrongs, face your mother. Avenge my sister and parents, step forward when no one else will."

I turn to her sharply, hoping I misunderstood her though I know I didn't.

She rolls her eyes with a smile. "Desperate, grand thoughts."

A chill is on the breeze, and I glance around, on edge. We're away from Faerie, but it's never safe to utter those sorts of things aloud. "Let's go inside."

Wallen appears to take the reins, and we step into the foyer. Thanks to the fire in the hearth, it's warmer than when we left—a fire that shouldn't be burning.

I narrow my eyes at the flames. "I didn't light that."

"Mr. and Mrs. Fletcher said they would return late this evening," Alice says. "They must be back."

Uneasy, I take Alice's cloak.

"Alice," I begin carefully, feeling we must broach the subject she brought up outside. "You know you must never—"

"You've returned," a female voice says from the hallway, making us both swing around.

I shove Alice behind me, hoping to shield her from my mother even though it's an impossible task.

The queen of West Faerie notes our position, and she slowly raises a dark eyebrow. Her impartial gaze lands on me, and then it slides to Alice.

Recognition shocks her, and she takes a step back as if she's seen a ghost. And yet, she doesn't look altogether surprised. Livid, she turns to me. "Where did you find her?"

I'm about to tell her it's not Alice, but my magic stunts me. After all, she is Alice—just not our Alice.

"It's not *her*," I say instead. "That girl's name was Eleanor. This is her sister, *Alice*."

My mind races. How is Mother here? How did she know?

Anger kindles in my core when I realize it must have been Sabine. Foolishly, I trusted her with too much.

Narrowing her eyes, Mother studies Alice, likely taking note of her champagne blonde hair and sky-blue eyes. Behind her, Ian ambles into the room, a wicked look of satisfaction spreading across his face as his eyes travel between Alice, my mother, and me.

"How are you here?" I demand, finally recovering from the shock. "You can't set foot onto human property without their permission—the magic won't allow it."

An ancient agreement was made with the local humans long ago, at the time the bridge was constructed. Our magic still obeys the bargain.

"This isn't human property," Ian says. "It belongs to you, and your mother is your sovereign. Therefore, she can come and go as she pleases."

"I gave Alice the deed today," I argue.

"It wasn't properly notarized," Mother says impatiently.

"Of course it was. I had Wallen—" I stop short, my mind reeling.

It wasn't Sabine who betrayed us.

She smiles. "Yes?"

My tongue suddenly feels too thick, and I try to swallow. "Wallen?"

"He is a loyal subject who tells me when my son is stepping over the line. I've put up with your ridiculous nightly escapades, but your attachment to this girl is going too far. I've come to take care of it."

"You knew?" I ask, aghast.

All this time, I foolishly believed I kept the Highwayman's identity a secret.

She clenches her fist with prideful anger. "Is there anything that happens in my kingdom that I don't know about?"

"There is not," I say dully, coming to terms with it.

No matter how we try to defy her, we are helpless to

right any real wrongs. We only do what she allows, until she doesn't allow it anymore.

Mother looks back at Alice, her expression becoming slightly haunted. "The resemblance is unsettling, isn't it? I suppose our Alice was, in fact, young Eleanor."

"How dare you call that girl yours?" I demand. "You threw her away."

"You sound like your father." Her eyes spark with bitter memories. "He loved that ridiculous human more than his own offspring."

She says it like she believes it, like it's a shard of ice lodged deep in her heart, but I know it wasn't true. I was old enough to remember, and though Father treated Eleanor like one of his children, he did not show her favor over us.

"Were you jealous of the girl?" I ask quietly. "Did you honestly believe Father valued her more than the children you gave him?"

"You are a fool if you don't think he preferred her. If not more than you, his precious first-born son, then certainly more than your sister. Sabine understands that, even if you cannot."

"And how many times have you told her that lie?" I ask, sickened at the thought of Mother poisoning Sabine's mind—and disgusted with myself for allowing it to happen.

"Don't pretend to care. You abandoned her, didn't you?"

It's an intentional barb, and it hurts just as intended. I close my mouth, too ashamed to respond.

Beside me, Alice stays still and silent, watching my mother as if she is a predator about to attack.

"Is she always this quiet?" Mother asks Ian when her attention returns to the girl.

"She's never spoken to me." Ian watches Alice with an eagerness that makes me want to throttle him. "But maybe she would warm up to me if I wore a mask."

I move forward, but Alice grabs my wrist, silently begging me to remain calm. I stare Ian down, itching to make him bleed.

"I suppose I can grow accustomed to her presence," Mother says. "You may claim her if you wish, Ian."

"*No.*" I step fully in front of Alice.

Mother gestures around the entry. "She's an untethered human on Fae property. You know the laws. If Ian wants her, he is well within his right to claim her as his illanté."

"We're not in Faerie!"

She smiles. "We've already been over this, Brahm. The magic loves loopholes. But I think you already know that."

I must claim Alice first—it's the only way.

"Brahm," Alice begs, her blue eyes wide with fear. "*Please.*"

"I can't do that to you," I say desperately.

Ian walks forward, smiling like a greedy boy about to steal a toy. "I can."

"Brahm!" Alice says urgently. "I choose you. I vow to be your illanté."

My magic responds against my will, intrigued by the bargain despite my revulsion.

Mother laughs, taking delight in my turmoil. "You do realize this is a binding agreement, don't you, Alice? As an illanté, you will be little more than a pet, lower than a servant. Bound forever and never able to marry or return to your life here in Kellington."

Panic fists over my heart. "No!" I snarl.

"I agree," Alice says quietly.

"Very well." Mother smiles. "Brahm, I bind this girl to you."

I feel the magic lock into place as the bargain is made complete, helpless to fight my queen.

Mother watches us with grim satisfaction, finding pleasure in my horror. Alice doesn't realize she played right into her hand. By vowing to be my illanté, she used herself as my mother's tool to wound me.

"It's better this way, Brahm." Mother smiles as she steps toward the door. "Your human knows her place—it's time for you to learn it as well. Consider this your only warning—stop your ridiculous attempts at defiance. It's becoming embarrassing." With a sweep of her hand, she prepares to leave. "Come along, Ian."

Rushing forward like a ferret, the count opens the door, letting in the winter chill. "Your Majesty."

And with that, the queen of West Faerie slips into the night.

I'm left grasping for a solution, begging my magic to release Alice from her vow. But it doesn't waver, and why would it? Though Alice became my illanté, she made the agreement with my mother.

Unable to look at her, I turn toward the hearth. I press

my palms to the brick, racking my brain for an answer but finding none.

"You don't know what you've done!" I finally cry, turning back.

"You know it was the only option." Alice stares at the floor. "And I don't regret it."

"Yet," I say darkly, rubbing my hands over my face. "But you will."

20

ALICE

Brahm is angry with me, and understandably so. But his mother gave us no choice. She knew it; I knew it. The only one in the room unwilling to accept it was her son.

"I would rather be your illanté than Ian's," I point out.

"She couldn't make you accept him."

"Regina already explained how that works," I say. "She would have threatened you, tortured you, done *something* to you, and I would have agreed to make it stop."

"Better me than you." He shoves his hand through his hair, disheveling the dark strands.

He looks ridiculously handsome when he's agitated, and I'm bound to him now. But not as an equal.

In one fell swoop, his mother destroyed us. This morning, I asked for this, but now I'm scared.

"How did you know you could initiate the illanté agreement yourself?" he asks. "How did you know it would work?"

"I didn't, but I remembered the first day when I spoke

with you in your foyer, when I started to make that vow
—you cut me off. I wondered if I'd almost initiated it by
accident." My muscles begin to tremble, and I suddenly
go lightheaded. "I need to sit down."

I lower myself to the floor, pressing my forehead into
my hands.

"Alice!" Brahm drops onto his knees next to me,
taking my shoulders.

"I'm fine," I lie. "I just need a moment."

Like I weigh nothing, he scoops me onto his lap,
holding me tightly. "Somehow, it will be all right," he says,
though it sounds like he's trying to reassure himself.
"We'll find a way to break this."

"You said there is no way," I say quietly.

Brahm's answering silence tells me it's true. We stay
like this, clinging to each other.

"There must be," he says suddenly. "Otherwise, I
couldn't promise it."

"Death," I say darkly. "Yours or mine."

It all happened too quickly. How long was his mother
here? Five minutes? It was ten at most.

Proof, yet again, at how quickly your life's path can
change.

But this contact feels good—it dulls the whispers of
panic that flutter at my mind.

And I want more.

I turn my head to look at Brahm, hesitating only a
heartbeat before I place a testing kiss to his mouth.

Brahm goes still, his arms like iron around me.

"I'm terrified," I admit softly. "But I'm grateful it's you,
and I'm glad today wasn't our last."

I press my lips to his once more, slowly this time.

"Kiss me like you did when we fled into the night," I say quietly when Brahm doesn't respond, my words feathering across his lips. "At least for now, let's focus on something pleasant."

I expect him to refuse—I know this isn't the right time.

But Brahm suddenly claims my mouth in a kiss that steals my breath. His lips move against mine, giving and taking, guiding and teaching, making me realize he's far more practiced than I am.

I've never experienced this sort of intimacy before, feeling so close, so connected. Brahm's lips and breath are hot against my still-cool skin; his jaw is smooth and firm.

A flame lights in my chest, the warmth burning away my lingering anxiety, and I wrap my arms around his neck.

Brahm lets out a dark sigh, and his fingers twine into my hair. The gentle tug takes me by surprise, and I draw in a startled breath, curling my fingers around his shoulder and pressing myself against him.

With a growl deep in the back of his throat, he deepens the kiss, making me nearly dizzy. Tasting, touching, wanting, needing—my thoughts are reduced to sensation.

After several minutes, Brahm lies back, taking me with him, rolling so I'm below him. He lies beside me, propped on his elbow, his free hand cradling the back of my head. The hard press of the wooden floor is a contrast to his soft exploratory kisses, and it nearly makes me lose my mind.

And then…Brahm pushes away. He sits up and presses the heel of his hand to his forehead. And though his eyes are dark with desire, his expression is tormented.

I blink at him, breathing hard, blood surging through my veins like I've been running.

Brahm helps me sit up, and then he stares at the dancing flames in the fireplace.

"What's the matter?" I ask softly, tugging at the long skirts that are now twisted around my legs. I feel I did something to upset him, but that doesn't seem right. He was fine until just a moment ago.

"We can't do this," he finally answers, his tone flat.

I hug myself, waiting for him to continue. When he looks up, I long to brush his messy hair back into place, but I know he wouldn't welcome my touch now.

"I'm not allowed to court you," he says, "so I can't touch you like you're mine."

I sit up straighter and smooth my skirts, unsure how to respond.

"This is wrong, and I would be as wicked as Ian if I let it continue." Brahm pushes himself to his feet and then offers me his hand. With regretful eyes, he says, "I'm sorry."

"For kissing me?" I demand, fighting back a horrified laugh as I avoid his face. "Or telling me you won't kiss me again?"

Looking as frustrated as I feel, he says, "Both."

"Are you telling me I've just agreed to a life of complete spinsterhood?"

"I didn't want this for you," he says, his voice raw. "I tried…"

"I know," I answer quickly, sensing he's on a precarious ledge. "This isn't your fault."

"My mother used you to attack me. For that, I am deeply sorry. But I swear, I will show you the honor you deserve."

I try to offer him a grateful smile, but inside, I'm sobbing.

My future looks very bleak indeed.

IT'S TAKEN several days for the sun to melt most of the snow and ice from the roads, but they're now clear enough to pass by carriage.

Goodbyes must be said, and they're even more difficult than I expected.

"What do you mean you're going back to Lord Ambrose's estate?" Mrs. Fletcher exclaims, horrified.

I don't want to tell her what's happened. She won't understand, and she'll worry too much.

Thankfully, Brahm walks into the room, saving me from the conversation. "Are you ready, Alice?"

Neither of us expects Mrs. Fletcher to turn on him like a mother badger. "You're not taking her! Alice has no obligation to you, and you will not manipulate her into thinking otherwise. Leave her be—go back to Faerie without her."

"I'm afraid the matter is out of my control." Less concerned about upsetting her than I am, Brahm waves his hand, making the air spark. "I tried to return Alice, but things didn't go as planned."

Mrs. Fletcher's gasp mirrors my own, but it's not his magic that startles me—it's what Brahm has revealed.

"What did you do to her?" Mrs. Fletcher demands, her eyes on the glowing cord between Brahm and me.

The cord wraps around Brahm's wrist before it travels to mine. Lifting my hand, I study it. I can't feel the golden braid against my skin. It's not cold nor hot, heavy nor light, and I wonder if it's merely an illusion.

Brahm mentioned a tether, but I thought it was a visual representation of the magic—not an actual *tether*.

"This was Alice's doing, not mine," Brahm says. When he lowers his hand, the golden cord fades.

Brahm watches impassively as my fingers go to my wrist. His eyes seem to remind me that I asked for this.

"Release her!" Mrs. Fletcher commands.

"I cannot. The agreement was made between Alice and my mother."

When Mrs. Fletcher begins to panic, I set my hand on her arm. "I'm all right."

"You're not all right!" Her hands flutter at her waist. "You're shackled to one of *them*. Do you have any idea what—"

"It's your choice whether you and your husband remain at your posts now that Alice is leaving," Brahm says, apparently done with the conversation. "I will continue your pay if you stay. Otherwise, I will give you a small sum to thank you for the trouble of returning so briefly."

Mrs. Fletcher's eyes flash. "I don't want your filthy money."

"Mrs. Fletcher!" I say, aghast.

Calmly, Brahm holds up a hand, telling me it's all right. "She's no less upset than I am, but what's done is done, and there's no changing that."

Mrs. Fletcher suddenly turns to me, growing frantic. "I don't understand. What happened? He was giving you back your home! He had all the furniture returned."

I glance at Brahm, unsure how to answer.

She turns to the marquis, pressing her hands together in a plea, changing tactics. "Please, Lord Ambrose, I beg you. Don't take her."

I know Brahm well enough to see his distress under his careful mask. Instead of responding to her begging, he says, "Gustin will be released by the end of the day. However, he is not welcome here. Do not allow him into the house."

Shocked, I turn to Brahm. "You're releasing Gustin?"

He crosses his arms, giving me a curt nod, making me think he's not telling me everything.

"Why now?" I demand.

"Are you ready to leave?" he asks.

"Brahm!"

Mrs. Fletcher peeps in surprise, and I realize I probably shouldn't have used his given name in front of her. The housekeeper looks like she's about to faint, and I'm sure she's imagining all sorts of improper things.

Brahm glances at her before he turns back to me. "The coachman is waiting."

"The coachman?" I ask, realizing we haven't discussed what happened with Wallen. It seemed he and Brahm were close, and I'm afraid he feels the deception keenly.

Though in the last several days, we haven't discussed

much of anything. While we've waited for the snow to melt, I've been sleeping in the bedroom I grew up in, pretending my life hasn't changed dramatically. Brahm has taken up a guest room on the opposite end of the hall.

With the furniture back in place, and Mrs. Fletcher buzzing about, instructing the new maids and footmen on their duties and chiding the young houseboy, it almost feels normal again.

Brahm might as well be a friend of the family, here for a holiday visit.

But today, everything changes.

"The man I hired when I believed you'd be staying here," Brahm explains.

Mrs. Fletcher's confusion grows.

I turn to her, opening my arms for an embrace. "Perhaps I will be able to visit occasionally," I say, glancing at Brahm to see if there's a chance. When he nods, I turn back to Mrs. Fletcher. "Unless you're going to leave Kellington?"

Stepping in to hug me, she eyes Brahm with suspicion. "We'll stay. For now, at least."

"I'm glad I got to see you," I say as she squeezes her arms around me.

"Take care of yourself," she whispers. "The Fae can't be trusted."

"I'll be careful," I promise.

Fifteen minutes later, I look out the carriage window, waving to Mrs. and Mr. Fletcher as the horses cut through the already melting snow.

And then we're exiting the drive, and I feel as if I'm leaving my childhood behind—this time, for good.

21

ALICE

"You avoided my question," I say to Brahm as we cross the bridge. "Why are you releasing Gustin now?"

Brahm crosses his arms, studying me with slightly narrowed eyes. "When you became my illanté, you completed a bargain he tried to initiate when he realized he'd lost the estate."

His words are ominous, and I sit up a smidgen straighter. "What kind of bargain?"

He doesn't want to tell me—the set of his jaw makes it obvious.

"Brahm," I say in a warning voice.

"Gustin offered you instead—a straight trade."

I stare at him. "He *offered* me?"

Brahm nods slowly. "I believe he intended a marriage contract, perhaps not knowing the Fae do not marry humans. You are fortunate he made the offer to me and not one of my peers."

Peers like Ian.

"Gustin attempted to trade me for the estate?" I ask icily. "As if I am property to add to a wager?"

"I'm afraid so."

I felt betrayed when Gustin lost our home, but now I'm livid. I knew we weren't close, but how *could* he?

"I didn't want to tell you," Brahm says quietly. "I'm sorry you had to find out."

"It's painful, but the truth is never something to apologize for sharing," I say. "Though I can't say I'd mind if you let him languish for a few more months in the debtor's prison."

"I'm afraid I cannot. I felt the magic complete the bargain as soon as we were tethered. Whether we like it or not, your brother is a free man." He smiles darkly. "A free man without a copper to his name."

A tiny part of me worries, but the rest of me brushes the concern away. If nothing else, Gustin is scrappy. Like a cat, he always seems to end up on his feet.

Let him figure out his own troubles. I have enough of my own to tend to.

MY RETURN to the Ambrose estate lacks any sort of fanfare. I step out of the carriage, peering at the manor that is now my home. I remove my cloak—it's much too warm for it in the spring woods.

The remainder of the drive here was nearly silent. I didn't know what to say, and it's obvious Brahm didn't either.

I hadn't realized our relationship would change this quickly.

The newly hired coachman, a human man named Darren, unloads my nearly empty trunk as he peers at the grounds, looking as if he expects to be spirited away and never seen again—a legitimate concern.

He will return to my family's estate after this. I overheard the conversation between him and Brahm before we left. Apparently, Brahm will keep him on staff so that he may be of use to Mr. and Mrs. Fletcher.

Though Brahm originally planned to sell the property when he won the wager, he seems to have no intention of it now.

He hasn't mentioned putting it in my name again, however. And why would he? What does a pet need with property?

Regina appears on the entry steps, leading a footman. He eyes me with curiosity, looking as if he's wondering why I'm back.

Do they know? Brahm said they cannot harm an illanté, so perhaps the tether is visible to them? Have I been branded like a cow, the magic proclaiming that I am Lord Ambrose's property?

The thought doesn't settle well.

Better Brahm than Ian, I remind myself.

"What happened?" Regina asks Brahm quietly, frowning at me. "Why have you brought Alice back, and why is she—"

"Later," Brahm says, gesturing for me to lead the way up the stairs. "Prepare Alice's room. She will be living with us now. Tomorrow, would you go into Corrinmead and bring back a selection of linens? She may choose whatever she likes."

"Of course," Regina says.

"And order several more gowns while you're there. I doubt she wishes to continue dressing like a garden maid."

Regina nods, glancing at me with something that seems a little too much like pity for my liking.

Brahm turns to me, looking terribly solemn. "What else would you like, Alice? Perhaps a private sitting room? A garden?"

I stare at him, dumbfounded.

"A studio," he says, acting quite strange. He turns to Regina once more. "Find somewhere appropriate, with plenty of natural light, and stock it well."

Even Regina looks bewildered. "All right."

"I have business to attend to," he says. "I assume you can make sure Alice is settled?"

Slowly, Regina nods.

"Whatever Alice wants—anything at all—make sure she gets it." Bowing his head toward me in a respectful goodbye, Brahm excuses himself and walks into the manor.

"Did you quarrel on your way here?" Regina asks quietly.

With a sigh, I say, "We barely spoke at all."

MY SECOND MONTH at Brahm's estate passes far more quickly than the first. The illanté tether has given me a new sense of freedom. The staff now ignores me as I explore the estate and grounds, and I feel less vulnerable without their constant attention. More importantly, the housemaids no longer see me as a threat—they barely look at me at all.

Though I never leave the safety of the iron fence, the woods inside the property are lovely and strange. I never know what I'm going to find, from pint-sized pixies that sleep in folded leaves to little birds with thick, icing-pink plumage.

On my daily walks, I find bundles of gifts. They always contain the same things—pretty rocks that sparkle in the sun, glittering pinecones, and intricate flower chains. I have no idea what creature leaves them for me.

Regina ordered four new gowns, each lovelier than the last, and my studio is big and bright. Even though I grew up as the daughter of a lord, I've never been so spoiled in my life.

But it's hard to enjoy it all when no masked bandit visits me in the evenings, and I only see Brahm at meals. He's distanced himself, speaking to me in a careful manner, asking questions about my day and acting as disinterested as a distant male relative might.

So this evening when there's a knock at my door, I expect it to be Regina and not Brahm. When I find him standing in the hall, I let out a surprised noise that makes his lips twitch so briefly, I think I might have imagined it.

Crossing my arms, I narrow my eyes at him. "Are we speaking now?"

Looking as if he's suppressing a long-suffering sigh, Brahm says, "When did we stop speaking? I believe we had a conversation about water sprites at dinner only an hour ago."

I found the creatures in the pond, peering up at me from under a lily pad. Apparently, in typical situations, they will call a human to their death. I, however, am safe because of the protection the tether lends.

"What would happen if they tried to hurt me?" I asked Brahm, sorting a pile of spring peas with a tine of my fork.

"It would go badly for them," he answered cryptically.

I've tucked the information away, adding it to my growing book of mental Faerie knowledge.

Returning to the present conversation, I ask, "What do you need, Lord Ambrose?"

Irritation flashes over Brahm's face for just a moment. Even now, he hates it when I use his formal name. It gives me assurance that he might be as torn up about our relationship—or lack thereof—as I am.

"Tomorrow is Mother's monthly masquerade. We will leave in the morning. I've already informed Regina, and she said she has ordered something suitable for you to wear."

I stare at him, processing that last bit of information. "I'm going to the masquerade?"

"As my illanté, you will be expected to attend."

I'm ashamed of the fear that makes my heart stutter. The idea of facing Brahm's mother again, and in her lair…

"It will be fine," he says, reading my horrified expression. "The illanté agreement will protect you."

"Will it?" I ask, uneasy. "I made the bargain with your mother, not you. What if she decides to…"

I don't need to finish the thought. We both know what Queen Marison is infamous for.

He shakes his head. "You and she agreed to the arrangement, but you are my illanté. The tether between us proves it. She can't hurt you."

I slowly nod, wanting to ask him about the tether. Sometimes, when I'm nearing the iron fence, I think I feel it on my wrist, tugging me back. Warning me that I'm not allowed to wander that far.

"I've never been to a masquerade," I say instead. "Is this one anything like the ones the humans throw?"

"I have not attended a human masquerade, but I imagine they are similar."

"So...you'll wear a mask?" I bite my bottom lip, trying not to grin.

Brahm lowers his voice. "Have you missed it?"

I give him a vague shrug.

Looking as if he doesn't want to smile, he clears his throat. "Be ready to leave midday. I want to arrive in Auvenridge before dark."

He then turns down the hall, deciding the conversation is over.

I lean my shoulder against the doorframe, watching him disappear into his room. With a sigh, I close my door, wondering what Auvenridge will be like.

Terrifying, most likely. And lonely, if this month is any indication.

IN WALLEN'S ABSENCE, an estate footman drives our carriage to Auvenridge. I watch out the window, eagerly taking in places of West Faerie I've never seen.

We leave the Rose Briar Woods and begin to climb into the mountains, traversing a road that's too narrow for two carriages to pass side-by-side. When we meet traffic coming down, one of the coachmen must find a wide spot in the road and wait for the other to pass. It puts us horrifyingly close to the edge, though Brahm doesn't seem even remotely shaken.

We've left the roses and raspberries in the lower forest. Here, wild flowering cherry trees grow amongst gray-blue spruces, filling the mountainside with showy pink blossoms. Bleeding hearts grow at the base of their trunks, with their cool foliage spreading like a carpet along the spongy ground. The white and fuchsia flowers drip along graceful, arched stalks, drawing humming-birds and butterflies.

Just as Brahm warned, the trip takes several hours. I'm almost asleep when the road suddenly evens out, and the change in terrain jolts me from my dozing.

Yawning behind my hand, I look out the window.

Old stone cottages line the road. Ivy grows up their walls, and the roofs are made of thatch or wooden shakes.

As we go deeper into the city, the cottages become businesses, all built out of the same stone. We pass a clock tower in the main square. It's a grand thing, elaborately carved. The artist crafted an owl to sit at the very top, and it now surveys the comings and goings in the square—its eyes blinking and head moving like a live creature's.

There's a bookstore and a patisserie. Another shop

appears to sell concoctions. Past them is a chandler whose window is filled with hand-cut candles in a dazzling array of marbled colors.

A Faerie peddler sells wooden flutes on the street, and the stand next to him is filled with crystal figurines that seem to be lit from within. Some hold roses; others contain things more ghastly.

The strangest of all, perhaps, is the puppet shop with marionettes hanging from a dead tree outside the door. Though their hand-painted faces smile at those passing by, there's something ominous about them.

I sit back in my seat, hiding from their watchful eyes.

The carriage pauses at a gate in a trimmed hedge. The living fence is at least twelve feet tall, with small pink flowers blooming between thick, oval-shaped leaves. The overhead sun is shadowed for several seconds as we pass under the arch.

"Have we entered the castle grounds?" I ask Brahm, marveling at the formal garden we've entered. More hedges grow, these much shorter. They create flower beds in geometric patterns—squares cut by triangles and circles, each balanced and perfectly planned. Spring flowers bloom in pastel rainbows—lavender irises and pale orange tulips, creamy daffodils, pink peonies, and sunny ranunculus.

Apple trees dot the garden, filling the area with even more color. The flowers cling to the branches like white wedding gowns, each individual blossom blushing at the center.

Petals drift through the air, but they never seem to

land on the ground or mar the tidy perfection of the groomed beds.

Does the fruit ever ripen? Or are the trees caught in a season of eternal bloom?

There are fountains, birdbaths, and colorful glass orbs tucked into the designs as well. Paths lead further into the garden, tempting people to follow them and see where they go.

It's all exquisite and lovely. But as I take it in, I realize something quite strange.

"There are no roses," I muse aloud.

The flowers are common to formal plantings, often the crowning jewels of the garden. It's bizarre not to see even one.

"Mother dislikes them," Brahm answers, his tone strange.

My mind travels to the rose-filled conservatory, and I believe there must be more to it. Brahm, however, seems on edge, so I won't ask him now.

The carriage slows, and I clasp my hands in my lap. We must be close.

"It will be fine," Brahm assures me. "You have nothing to fear now that you're an illanté."

"Then why do you look so on edge?"

"You've met my mother," he says. "Does it seem like family celebrations are enjoyable occasions?"

I want to tell him that doesn't ease my concern.

"Brahm…" I say instead, panicking a little when the carriage comes to a stop. "What exactly is my place? How do I behave? I don't want to embarrass you or cause you trouble."

He huffs as if he couldn't care less.

"I'm serious."

With a sigh, he says, "You are expected to stay by my side. Very few people will talk to you, but if someone does, and they make you uncomfortable, you have no social obligation to respond. Because you are lovely, most will assume you are my mistress. Our relationship is none of their business, but it will make them wary of the power you wield nevertheless."

The carriage door opens before I can respond, letting in cool, dusky sunlight.

"We have arrived," the footman says needlessly.

Brahm steps out first, and then he looks back, offering me his hand. I duck as I step down, and when I look up, I nearly freeze.

Dozens of Faeries mill around the garden entry, watching Brahm with avid interest. Chatter fills the courtyard when they see me, all of them whispering amongst themselves in small groups.

"Your Highness," says a short man in a red waistcoat. His hair is snowy white, and his eyebrows are bushy. "Welcome home. Your mother requests that you dress accordingly."

My eyes move to the red velvet pillow he holds. A golden crown sits atop it, shining as if it has been polished.

Brahm averts his gaze, looking vexed. After a moment, he snatches the crown from the pillow and places it on his head.

The crowd claps as if he performed an amazing feat.

Several nearby women swoon, clutching onto each other as they gaze at him.

When they catch me watching them, they promptly look away.

"Dinner is at ten sharp," the man in the waistcoat says, following Brahm as he begins walking up the wide steps that lead into the castle's grand entry.

"Yes, I'm aware." Brahm turns back to make sure I'm behind him. "It's the same every month."

"The masquerade will begin at twelve," the man continues.

"Alice, this is Phineas," Brahm says. "He will fetch anything you desire."

Phineas turns to me as if startled. As he stares at me, his jaw goes slack, and his bushy white eyebrow twitches. "A…Alice?"

"That's right…"

"Forgive me," he says suddenly, shaking himself. He then bows low and continues walking, hurrying ahead to get the door before Brahm can reach it. "As Prince Brahm said, I will fetch anything you desire, at any hour of the day. You need but ask."

"Thank you, Phineas," Brahm says. "Please tell my mother I have arrived."

"Of course, Your Highness." The man bows one more time before he bounds off.

"He's usually running five errands at once," Brahm says as we enter a grand foyer that boasts no less than five staircases. "He's always late for something. If you do make a request, you'll likely receive it in a week."

"He's certainly spry for someone his age."

"He's not old," Brahm answers, leading me up the first winding staircase on the left. "He's nearly my age."

I stop mid-step, baffled.

"Mother cursed him several years ago," Brahm explains. "She said if he was as slow as an old man, he might as well look like one."

I merely nod, not sure what to make of that.

After taking a few more twists and turns, we venture through a window-lined colonnade that looks down at the gardens on both sides. It ends in a single red door.

"Where are we going?" I ask.

Brahm doesn't answer right away. When he does, his voice is stiff. "My quarters."

He opens the door, letting me go in first. We're now in a narrow, circular stairway. The stone steps twist as they rise, and windows occasionally dot the area to let in light. But it's almost dark outside now, and it's difficult to see.

I trip, stumbling back into Brahm. He catches me by my waist, and my neck ends up dangerously close to his mouth. My pulse quickens, both from the fall and the feel of his warm breath against my skin.

"Careful," he murmurs, holding me until I get my footing.

Swallowing, I continue.

He raises his hand, and suddenly, sconces on the wall come to life, filling the space with warm light. "Better?" he asks.

Not trusting my voice, I nod.

We finally reach the top of the stairway, where another red door waits for us.

"Another hall?"

"The castle is like a labyrinth," Brahm says, apologizing. "But we're almost there."

Though the space is clearly a walkway to another part of the castle, it's wider than the glassed-in colonnade we traveled a few minutes ago. Tall, fern-like plants grow on stands placed in front of the narrow windows. They have long, white fronds, and they appear to move despite a lack of breeze.

"What are those?" I ask.

"Cloud Elosia."

"Are they...breathing?"

"They are—I don't recommend touching them."

I give the plants a slightly wider berth. "I hadn't planned on it."

And finally, we find the end of this hall, which, no surprise, ends at a red door.

"Someone likes that color," I comment.

"We're in the scarlet wing." Brahm produces a key and then enters the room. "All the doors are red in this part of the castle, just as they are black in the ebony wing and blue in the sapphire wing. It's easy to get turned around. Sometimes, the doors are your only clue as to where you're at."

When I follow Brahm into the room, I find it's actually a suite.

We walk into a marble entry with a tall ceiling and a chandelier flickering with orbs of firelight. There's a small private sitting area to the right and a study to the left.

I follow Brahm into a large entertaining space, where a fire already burns in the massive stone hearth.

"I have two guest rooms," he says, tossing his crown on a side table, obviously eager to be free of it. "But Drake began to use one for plant storage, and it's so overrun with rose canes, you can't even find the bed."

"Out of the entire castle, he decided to turn one of your rooms into a conservatory?" I ask.

Brahm turns back. "Out of the entire castle, my room was the only place he *could* turn into a conservatory."

"Oh," I say softly, wondering at the bite in his tone. It didn't seem to be intended for me.

We enter a large bedchamber. Along with several heavy chairs, chests, and armoires, there is a massive bed encased in dark, glossy wood, with a thick, tall headboard.

"I don't know how I'll climb in," I say nervously.

Brahm gives me a sideways look. "You won't—that's my bed."

A nervous laugh flutters in my chest, but I hold it back.

He walks across the room and opens a door. "This will be yours."

I stand at the threshold, surveying the room. Everything inside is petite and feminine—the bed, the chairs, even the little table and the tea set that rests upon it.

I give Brahm a questioning glance.

"In Faerie, it's traditional for the royal suites to have two marital rooms. This is what's known as a queen's room. That's why it's off the main bedchamber."

Suddenly, it feels as if the space has shrunk. "Do married Fae often sleep in separate chambers?"

"No," Brahm says from very close, drumming his fingers on the doorframe.

Slowly, I drag my eyes to his. "Then why…?"

"It began as a place for a woman to retreat to—her own space. If she wanted to rest during the day, she could close herself inside and not have to worry about the maids and staff bustling around in the main area."

"And now?"

"For many, it's a room used for young children—a nursery of sorts. For others, it's a convenient spot to lodge a mistress."

I open my mouth to tell him how reproachable that is, but he cuts me off.

"I didn't say I approve," he says with a laugh that I seldom hear.

It catches my attention and makes my heart miss a beat.

"So, what you're telling me is that you're giving me the mistress room," I say coolly.

Brahm raises his brows. "If you'll remember, this illanté business was your idea, not mine. Would you rather sleep with Drake's roses?"

I smile, shaking my head. "No."

"It's the safest room in my suite," he points out. "The only way someone can get to you is through me."

I walk in, surveying the space. It's lovely, with roses stitched onto the coverlet and gossamer curtains covering the windows. It's a dainty room, a pink room.

"For a man who claims to be indifferent to the flower, you're certainly surrounded by them," I say.

"This was my mother's room once," Brahm answers

carefully. "When she and my father were first married. Before her eldest sister died and she became queen."

"I thought you said your mother hates roses?"

"She hates them now, but there was a time she adored them. They represented Father and the woods where he lived. It's hard to believe, but they were happy in the beginning."

"Wait." I turn toward Brahm. "Before her sister died and she became queen?"

"Mother was second in line to the throne. Winnalynn was in front of her. She died before having children, and the crown passed to our family."

"Did your mother kill her?" I ask bluntly.

Brahm is quiet for several seconds. "I don't know."

Now that I'm aware this was the queen's personal room, I don't know how comfortable I'll be sleeping here. Maybe I should brave the real roses.

"We leave tomorrow morning?" I ask, deciding I can manage one night.

"That's right." Brahm walks back into his room, leaving the door open.

I follow him partway, hovering between the rooms.

"We need to prepare for dinner," he says. "Mother gets fussy if people are late."

I watch as he loosens his cravat. "You make her sound like a toddler."

He raises his eyebrows as if finding that idea humorous. Walking to the armoire, he unbuttons his waistcoat and then tosses it aside.

"What are you doing?" I ask nervously.

Next goes his shirt.

"I already said—I'm preparing for dinner."

I gape at Brahm rather shamelessly, letting my eyes rove over his broad, muscled shoulders and strong back, and it strikes me again that he's not a slender and slight man as I'd assumed most Faeries to be. He's built like a warrior.

My mind wanders a little further, to the night he came to me covered in blood. I touched him, ran my hands over his skin. At the time, I was able to put these thoughts aside and focus on my task, but now...

I should probably retreat into my room, but I'm having trouble convincing my feet to take me away.

Brahm turns back, holding a black doublet. I avert my eyes, pretending I wasn't admiring him.

He pauses, making me think I wasn't stealthy enough.

I turn quickly, ready to hide in my room and pretend I don't still want him as badly as I do.

A strange tug at my wrist catches me off guard, and I turn back, questioning it. When I glance down, I realize the tether is once again visible.

"What are you doing?" I ask him, my voice hitching.

Brahm looks as conflicted as I am.

"Is it always here?" I ask nervously, gesturing to the golden cord with my free hand.

"It is."

"So, it's not an illusion that you created for Mrs. Fletcher?"

He shakes his head.

"Can you...manipulate it?"

Brahm's dark eyes are on me, his expression giving

away nothing. He steps forward, pulling the cord as he walks, shortening the length, drawing me toward him.

I stumble as my knees grow wobbly. I feel like a newborn sheep on a lead, clumsy and suddenly unsure.

Too soon, we're standing face-to-face, close enough I could touch him.

Close enough he could touch me.

I pretend I'm not affected by this nearness. Unfortunately, my mind travels to the last time we kissed, the way he held me and made me feel wanted.

I've told myself to forget it, that we cannot be that to each other anymore. I thought I was the only one truly struggling, but the look in Brahm's eyes says otherwise.

We study each other, neither daring to voice our thoughts aloud.

"You're making this very difficult," he finally murmurs.

My pulse quickens. "What?"

He takes another step forward, putting us so close I have to look up to see his face. "You keep looking at me like you still want me."

"I'm not sure I can stop."

"Alice," he says raggedly.

My eyes drop to his chest. Hesitantly, I touch my fingers to his skin, emboldened by the way his muscles tighten under my touch.

"You're beautiful," I murmur, the words oddly regretful.

He groans softly, his hand raising and then pausing mid-air as if he can't decide whether to take hold of me or nudge me away.

"I don't think I can live like this," I say quietly, drawing my hand back. "Living with you, belonging to you, but never able to touch you..." I shake my head.

Brahm's chest moves with his quickened breath.

"It's too cruel." I turn to walk into my room, desperately grateful that he loosens the tether and lets me go.

22

ALICE

I've never seen so many beautiful people in my life.

I touch my hand to my stomach, trying to soothe my nerves. Faeries look at Brahm and me as we enter the dining room. They bend their lovely heads together, whispering speculations, their eyes sliding over the fine sapphire gown Regina commissioned for me.

It's now that Brahm's people will decide what kind of illanté I am. I'm obviously not a servant or a drudge in such a gown, so I must be Brahm's mistress or one of those pampered pets Regina mentioned.

Either way, we are the subject of gossip, and I have no doubt Brahm's name will pass nearly every pair of lips before the night is over.

The dining room is a massive space, though its name makes it sound deceptively small. There are dozens of round, cloth-covered tables, each with ten chairs. As Brahm leads me toward the front of the room, I peek at the place settings. The plates and utensils are silver, and the drinkware is cut crystal. A teacup sits atop each plate, with a large, multi-petaled red flower resting in the bottom.

The tables have several steaming porcelain teapots at their centers, all nestled amongst boxwood and rosemary garlands. Place cards with scrolling names written upon them inform guests where they are to sit.

With growing dread, I realize that most names have titles attached. Not only is this the largest gathering of Faeries I've ever been amongst, but they are the most powerful citizens of West Faerie.

I return my attention to the front of the room, where Brahm's family is already seated.

Queen Marison watches us with narrowed eyes, and a small, twisted smile graces her lovely face. She is truly a beautiful woman, looking somehow timeless. She and Brahm share the same hair color, but her eyes are green.

Ian stands behind her, resting one hand on the back of her chair. He speaks with a man who came to give his greetings to his monarch, smiling like he's already the queen's new consort.

To the queen's right sits a woman so beautiful, she looks as if the sun lent her its light to wear as a cloak. Her hair is golden and long. Her lips are the color of the roses her mother now despises, and her lashes are dark. She's dreadfully intimidating, especially when she watches me with an expression that says she resents my presence next to Brahm.

I lean close to him as we walk. "Is the blonde woman, perhaps, one of the women whose hearts you mentioned stealing?"

"Worse," he says. "She's my sister."

Softly, I ask, "And why does your sister look as if she'd like to behead me?"

"She always looks like that when she sits next to our mother. Try not to take it personally."

My eyes shift to a man dressed in full black who stands just behind the table. He's leaner than Brahm, but just about the same height, and they share similar hair and eyes. He's startlingly handsome, with a dark, haunted expression.

And he watches me intently.

I feel as if I've become the ghost of my younger sister —a girl this family knew far better than I ever did.

"Is that your brother?" I whisper. "The one who grows the roses?"

"That's right. I won't be able to introduce you, but his name is Drake."

"Why can't you introduce me?"

Before Brahm can answer, Ian interrupts.

"Wasn't Brahm the one who said he'd never take a pet?" the count asks the queen offhandedly. His nasty smirk makes my skin crawl.

"Yes," Queen Marison responds, pulling her eyes away from me as if bored. "He said it was an 'appalling tradition' that he wanted no part in."

"Have you changed your mind now that you've found one who appeals to you, Brahm?" Ian asks snidely. He then slides his eyes over me, making me want to hide behind Brahm's back. "You've certainly decorated her, haven't you? Is she a pet or a doll?"

"Enough," Drake says through gritted teeth, making everyone at the table jump, including his mother.

No one responds to him, but Ian shoots him a guarded look before returning his attention to us.

"Sit down, Brahm," Queen Marison commands, gesturing to the empty spot next to Brahm's sister.

One empty spot.

"Move down," Brahm commands the others at the table. Though they look like high-titled Faeries, they scurry to do the prince's bidding. Satisfied, Brahm pulls out the chair next to his sister for me.

People watch the display. Their murmurs are like a flock of birds winging about the room, and they make me anxious. I reluctantly lower myself into the chair.

The queen watches without a word, but I can feel the weight of her stare.

"Alice, this is my sister, Sabine," Brahm says. "Sabine, this is Alice."

He then gives her a look that plainly says, "Be nice."

"Hello," I say quietly, terrified of the pretty Fae woman.

The princess turns in her chair, assessing me. "I don't know what all the fuss is about. You do resemble the girl, I suppose, but your hair is clearly wrong."

I twist my hands in my lap, forcing myself to give her an answering smile.

"I'm sure you have no idea, but you're quite fortunate to be tethered to Brahm," she says. "He is the kindest master you could ask for—do not forget that."

"That's enough, Sabine," Brahm says shortly.

The princess's eyes move beyond me to her brother. "It's been a month. Are you still in a foul temper about it?

If you've grown tired of her, give her to Ian and be done with it."

"No," Drake says from behind us in a rough, oddly unpracticed, voice. "Not Ian."

Both Brahm and Sabine turn to look at him, their shock apparent.

Brahm's face contorts, looking like he's fighting something before he finally surrenders.

Looking defeated, he turns from his brother without acknowledging him and leans forward to speak with Sabine. "I have no intention of giving Alice to Ian or anyone else. She's mine, and I am hers, and it will remain that way."

Though I didn't like Sabine's use of the word "master," my heart dances when Brahm claims we belong to each other. But the announcement must be a dangerous one.

People in attendance shift and whisper once more, and from the way Queen Marison's eyes flash, I know Brahm crossed a line.

Suddenly, the queen laughs. The sound is sweet and bright, but a mockingly benevolent smile passes over her lips. "It's so like you to cherish your first pet, Brahm. If I'd known it would please you so, I would have gotten one for you sooner."

Brahm's hand fists around his napkin.

"But I'm afraid you must remember her place," Queen Marison continues, "lest you give her too much leash and make her unruly. Alice, stand with Drake while we eat."

Except for Sabine's sharp inhale, the room is silent.

As I begin to stand, Brahm catches my shoulder,

making me pause. "It's my choice whether or not I bring my illanté to dinner, is it not?"

The question echoes in the room, the hush making it sound much louder than it actually was.

His mother's eyes flash, and a terrifying smile tugs at her crimson lips. "Are you defying me, Brahm?"

"He's not," Sabine says before Brahm can answer, knocking his hand from my shoulder and urgently pushing me to my feet. "She's going."

I immediately rise, not daring to look at Brahm, knowing what's at stake.

Brahm begins to argue, but Sabine hisses to him under her breath, "What do you think will happen to her if you're *dead*?"

That's all it takes for Brahm to relent. Jaw rigid, he sits back in his chair, staring straight ahead.

Hating that I'm on display, and terrified for Brahm, I join Drake. The prince watches me, looking almost as angry as his brother. But when he meets my gaze, he looks away.

He's the only one. Too many eyes are on me. Some of the attending Fae nobles look like they're enjoying the display, but most appear uncomfortable.

And a few seem as quietly outraged as the royal siblings. The queen was purposefully baiting Brahm, but why? Does she want an excuse to execute him? How could she feel so venomous toward her own blood?

"Evony," Queen Marison calls into the room, looking somewhat displeased that Sabine convinced Brahm to stay quiet. "Come sit by my son. He has regretfully lost his dining partner."

My stomach falls when a beautiful woman stands.

Sabine stares at Brahm, begging him to stay silent. Thankfully, his stony expression is his only response to his mother's manipulations.

The Faerie walks to the front of the room, looking terrified of her queen. She averts her eyes to the floor, glancing at Brahm only briefly as she approaches the table. Her long auburn hair falls around her shoulders in soft, uniform curls, vibrant against her white gown.

She looks like a reluctant bride, and the thought makes my stomach knot.

Resigned, Brahm pulls out my recently departed chair with a heavy sigh, mannered to a fault.

Evony's eyes flicker to him, her face soft with sympathy as she takes my place. Soon, their backs are to me, and all I can see is the two of them together, making a handsome pair.

And then, the meal begins.

It doesn't take long before I grow fatigued from remaining in the same position. Drake barely moves. He doesn't fidget or shift, likely used to standing for long periods of time.

The meal stretches on, each tiny course followed by another, until my feet ache from standing, and my muscles protest the uncomfortable position.

When dessert is finally served, I hide a yawn behind my hand, shifting my weight from one leg to the other.

The queen's gentle laughter becomes harsh and grating as the night wears on. Again, she waves a serving-man over, commanding him to refill her empty chalice with the ruby red wine most drink in moderation.

I've heard tales of Faerie alcohol. If half of them are true, the queen might be dead by morning. Though I suppose the Fae are immune to the drink's extreme potency, and we aren't likely to be fortunate enough to get rid of her so easily.

"It's almost midnight," Drake says so quietly I almost can't hear him. "The masquerade will start soon. If you're careful to stay out of the queen's line of sight, you might be able to slip away undetected."

He looks straight ahead as he speaks, making me believe I should do the same.

"What about you?" I ask softly.

The prince looks over so sharply, I'm sure it must have drawn the attention of at least a few people in the room. His dark green eyes are wide, and his mouth hangs open.

Startled, I stare back at him, unsure what I did wrong. After a moment, I say, "I'm sorry."

Looking as if he's thinking a thousand things at once, he drags his attention to the wall across the room. After a long moment, he says in a jagged voice, "We'll go together."

I watch Drake from the corner of my eye, growing concerned. He's gone pale, and his hands appear to tremble despite the way he clenches them at his sides.

As soon as the queen rises, others follow her lead. Immediately, Brahm leaves his dining companion and turns toward me.

"Brahm," Queen Marison says harshly, her voice slightly slurred. "Escort Evony into the ballroom."

"I—"

"Your *human* will be fine on her own," she says, stumbling against the table when she loses her balance.

"I'm all right," I say to Brahm quietly, jerking my head toward the doorway, telling him to go.

Those who are still in attendance pause halfway out of the room, watching the exchange.

Brahm's eyes find mine, their deep brown depths sparking with defiance. I shake my head subtly, begging him not to fight.

Brahm's gaze moves to Drake. After a long moment, he relents. Turning his eyes away, he stiffly offers his arm to Evony. I watch as she slides her hand into the crook of his elbow, feeling like a part of me is dying.

Satisfied, the queen collects Ian and sweeps Brahm and Sabine from the room, forgetting all about her second son and Brahm's illanté.

Drake clears his throat next to me. "We should go... while she's preoccupied."

He pauses, perhaps debating whether he'll offer his arm. After several seconds of indecision, he lowers his head and begins walking to an unimposing door off the side of the room—the same which the serving staff used throughout the meal.

I follow him, feeling small.

If it was Queen Marison's goal to put me in my place, she certainly accomplished her task. I've never felt so insignificant in my life.

"I'll take you to Brahm's rooms," Drake says as soon as we're in the empty hall, still not looking at me.

I follow without speaking, sensing I unnerve him.

The halls feel longer and darker without Brahm.

I know little about his brother, except he tried to save my sister when he was just a child, and he paid dearly for it. He also seems bizarrely fond of roses.

We pass the colonnade, and I follow him up the winding stairway, growing more uneasy with every step.

A shadow cloaks Drake. It's not visible, but it's there all the same. Whether it's sadness or something more sinister, I don't know.

Perhaps I was a fool to go with him, but what choice did I have? My only alternative was to wander the castle and hope something worse didn't find me.

Besides, Brahm said the illanté tether will protect me. It seems as good a time as any to see if he's right.

When we arrive at the last scarlet door, Drake pauses as he reaches for the handle. Slowly, he lets his hand drop, and then he turns to me.

As if it's painful, he forces his gaze to mine. I stand very still, my heart beating too quickly.

"I've only overheard bits and pieces of the story," he says roughly. "You're Alice?"

Slowly, I nod.

"And she...*my Alice*...was your sister?"

"Yes."

He closes his eyes when I answer, making me think it's difficult for him to carry on a conversation. "What was her name?"

"Eleanor," I whisper.

He swallows hard, taking a moment. "And apparently you can talk to me."

Confused, I say, "It appears that way..."

"Of course you can—you're human," he says darkly, rubbing his hand over his face.

Suddenly, he laughs. It's an agonized sound, seeming to come from the darkest, rawest parts of his very being.

He leans against the door and rests his head on the wood. "I haven't had a conversation with a person since I was ten."

His words confuse me until I remember what Brahm said when we entered the dining hall.

"Brahm told me he couldn't introduce us," I say carefully. "I assumed it was merely a way of saying he wouldn't have a chance..."

"He meant he *couldn't*. Years ago, after Eleanor, Mother decreed that no one was allowed to speak to me. The command was sealed with magic, impossible to fight." He huffs out a scoffing breath. "At least if you're Fae."

Ten years—that's how long he's lived as an apparition in his own home.

"Why didn't you leave?" I ask, aghast. "You could have gone somewhere your mother doesn't have jurisdiction."

"I'm tethered—same as you. This silence is my punishment, my prison."

Overwhelmed, I fall quiet, staring at the floor between us.

"I must ask you something," Drake says heavily. "But I'm afraid of the answer."

Gently, I say, "But perhaps it would be worse to pass up the opportunity?"

He looks at me again, his heart bared and bleeding. "Did Eleanor find her way home?"

After all this time, after everything he's been through, Drake wants a confirmation that my little sister made it back—that he was successful. That everything he lived through was for *something*.

How can I tell him?

"I'm sorry," I say softly, shaking my head.

A deep, guttural sound escapes him—like a sob wrenched with a moan. He slowly slides down the door and sits on the floor, one knee drawn to his forehead, looking like a man destroyed.

Unsure what else to do, I sit on the floor across from him, fighting with my many layers of skirts.

"Why roses?" I ask softly.

Drake meets my gaze. "Alice—" He shakes his head. "*Eleanor* loved them. Everyone says she knew what they were when she arrived—she pointed to them and called them by name."

"How old are you?"

"Nineteen."

"So, you must have been about four when Eleanor came to your family." I swallow, feeling lightheaded. After all these years, I have answers, but they only add a layer of heartbreak.

Drake stares at his hands. "Probably."

"We're the same age."

"Do you remember her?" he asks quietly.

"A little," I say with a sigh. "Just fleeting memories—nothing substantial. But...I think I know why she liked roses."

He looks up, desperate to know more about the friend

SHARI L. TAPSCOTT

he lost so long ago. And maybe talking about her—or talking to anyone about anything—is cathartic.

"My grandmother grew roses," I say. "The horticultural society in Davon even gave her an award for a hybrid tea rose she created. Some of my earliest memories are of walking with her through her gardens. Maybe when Eleanor was little, roses subconsciously reminded her of home."

"She liked visiting Father's rose woods the best," Drake says with an absent nod, looking as if he's lost in memories. "But when we were here, as we were most of the time, her favorite place was the garden Brahm planted for her. It was a secret spot, hidden in the hedges, the entrance concealed behind a massive weeping spruce."

"I didn't see any roses on the castle grounds."

"The queen had them removed."

That's twice he's referred to his mother that way. Does he no longer claim her? Not that anyone could blame him.

"Thank you," I say softly. "Thank you for loving Eleanor, for risking all you did for her."

Drake watches me, and his eyes grow glossy.

"I think..." I blink several times, overwhelmed by his reaction to my words. "My parents would have been so relieved to know she had you caring for her."

Drake studies me for several long seconds, and then his eyes move behind me. "Brahm."

I turn, relieved to see him this soon but anxious about what his early arrival could mean. "You're back already?"

Brahm strides down the hall, looking heartbreakingly

238

handsome in his dark, formal doublet—looking like a prince.

Though he seems agitated, he offers his hand as I scramble to my feet. "I see Drake helped you find your way."

"He did."

Looking at me, he says, "I hope he knows how grateful I am that he didn't leave you alone."

I glance at Drake, my heart twisting over the strange situation. The younger prince merely shrugs as if accustomed to hearing words meant for him directed at other people.

"Your mother let you leave?" I ask Brahm.

He shakes his head. "I told her I was feeling ill, and I excused myself."

"I thought you couldn't lie."

"I can't." He brushes my hair behind my ear. "But I'm better now."

Belated tears sting my eyes.

"You're all right?" he asks quietly.

I nod, trying to stay composed. This poor family. How have they survived all these years?

Drake bows his head, silently excusing himself, and begins down the hall.

"Thank you," I call to him.

Drake's eyes cut to his brother to see how he will respond.

"You can talk to him," Brahm breathes, saying it as if it was something he knew but only just remembered.

"I can."

Drake hesitates for another second, and then he

continues, eventually disappearing into the door that goes to the stairwell.

Brahm ushers me inside before he turns to me. "Did you speak with Drake?"

"I did."

"And...he spoke back?"

He looks torn, and I have no idea what answer would ease his anguish. "He did."

Brahm lets out a long sigh. "I am envious of you, Alice."

"He spoke at dinner," I point out. "How is that possible?"

"Drake has always been able to talk—that was never taken from him. But no one could answer. Eventually, he fell quiet."

"Forgive me," I say darkly, "but your mother is a wretched person."

He laughs under his breath. "I am aware."

I look up at him solemnly. "Don't give her a reason to hurt you."

"You sound like Sabine."

"Then maybe I will get along with your sister."

"I'm sorry for tonight," he says, reluctantly stepping away.

"Don't apologize for something that's not your fault."

He sits on a bench near the fire, staring at the dancing flames.

"I am disappointed about one thing, though," I say, joining him.

He turns from the flames to face me. "What's that?"

"I didn't get to see you in your mask," I tease.

"It isn't the same one you're accustomed to."

"I believe I would have still liked it."

"I'm sure I would have liked yours as well." He shakes his head, averting his gaze. When he looks back, he wears a smile. "We can still go. You said you've never attended a masquerade, and I hate to disappoint you."

Suddenly serious, I sit up. "Brahm, no."

"It's fine. Mother is too fond of her drink. You saw how tipsy she was at dinner. She was almost passed out when I was leaving the ballroom. She'll never know, and no one else will care."

"Then why does it feel like such a bad idea?"

He laughs. "The choice is yours, but I promise it will be all right."

"If I go, will I be sent away again? Will I be commanded to stand in a corner and forced to watch you spend the evening with Evony?"

Brahm's expression darkens with the memory. "The only one who outranks me is already incoherent."

I hesitate. "Regina did go to all that trouble of ordering me this gown..."

Brahm's eyes dip to the sapphire creation just long enough for me to feel the weight of his attention, and then he meets my eyes once more. "She did."

"Maybe we'll go," I say. "But only for a little bit."

23

BRAHM

I have two reasons for attending the masquerade—the first is that the people, including my own brother, need to see I will not bow easily. The second is purely selfish.

I want to show Alice more of my world. Some of it is ugly, yes, but not everything. She's experienced too much of the dark side of Faerie and so little of the magic that often lures humans here in the first place.

I wait for Alice by the fireplace, straightening the uncomfortable half-mask. The molded gold creation always feels foreign when I'm used to the soft fabric I use as the Highwayman.

But I doubt I will ever don that mask again.

Even the thought of my alter ego fills me with revulsion. Mother knew the entire time. Like an indulgent parent, she let me play the part for a while, allowing me to think I had some control over my life.

It plagues me, along with Wallen's deception. My valet

disappeared after Mother arrived at the Gravely estate, somehow slipped away like a snake in the grass.

I thought I might see him here, skulking close to Mother's side, but there's no sign of him. No one has seen him either—at least no one who is willing to admit it to me.

The inner chamber door opens, and I turn. Alice looks lovely in deep blue. The bodice hugs her delicate curves before the skirt flares at her hips. The material is sumptuous velvet, and the cut is flattering but modest.

Regina chose well. It only takes one look at Alice to know she's beloved—not a servant or a pet, not a mistress or a casual plaything.

It's likely the dress that first agitated Mother at dinner. Alice didn't realize it, but she wore a quiet battle cry, a proclamation that I refuse to treat her as anything less than my equal.

"Can you tie the ribbon for me?" she asks, holding her mask to her face.

I close the distance between us and fumble with the delicate ties, trying not to catch her hair.

"I'm sorry," I murmur, feeling clumsy.

Alice turns when I'm finished, smiling under her ornate, black mask. Like mine, it covers the upper half of her face and leaves her lips and the graceful curve of her jaw visible.

Her blue eyes sparkle at me, making me believe she's already enjoying the intrigue that surrounds the masquerade. "I would think you'd be used to tying such things."

I smile. "These are different."

She studies me. "But you're just as dashing in this one."

"Am I?"

"I was doomed the day we first met," she says, not quite meeting my eyes. "How couldn't I fall for you?"

"I dragged you into the brambles," I say skeptically.

"You saved me." She lifts her eyes, and my heart stutters.

Alice doesn't realize it, but I was doomed that day as well. One smile from her was all it took to capture my attention.

And she still has it, though I tried to pull back after Mother cornered us into the illanté agreement. But today, we've trampled the line I created between us. It might as well be drawn in sand for how stable it is. Though I knew staying away from Alice would be impossible.

She's right—the arrangement is cruel for both of us. My convictions are strong, but she makes me weak.

I'm afraid we will eventually fall into each other's arms, and I will be no better than the Fae I've so despised.

But that's a worry for another day.

Tonight, we'll dance together in the candlelight and pretend the rest of the world isn't waiting and watching for our imminent demise.

THE BALLROOM IS awash in firelight. Thousands of flames flicker from the tapered candles burning in the golden chandeliers fixed to the high ceiling. They lend a moody ambiance, just enough light to see by.

The glass skylights reveal the night sky. The moon

hangs above us, a pale and lonely guest of honor, and its dim glow passes through the glass.

Clutching my arm, Alice stares up at it. Her long blonde hair falls down her back, silver in the light, just as it was the first night we met. She could be a Faerie for how lovely she is, with only the tips of her ears betraying her heritage.

The proof of our tether shines like a golden bracelet around her delicate wrist, visible only to those with magic unless it's coaxed to light. Like a wedding band, it proclaims she is mine.

Unlike a wedding band, it also warns I must keep my distance if I care about Alice's virtue.

And I do, though a dark part of me voices its displeasure far too often, especially when Alice says things like she did earlier in my quarters.

Especially when she touches me.

Tables line the edge of the room. Beyond them, doors are open to the night, letting in the mountain air and the perfume of the night-blooming vines that climb the outside walls.

People freely go between the garden and the ballroom, some pausing by the great fire urns that are placed near the doorways to chase away the mountains' evening chill and warm their hands.

"You have a masquerade every month?" Alice asks, her attention moving to the wall of open doors.

"Every month," I confirm, hoping to hide my weariness.

Even though I'm finding it's far more pleasant to

attend with Alice on my arm, in the past, the balls have been tedious affairs I would have rather missed.

"I suppose it's cold in winter," she says absently.

"We have no winter," I remind her.

She turns back to me, surprised when she realizes her mistake. "Of course."

"There's a winter court, though," I tell her. "Tunder, in North Faerie. The palace is made of ice."

"That must be frigid," she says with a laugh, allowing me to escort her onto the dance floor.

"Mmm." I turn and take her waist. "I've only been once. If I weren't Fae, I would have frozen to death."

A strange expression crosses Alice's face, but she appears to brush the thought away as she sets her hand on my shoulder.

"What is it?" I ask.

"I don't suppose I'll ever be able to see it. No human could."

"They have illantés as well. They're protected by magic."

She slowly nods.

"But you're right—I don't have that kind of power. I can protect you from goblins...but not ice."

We fall into step with the other couples, and Alice easily picks up the foreign steps as she follows my lead. A quartet of players sits on an elevated dais in the corner. They create a dark, haunting melody with their stringed instruments, setting the mood.

"What other courts are there?" she asks.

"There are five high courts, of which Auvenridge is one. Eilonwy in East Faerie is another, as is Tunder."

"And the other two?"

"They're both in South Faerie. The Sionna court rules the archipelago, and the Cavonshim court rules the southern mainland. Then there are several lesser courts scattered amidst the human territories. Though they are self-governing monarchies, like the high courts, their territories are smaller, usually confined to small land features, such as valleys, forests, or islands."

"I've read that in the past, in some places, Faeries and humans coexisted," Alice says. "Is it true?"

"Are you speaking of the fairies of the warring kingdoms of Draegan and Renove?"

She nods.

"Fairies are another high race of Faerie, originally from a small court in northern Evelsa, high in the mountains. They're shapeshifters—highly attuned to the natural elements, arguably the most powerful of our kind. They can live hundreds of years. They believed humans and the Fae should live together—supporting one another with natural talents. But when the tragedy befell Draegan and Renove, their ideology was shunned by most. After that, the fairies all but disappeared."

"Where did they go?"

"Many still reside amongst humans, usually preferring the outskirts of small hamlets and villages, where they can quietly live their long lives. I'm sure many reside in our courts as well, and we simply don't know it." I carefully steer Alice clear of another couple, pulling her just a touch closer as we maneuver around the dance floor. "It's rumored that many have returned to Draegan and Renove now that they're back on the map."

"Have you been to the isle?" Alice asks, her eyes lighting. "Have you seen the healed rift between the kingdoms? Or visited their medieval villages?"

Trapped under a curse for more than a hundred and thirty years, separated from the rest of civilization, the sister kingdoms' people lived as if frozen in time. People say that visiting their isle is like taking a holiday in history.

Laughing, I shake my head. "I have not."

"Maybe we'll go someday," she says, grinning up at me.

I smile back, intrigued by the idea of traveling the world with Alice by my side. "Maybe we will."

We dance until it's late, well past the hour I usually excuse myself.

I'm lulled to a state of complacency, paying little attention to those around us. So when Alice's hand tightens on my shoulders, it takes me by surprise.

"Brahm," she says urgently.

"What is it?" I ask, falling out of step. I follow her eyes, and then I nearly laugh. "They won't bother you."

"They're goblins," she hisses.

"I'm aware."

"What are they doing here?"

"A few always show up—they come for the food."

And sure enough, the beasts linger in the shadows near the refreshment tables, likely thinking they're stealthy. They wear an odd assortment of pilfered items. One is in a waistcoat that falls to his knees. Another wears a human maid's cap, along with a wreath around his neck that he must have stolen from a lamppost in the garden.

They've adorned themselves with other bits and trinkets as well—jewelry that catches the light, bunched up stockings worn as ill-fitting gloves, and ribbons tied around their necks like chokers.

I watch with disinterest as one sneaks to a platter of tartlets and tilts it into a grubby bag—tray and all.

The creatures near him shake with laughter before they make their way down the table, stealing anything and everything that will fit into the bag.

"Shouldn't we tell someone?" Alice says, aghast.

"No one cares," I assure her.

She looks back as if she's going to scold me. "You said they are dangerous."

"They are dangerous—if you're an untethered human. They wouldn't dare touch you now."

"If you'd confronted them in the woods, would they have known you are their prince and run away?"

"Yes, though it's likely they would have caused trouble when they saw I was alone. They're wicked opportunists. They'd try to dispose of me if they thought they could."

"But they can't hurt me now?"

"The tether would likely kill them if they tried, and they are aware of that."

Alice looks as if she's thinking about it. "You're certain?"

"I am."

Nodding to herself, she suddenly marches toward the refreshment tables, her arms swaying with determination.

Startled, I hurry to catch up with her. "What are you doing?"

One of the goblins spots us and nudges his friend in the ribs. Quickly, the small monsters dart under the tablecloth.

Instead of answering me, Alice pulls up the cloth and leans over.

Stupefied, I watch as she grabs one of the goblins by its flabby arm and yanks it out from the protection of the table.

"No, not you," she says almost immediately, shoving it away and going back for another.

The goblin shrieks and runs for the closest door, drawing the attention of nearly everyone in the ballroom. Even the players go silent as Alice drags another goblin from under the table.

The others cower in the corner, squealing like terrified piglets.

"*You*," she says darkly, bringing the goblin into the light. He wears a woman's corset on his bulbous body, along with several satin ribbons and an assortment of jewelry.

His eyes go wide with terror. He could easily shred Alice's exposed skin with his sharp, jagged talons, but he doesn't dare.

"Give me back my grandmother's ring," Alice demands, pointing at the band that hangs from a piece of leather around the goblin's neck. "*Now.*"

Shaking, the monster quickly does as it's commanded, thrusting the ring, leather and all, into Alice's hand. It then prostrates itself on the floor, babbling a string of guttural nonsense that can be nothing but a desperate plea for forgiveness.

Alice kneels in her elaborate ballgown, looking down on the miserable creature. "Do you know what I am? Do you know who I belong to?"

The pathetic creature nods.

"Good," she says hotly. "Then you know why you will return to your lair or den or whatever your kind hole up in, and you will fetch every last thing you stole from my trunks and return them to Prince Brahm's estate. Do you understand?"

He nods, nearly smacking his forehead on the ballroom floor.

Alice stands, wiping her hands, likely regretting touching him. "Get out."

The goblin stumbles to his feet and runs from the room as if a dragon is on his heels.

When Alice turns back, she goes still. Perhaps she didn't realize she'd drawn such a crowd.

People gather around us, amused by the display. They watch Alice, wondering if she's something a little different—something they could embrace.

Mother would be livid, but she's passed out on her throne, fast asleep like she always is by this time of night.

Alice scans her audience, and then she straightens her spine and walks to my side. Concealing a grin, I offer her my arm. "Would you like to wash your hands?"

"Very much, thank you," she answers primly.

Leaving Alice's spectators behind, we go into the garden.

24

ALICE

I've made a spectacle of myself, but I can't say that I care all that much. I got my grandmother's wedding band back.

Brahm looks like he's trying not to laugh as he leads me to a moonlit fountain. I pause to rinse my hands, scrubbing them together in the frigid water to rid myself of the goblin's unique aroma.

Once I'm satisfied they are as clean as possible, we continue past the manicured beds instead of returning to the ballroom. In the distance, the players begin their music once more.

Eventually, we end up in a small alcove in the hedge, a spot of quiet respite, with a statue of a winged woman at the center of the planting. Her face is turned toward the sky, with her hand extended, looking as if she's crying. At her feet appears to be the recently deceased form of a loved one.

"This is a lovely spot you've brought me to," I say with a smile.

Brahm fetched my cloak before we left the ballroom, and he drapes it around my shoulders now. "No one comes here."

"I wonder why," I say lightly.

A glimpse of painted wood in the hedge catches my eye. It's hidden behind the plantings, but a tiny handle is just visible. I cross the space and pull back the limbs of a weeping willow, revealing a small blue door. "It's tiny," I say, wondering if it's meant for pixies. "Where does it lead?"

"We can find out if you'd like."

"You don't know?" I kneel to examine the door, and my skirts bunch up around me. A child could fit through it if they crouched, but we would have difficulty. "I see a problem."

"You see a *human* problem."

"Forgive me, but that is how I tend to look at the world. How do you pass through?" Then I'm struck with a disconcerting thought. "Do you shrink yourself to fit?"

Brahm laughs, wickedly amused by the idea. "Certainly not. You only need to touch it, and it will spirit you away. It's a gate to the human world—it leads to a fairy ring somewhere. But since the rings never show up in the same place, it's impossible to know where you'll end up. They're old magic, and very few utilize them anymore."

"So, if we were to touch it, it could take us anywhere in the world?"

"That's right, but only tonight."

"Why tonight?"

He nods toward the sky. "It's a full moon. All of Faerie,

and its inhabitants, are at the height of their power when the moon is full."

Slowly, I stand, backing away from the door and letting the willow fall into place. "I don't think I'm that adventurous."

"I was terrified of them as a young boy," Brahm says. "But after Father died, I was desperate to escape. I used one the full moon after his death."

"Where did it take you?"

"To the woods just beyond the bridge." He scoffs, disgusted. "It could have taken me anywhere, and I ended up right outside West Faerie."

"Truly?"

He nods.

"Did you resent my sister?" I ask him quietly. "If Drake hadn't tried to help her, your father would still be alive."

Slowly, he shakes his head. "I believe Drake did the right thing. But often, I wish it had been me and not him. I was older. Maybe I could have slipped her away without Mother ever realizing who was to blame."

"It's not your fault." I step close, wanting to offer comfort but unsure if he'd welcome it.

"I know that."

After a moment, he wraps his arm around my waist and pulls me into him. His mask makes him look too otherworldly in the light of the full moon, and for the first time, I think I can truly believe he is a prince of West Faerie.

Our gazes meet. Brahm's eyes fall to my lips, and heat dances across my exposed skin despite the nighttime chill.

I tilt my head toward him in invitation—waiting, wanting, needing so very much.

Brahm lowers his head slowly, almost as if he's about to change his mind. I hold my breath, silently urging him forward.

Please kiss me, I beg him with my eyes.

"Alice," he breathes, beginning to shake his head.

Gently, I press my hands to either side of his face. "It's all right."

He pauses, searching me for signs of hesitation—and finding none.

I slide my hands down, letting them rest on his shoulders, counting the seconds as I wait. Tension grows between us, drawing us closer.

My eyes flutter closed when his mouth brushes against mine. Though the kiss is sweet and short, it's followed by an oh-so-slow retreat that leaves me swooning.

But when I think we're going to part, Brahm kisses me again, firmer this time, his lips lingering just a little longer before he draws back. I lean into him and loop my arms around his neck, pressing close.

"Alice," he says, this time breathing my name like its precious air. He flattens his palm against my back, dragging me against him, and his other hand grips my waist firmly.

I pull off his mask, needing to see him, and then I remove mine. We come together once more, the time for hesitating long past.

I'm lost to Brahm, my heart full to the brim. I kiss him back, meeting his growing intensity, feeling the air crackle with magic around us. It sweeps over my skin, addictive and new.

Perhaps Brahm was holding back before, or maybe it's the full moon, but it does feel magical in Faerie tonight. The garden is alive around us, and I'm suddenly aware of it.

When we do part, Brahm's eyes fall to my finger. I discarded the filthy leather when I washed my hands, and then I slid on grandmother's ring.

"You seemed happy to have it back," he says quietly.

I look down at it now, rotating the gold band around my finger. "It was special to my grandmother. She wore it every day, even though she'd lost grandfather before I was born. She spoke about him like they'd only parted the week before—like she still loved him as much as she did the spring evening they exchanged their vows. It always seemed so beautiful to me, so pure."

Brahm is quiet, waiting for me to go on.

"The ring technically belonged to Gustin, but I smuggled it into my things," I admit, giving him a guilty smile. "Like everything else, it was supposed to be auctioned to help pay the debt. Forgive me, I suppose I stole it from you. But I couldn't bear to see the token of their life together sold off to the highest bidder."

A strange look crosses Brahm's face. "We should fight for the things that are precious to us, shouldn't we?"

Slowly, I nod. "I believe so."

"You're precious to me, Alice." Brahm pauses. "The most precious thing in my life."

I stare at the ring, letting his declaration heal

wounded parts of my soul. I've never been precious to anyone. Not Mother or Father, and certainly not Gustin. Grandmother loved me, but even she worried over Gustin's growing recklessness too much to give me much time. I was always there, quiet and obedient, never demanding anyone's attention...and therefore never receiving much of it either.

And now here I am, in an enchanted garden, hearing words I've been so desperate to hear, and from a prince of Faerie.

I'm precious.

I'm not just Eleanor's sister or Gustin's unfortunate problem. I'm not the quiet daughter of poor Lord and Lady Gravely or Prince Brahm's illanté.

Tears blur my vision, but they don't fall. Even if we can never be anything more, this is enough. For the first time in my life, I feel cherished.

"I want to take you somewhere," Brahm says quietly, suddenly looking very sober.

Nodding, I loop my arm through his, allowing him to lead me wherever he wants. We meander through the garden, startling drowsing flowers. They bloom when they spot us, putting on a show.

"That's the strangest thing," I whisper to Brahm, eyeing them with great interest.

After we pass, their petals fall around their heads as they drift once more.

There are pixies in the bushes, along with the creatures with the golden eyes. They're getting braver now, and a few let me glimpse a peek at their furry faces. They look a little like cats hiding amongst the flowerbeds. They watch us, terribly interested in our meanderings.

We walk until the gardens grow wild, and I begin to wonder if we haven't gone past the castle grounds. And then, we stop.

"What do you think?" Brahm asks, gesturing toward a tiny one-room cottage in the trees. It looks like a caretaker's shed, or perhaps a child's playhouse.

Overgrown trees nearly cover it with their limbs, and massive peonies spill light pink blooms onto the stone step.

Brahm pushes through the brush at the side of the small building, looking for something. A moment later, he returns with a key. After he unlocks the door, he pushes it open and gestures for me to go in first. "You'll have to lean down to enter, but I promise this doorway is passable."

"It's dark," I point out.

Nodding, Brahm extends his hand toward the cottage. Light suddenly glows from within.

"Such a useful trick," I tease him. "I think I'll have to keep you."

He laughs under his breath as I duck down and step inside. When I straighten, I inhale slowly.

There are books everywhere—stuffed into a tiny bookshelf, piled onto the floor, even stacked on a chair in the corner. There's an old coat-of-arms on the wall, and a group of hand-carved figurines that look like they were crafted by a child. An assortment of daggers and a short sword. A golden cup and a wooden plate. It's a strange collection of eclectic things, and yet it seems everything here was treasured.

"What is this place?" I ask, my eyes sweeping over the space.

"Father built it for me when I was young," he says. "Drake and Eleanor had their garden, and Sabine has a hidden room in the sapphire wing. This was mine."

The place where Brahm spent his childhood.

I venture deeper inside, looking at all the things he collected as a boy.

"May I?" I ask, pausing in front of a small silver box.

He's preoccupied with the contents of a basket, but he waves, giving me permission.

I open the box, wondering what he might keep in something so precious, and I nearly laugh out loud when I discover its secret.

"Acorns?" I ask.

Brahm glances over, smiling though he doesn't answer.

"Are they magical?" I prod. "Enchanted, perhaps?"

"They're just acorns."

Another container holds small rocks, and then I find a pile of pinecones.

"Why did you collect all of this?"

"The natural world holds its own sort of magic. Seeds, like acorns and those found in pinecones, contain raw energy. Rocks are connected to the earth."

"Do the Fae pull all their magic from the world around them?" I ask.

Brahm shakes his head, still shuffling through the

basket. "No. We have our own. Those things just act as a booster. They're more helpful when we're young and still clumsy with our magic."

"What did you use them for?"

"I enchanted trinkets, mostly."

"Like the things the Fae merchants sell in Kellington?"

He nods. "Nothing with true magic—just little charms, more amusing than useful."

"Gustin used a Faerie love charm on a girl he fancied once," I say absently. "She kissed him in front of the main square on Spring's Eve. Once she found out what he'd done, she punched him right in the face. He had a black eye for almost two weeks."

Brahm grins to himself, perhaps liking the idea of Gustin getting maimed. "Most of the charms the Fae sell don't have lingering effects."

"This one lasted all of two minutes," I say with a laugh, wondering where Gustin is now. I'm not sure I should care, but I do a little. I can't help it.

"What kind of charms did you make?" I ask Brahm, pushing thoughts of my brother aside.

"Mostly things to amuse Sabine and Eleanor. Little dancing dolls, flowers that never faded, candles that sparked and burned in different colors. Trivial things." He hums with pleasure, making me think he's found what he was looking for. "Sabine always liked it when I'd charm human trinkets—instruments, games, things of that sort. She wouldn't admit it to a soul, but she's desperately obsessed with your people."

I browse the books, hoping to learn something about

Brahm from the selection. But if I glean anything, it's that his taste is eclectic. He has everything, from journals to epics, to stories of heroic adventure.

"Are these all human authors?" I ask, running my finger over the printing date on the front page of *Birds of Prey: Falcons, Hawks, and Owls of Northern Illusa and the Arctic Hold*.

"Most." Brahm unwinds a spool of thin silver wire, snipping it into three equal pieces before he begins braiding it together. "The Fae of the high courts don't often write books. Our history is passed through songs and poems, recited by bards and court jesters."

"But you have your own language—I've seen it."

"It's archaic, rarely used anymore. Through time, we've adopted the human languages. Some Faeries still believe there's power in written incantations, but that's an outdated ideology." He gives me a look. "Often, random words are etched onto things sold to the humans to make them seem more magical than they truly are."

Laughing, I step up beside Brahm, watching as he creates two more braids from the whisper-thin silver. He then begins to twine them together, making an intricate twist.

"Silver doesn't bother you?" I ask.

He shakes his head, working deftly. "All metals respond to magic. Silver is an amplifier, and gold is a vessel for storing a surplus gathered from nature. Tin holds memories, and copper reacts badly."

"Badly?"

"It burns."

"And iron?"

Brahm cringes. "Iron is uncomfortable. It's hard to explain. It's similar to the sensation you get when you hit your elbow on something hard, but it's more intense and not as localized."

"So copper is your true weakness?"

He glances over as if amused by the question. "Should I be worried?"

Laughing again, I shake my head.

"What are you doing?" I finally ask, realizing Brahm came here with a purpose, and it wasn't just to give me a glimpse of his childhood.

He doesn't answer. Instead, he pulls on a thick pair of leather gloves and rifles through the basket once more. He chooses another tool, this one a long metal mandrel with an iron handle.

Using it to coax the silver to bend, he creates a loop in the braid.

Intrigued, I pull out the short stool and sit, waiting for him to explain what he's making and why he brought me here at this time of night to create it.

Next, he chooses a heavy pair of shears with a blunt tip. Eyeing the intricate braid with a solemn expression, he clips away the straight sections and tosses them aside.

He's left with a ring, and my interest grows.

After coaxing the ends to meet, he chooses another tool—this one long and narrow, with a sharp point.

I lean a little closer, realizing he's using magic now. Brahm barely touches the loose silver strands with the point of the tool, and they meld together as if soldered.

When he's finished, the braid flows in a continuous loop, impossible to tell where it once began and ended.

Satisfied with his work, Brahm slides the ring onto the mandrel once more, shaping it into a perfect circle.

He then runs his finger over and around it, polishing it, his magic shimmering slightly as he works. When he's finished, the silver gleams in the dim light.

The entire process takes him less than five minutes. When he's satisfied, he turns, looking somewhat unsure of himself. He studies the ring, rolling it between his fingers.

I wait, and my stomach grows anxious as the seconds stretch between us.

"Is it for...?" I ask.

He traces the metal band with his fingertip. "If you'd like it."

My pulse quickens. "It's beautiful."

"Rings have fallen out of tradition with the Fae," he says, still looking at the piece of jewelry he created so quickly. "Hundreds of years ago, they were used in marital binding ceremonies before we adopted the human tradition of weddings. A vow is sufficient now, without the added binding magic, especially amongst the people of West Faerie. Rings have lost their meaning, and some snub them altogether because of what they represented in the past."

"Because of what they represented?"

"The traditional binding ceremony is considered archaic. When you enter into it, the magic literally binds your existence to your partner's. You can't stray far without enduring physical pain, and when one dies, the other perishes as well. A ring seals the vow."

I nod, unsure what to say.

"But when you speak of your grandmother's ring, you make it sound as if it's a symbol of love. Of devotion and honor." He looks up, and his dark eyes meet mine. "Because of the illanté tether, we're bound for life, Alice. Perhaps there is a way to break the oath, but the truth is, I don't want to let you go."

My breath quickens, and I wait for him to continue.

"You and I will never be allowed to marry in Faerie. Even if we put aside the tether, it's forbidden for a Faerie to marry a human."

"Why?" I whisper.

"Because my people believe it dilutes our magic. Eventually, if we intermarried with humans, there would be no Fae left. We, as a people, and our magic, would cease to exist."

"But you said Fae men have human mistresses. Aren't children inevitable?"

He shakes his head solemnly. "There are charms and spells to prevent it."

"Oh," I say softly.

"If we're together, then I want our union to be legal, lawful, and right. I want a family, and eventually children...and you."

I swallow as my heart begins to race. "If we're together? But you just said..."

"Marry me, Alice," Brahm says softly. "Let's go into Valsta and elope. No one will marry us here, but that doesn't mean we cannot be married in human territory."

"You want to marry me?" I whisper, sure I must have misunderstood.

Brahm takes my hand. "We'll live in Faerie for a time, until we decide to begin a family, and then we'll leave. We'll go somewhere no one knows us. I'll live like a human, disguising myself."

"And what about your sister and brother?"

Pain crosses Brahm's face, and he looks down.

"You can't leave them," I say softly. "You would regret it your entire life—it would haunt you."

"This wasn't my choice, Alice. I tried to let you go. You know I did. But now that we've been tethered, I know my limits. I cannot stay away from you, not when I've come to love you like I do."

My fingers tighten around his. "Say it again."

Brahm brings a hand to my face, gently brushing his thumb over my cheek. "I love you, Alice."

I close my eyes, savoring the confession. When I open them, I find him watching me, waiting for my answer.

"I will marry you, Brahm. But we will remain here, keeping our vows secret so that you may remain close to your brother and sister." I look down. "Let people believe I'm your mistress—I don't care. We'll know the truth, and that's enough."

"If my mother finds out, she'll kill us both," Brahm warns.

"Then she mustn't find out."

"And if you decide you want children?"

"We'll cross that bridge when we reach it."

Brahm nods, letting me make the choice. He raises my hand and slides the ring over my finger. It feels like a promise, solid and substantial. Not a leash, not a shackle —a gift of love, freely given.

"It's not as lovely as your grandmother's," he says regretfully.

I admire the way the twisted silver gleams. "It's perfect."

Stepping back, Brahm takes my hand. "We'll leave as soon as we return to my estate."

25

BRAHM

"Have you gone insane?" Sabine hisses, looking over her shoulder to ensure we're alone. We're in her sitting room—I'm not sure who she thinks could be lurking.

"Probably, but it doesn't matter because I've made up my mind."

She shakes her head, looking more scared than angry. "If Mother even had an inkling of what you have planned—"

"Are you going to tell her?" I ask needlessly, mostly to make a point.

My sister's eyes flash. "Of course I'm not."

"Then how will she find out?"

Sabine crosses her arms. "I understand, all right? You're not like so many of our people—you're chivalrous, a man of honor, and I know why you're doing this. But…"

"But what? Do you want me to change who I am? Should I become a lecherous pig like Ian? Turn Alice into a—"

"Brahm," Sabine interrupts, pulling a disgusted face as she holds up her hand. "I do not want details about your relationship. Fine. Marry the human—but be quick about it. If you intend to return, you had better not linger outside Faerie. I'll do everything I can to keep Mother away from your woods for as long as possible."

"Thank you," I say heavily. "Sabine, I—"

"Yes, yes. You are so grateful and are blessed to have me as a sister," she says, eyeing me like I'm a nuisance. "I'm aware."

"I am."

Anxiety creeps across Sabine's features once again. "Please—*please*—be cautious."

"I will," I swear.

Suddenly, she chokes back a sob. From the horrified look on her face, I believe it's a surprise to us both. Swiping at her eyes, she growls, "I swear, if Mother tries to hurt you, I'll fight her."

"Sabine," I say slowly, at a loss. Never in my life have I seen my sister cry. "Don't say such things."

"I would though. I'm stronger than she is now—I know it. And you and Drake are all I have. If she so much as tries to lay a finger on either of you..." She blinks furiously, looking as angry as I am startled.

With a sigh, I step forward, awkwardly hugging her.

I've taken her strength for granted—and now her shield is cracking.

Even Sabine can only take so much of Mother's wickedness. She's been crushed under her heel, refusing to break. But no one is invincible.

"We'll return as soon as possible," I promise her.

Nodding, she struggles out of my arms, brushing the front of her gown as if it might be wrinkled. Avoiding my eyes, she regains her composure. "But seriously, Brahm. A human? Thank goodness you're not the heir. Can you even imagine?"

I laugh. "You're far more suited for the throne than I am."

Finally, she looks back at me. "Have a safe trip."

I pause by the door as I leave. "You have a good heart, no matter how you try to hide it. You know that, don't you?"

"Why are you still here?" she demands, turning away as she begins to cry again. "I don't want to look at you anymore."

I smile as I step out, but when I shut the door, I'm hit with a wave of guilt.

Our family is broken, and I have no idea how to fix it.

———

THERE'S freedom in the human lands. No one knows me here, and when I cloak myself in illusion, most can't even tell I'm one of the Fae. A few people give me questioning looks, likely suspecting. But when their eyes move to my ears, they look away as if perplexed.

We traveled through Kellington, across the ferry that goes to Thornborough, and now we're on our way to Valsta's capital city of Davon. We should arrive in just a few hours.

We're only a few days from the boundary of West Faerie, but it's far enough. Not many of my people venture this deep into human territory, and our chance of being detected has gone down dramatically.

"I have a question," Alice says across from me in the carriage, huddled under a thick fur blanket.

I watch the scenery pass beyond the window, intrigued by the snow. "All right."

"Back in the garden, when you made the ring for me, you said a marriage vow is sufficient without the added binding magic, especially amongst people in West Faerie. What does that mean?"

I sit back, giving her my full attention. "Long ago, my distant grandmother tricked the wealthy king of East Faerie into creating a betrothal between her daughter and his son, saying that the princess was with child thanks to the unscrupulous nature of the eastern prince.

"The king of East Faerie, being an honorable man, agreed to the marriage and promised a large sum of money as an apology for the heartbreak and shame the queen and king of West Faerie had to endure. After the agreement was made binding, however, he learned that the princess was not carrying his grandchild—or any other child," I explain. "Before the prince left his land to join our family, his father cursed him so that all his descendants, and anyone under their rule, would be forced to speak nothing but truth."

"So, your family has always been rather awful."

I smile at her teasing. "I think that sums it up well enough."

"And if you lie?"

"It's painful. Excruciating, really. And we're ill for days."

Alice thinks about it for several seconds, and then a mischievous smile spreads across her face. "So, if I were to ask you something, you can truly do nothing but answer me honestly?"

"Or avoid the question," I say with a smirk, doing just that.

Looking delighted, Alice bites the corner of her lip, likely trying to decide what she'd like to ask. Then she nods to herself and leans forward, resting her elbows in her lap.

"Were you attracted to me when you first saw me stranded in the middle of the road? Did I make your heart flutter?"

I match her stance by leaning forward. "Yes."

She grins, delighted. "Did you want to kiss me that night when we stood so close?"

I smile. "Yes."

Her expression becomes serious. "Did you feel bad for deceiving me?"

I begin to tell her that I did, but my stomach tightens, and I pause, forced to think about it. "Yes and no."

Alice's eyes widen with question.

"I liked getting to know you behind the mask, without my title or my identity getting in the way. For the first time, I was no one—and you liked me anyway. But I did feel guilt for deceiving you, yes."

Accepting my answer, Alice nods. Then her face brightens once more. "Did you think you'd ever fall in love with a human?"

"No."

"It would be easier if I were a Faerie," she says.

"Yes—but I like you exactly as you are."

Slowly, her hand goes to the side of her head. "Do you think my ears are ugly?"

I snort out a laugh, unable to stop myself. "No, I think your ears are very appealing."

"And the rest of me?"

I cross the carriage, claiming the spot on the bench next to her. I take her waist, sliding her toward me, pleased when she comes eagerly. "Everything about you is appealing, Alice."

She lets out a satisfied sigh when I kiss her. Then suddenly, she tilts her head back. "You said I was uncomfortable."

"That wasn't a lie," I laugh.

Her eyes flash with irritation, but when she tries to pull away, I clutch her closer. Moving my lips to her ear, I say, "You made me want things I didn't think I could have."

"You can have them." She turns to face me. "You can have me."

I nod, studying her as I brush her hair back from her face. "Soon."

Alice lays her head on my shoulder and tugs the blanket over us both.

I drape my arm around her back, and we travel the rest of the way to Davon like this, our fingers twined together, in peaceful silence.

Beyond the carriage window, farms dot the snow-blanketed countryside. Red-painted barns contrast the never-ending white, and smoke rises from cozy farmhouse chimneys. Cows and horses stand in the snow, looking impervious to the weather.

"I've never seen anything like it." I rest my cheek against Alice's head.

"You don't have farms in Faerie?" Alice asks.

I shake my head. "Not like these. Many grow gardens, and some keep chickens or ducks for eggs. But most of the meat that graces our tables is wild, and many refuse to eat it at all."

"Have you ever been this far away from Fae territory?"

"No," I answer. "We don't generally venture deep into the human kingdoms. We have no business there, and we're not particularly welcome."

The farms grow smaller the closer we get to the capital, and the houses become closer together. They group in little villages that outskirt the city, and eventually, large buildings begin to dot the roadways. We pass taverns, guild houses, inns, and craftsmen's shops.

As we venture deeper into Davon, cottages are replaced with tall boardinghouses that house many families of meager income and even larger, gated townhouses for the wealthy. More people travel the busy streets—men driving canvas-covered wagons, bringing produce from the warmer regions into the city; carriages, both public and private; and men and women on horseback, braving the gray sky and the chill. Bundled-up children run on the streets, their scarves flying in the air behind them, and people bustle between shops.

"So many humans," I murmur.

Alice laughs. "You do tend to run into many of them in *human* cities. Strange how that works."

A grand cathedral stands in the distance, its medieval

parapets towering over the rooftops. At the top of the hour, the bells ring, scaring a flurry of blackbirds into the air.

The carriage comes to a slow, bumping stop near the snowy entrance of a public garden. Shifting from under the blanket, I move to the opposite side of the carriage just before Darren opens the door.

"We've arrived in Davon, my lord," Darren informs us, letting in the afternoon chill. "Where would you like me to take you?"

"The city magistrate's office," I tell him.

He bows his head. "I'll ask for directions, and then we'll continue."

The door closes, and Alice shivers across from me, pulling the blanket over her shoulders. "It's cold."

A few minutes later, we continue our trip through the city, eventually entering an old section with large, stately buildings and meticulously planted landscapes. Bare-limbed trees grow encased in small, circular iron fences, and boxwoods line the streets, cut into spherical topiaries.

The shops in the square boast glass windows with striped awnings over their entries. Judging from the people on the streets, only the well-to-do can afford to shop in this district.

We come to a stop in front of a large stone building. The painted sign that hangs from the eaves states it's the local magistrate's office.

"I think we're here," I tell Alice.

A nervous smile flits across Alice's face, letting me know I'm not the only one feeling anxious.

"You're sure about this?" I ask her quietly.

Her smile is bright, and she clasps my hand. "Certain."

Darren opens the door, and this time, we step onto the icy street. Alice adjusts her cloak around her neck, trying to block the chill, and then she takes my arm as we start up the slick front walk. It looks like the snow was scraped away after the last storm, leaving a thin layer that melted during the warmer afternoon hours. Now there's a thin sheet of ice, making it more treacherous than walking through a drift of snow.

We're almost to the door when Alice slips. She grabs my arm to keep from falling, her feet sliding under her. I catch her, nearly going down myself, and we laugh like fools, earning a few disgruntled looks from the snobbish humans passing by.

Composing herself, Alice straightens. Her eyes sparkle, and her cheeks are pink from the cold. "It's slick."

"I noticed."

I open the heavy wooden door, and we're met with warm air. A woman at a receptionist's desk looks up, smiling serenely. "Good afternoon. How may I help you?"

The room smells like spices, apples, and parchment, with a hint of coal mixed in as well. The first fragrance likely comes from the small pot simmering atop the stove in the corner.

"We're here to see the magistrate," I say. "We would like to be married."

The woman's eyes travel between us. Her eyebrows raise in question as her gaze first travels over our clothes and then moves to the carriage that waits on the street.

I imagine she's wondering why people of our station

would rather marry quietly instead of having a large society wedding, with all the fuss and fanfare that comes with such an event.

But, proving to be professional, she quickly dismisses her confusion and opens a cabinet next to her chair, thumbing through several folders until she produces a piece of parchment. "You'll need to fill out the license, but don't sign it just yet." She nudges a quill and inkwell to the edge of the desk. "The magistrate is out, but I expect he will return soon. You are welcome to wait."

She then excuses herself and walks into the back room.

Alice stands next to me as I begin to fill out the license, saying nothing when the quill trembles subtly in my hand.

When I'm finished, we stare at the parchment together.

All that's left to do is sign.

26

ALICE

I let my fingers drift next to Brahm's, offering assurance as we wait. He looks nervous but eager, mirroring the emotions swirling in my own heart.

A few minutes later, the woman returns, taking the parchment and scanning it to make sure Brahm filled it out correctly. Satisfied, she places it next to a ledger.

"Would you like tea?" she asks. "Or if you're hungry, there's a nice café on the next block. I expected Magistrate Rodgers to return by now. He must have been delayed."

Brahm turns to me, letting me decide.

Even though I don't think I could eat right now, the idea of passing the time in the small, warm room is unnerving. "Maybe we'll browse a few shops and then return."

The receptionist nods politely, and we walk onto the icy entry once more, this time passing without incident.

We step into the first business—a tea shop that smells like rosemary and lemons. I browse the selections, intrigued by blends I've never seen offered in Kellington, such as lemongrass with rose, mint, and chamomile. There are exotic black teas as well, costing more per ounce than silver, from faraway places I've never even heard of.

The next shop is a working gallery, with a blown glass artisan creating his delicate figurines in the back of the room. We watch him for a while, and then we move to the next business—a shop that carries nothing but stationery.

Brahm pauses by a map of the Valsta Algora Alliance that hangs on the wall, and another customer strikes up a conversation about trade routes with him—something I'm not sure a prince of West Faerie knows much about, though Brahm carries his end of things well enough.

I smile as I walk through the aisles, taking in the assortment of hand-pressed papers, many of them flecked with tiny, dried flower petals or herbs. The shop carries dozens of quills and every imaginable color of sealing wax. There are envelopes, hand-painted cards, and decorative cork stamps that are designed to press into ink-soaked pads.

I pause near the counter, standing in front of a case filled with paperweights. Many of them are little animal figurines made of pewter—small rabbits, cats, a few owls, and a dove. Others are glass and brass, and a few seem to be made of silver.

"Would you like to see anything closer?" a man with a thick mustache asks, looking eager for a sale.

"I'm just browsing," I say, and then my eyes catch on a

letter opener next to a pewter rooster. I gesture to it. "Is that copper?"

The man pulls it from the case. "It is, yes. The scroll-work is quite exquisite."

That may be, but that's not what snared my interest. It's long, with one sharpened edge and a narrow, pointed end.

"How much is it?" I ask.

"Fifty-seven fluots."

That's robbery if I've ever heard it, but the inflated prices are a product of the shop's location and the clientele they cater to.

But I have the money with me. It's the leftover pay that Brahm gave me all those weeks ago for tending the conservatory plants.

"I'll buy it," I say.

"Lovely!" The shopkeeper beams. "I'll wrap it up for you."

"I'll take the little glass rabbit there as well," I say, pointing into the case.

The man's smile grows. "Of course."

A few minutes later, I meet Brahm by the door.

He gestures toward the brown paper bag the man gave me. "Did you find something you like?"

I nod, pulling out the rabbit.

He takes it to examine closer. "And what is its purpose?"

"It's a paperweight."

"All right," he says, clearly not understanding the point of that any more than a glass rabbit.

I laugh, taking it from him and carefully nestling it

into the bag. "I thought Sabine might like it. She has all those little figurines in her room at your estate, and I'm not above bribing her to like me."

Giving me a curious look, Brahm's smile softens. "She'll love it."

When I pull out the letter opener, Brahm's eyes go wide.

"Don't touch it," I warn.

He eyes the little tool with great distaste. "I wasn't going to."

"It's a precaution, that's all," I explain. "If a human is going to live in Faerie, with a mad queen as her mother-in-law, she must be able to protect herself somehow. I know you said the tether will keep me safe, but..."

I shrug instead of finishing the sentence.

"I understand—but now I must be extra cautious not to anger you."

I laugh, rolling my eyes as I slip the letter opener back into the bag. "I have no intention of using it on you."

Brahm's expression becomes serious. "I hope you don't have to use it at all."

WHEN WE RETURN to the magistrate's office, we find a blond-haired man with a short, trim beard speaking with the receptionist.

"Ah, hello," the woman says, turning to us as we enter the room. "Good timing. Magistrate Rodgers has just returned."

The magistrate scans the paper and then turns to us.

"All seems to be in order. All that's left is your signatures and the exchanging of vows, and then I'll notarize the license."

Brahm and I step up to the desk together. My hands shake, though I'm not having second thoughts. I want this.

"Shall we begin?" Magistrate Rodgers asks patiently.

Brahm's hand finds mine, and he interlaces our fingers. Together, we nod.

"Are you both acting of your own free will?" the man begins.

"We are," we both parrot obediently.

"And your father, miss?" he asks kindly. "Does he agree to this marriage?"

"My father is deceased, sir," I say. "I am now my own guardian."

"Very well. Do you"—he glances at the license—"Alice Elizabeth Gravely take Brahm Ambrose Severin to be your lawfully wedded husband? Do you swear to honor, love, protect, and cherish him through sickness and health, for better or worse, for as long as you both shall live?"

"I do," I say softly, feeling as if the butterflies in my stomach will carry me away.

"And do you Brahm Ambrose Severin take Alice Elizabeth Gravely to be your lawfully wedded wife? Do you swear to honor, love, protect, and cherish her through sickness and health, for better or worse, for as long as you both shall live?"

"I do," Brahm answers confidently.

"Then by the power vested in me by the Holy

Sovereign and King Balthus of Valsta, I pronounce you husband and wife. Brahm, you may kiss your bride."

Tears sheen over my eyes as Brahm turns to me.

I didn't wear a white gown. We had no flowers or girls in fluffy dresses. There were no wreath-decked aisles, no candles, and not even a family member was present.

But it's perfect because Brahm is mine, and I am his—officially, bound by something more meaningful than the tether.

Brahm kisses me softly, sealing the promise.

"If you'll now sign your names," the man says when we part.

We do as he asks, and then the receptionist steps forward to write her name as the witness. After Magistrate Rodgers signs the license as well, he seals it with his stamp.

"Congratulations," the receptionist says after the magistrate excuses himself. "We'll file the license. If you ever wish to see it, it will be kept in the records building next door."

After we say our goodbyes, we leave the office, officially married.

Feeling giddy, I sit next to Brahm in the carriage. After Darren closes the door, Brahm kisses our clasped hands, looking completely content. "So, Alice, how does it feel to officially be a princess of West Faerie?"

I blink at him, startled by the realization. "I am, aren't I?"

He laughs, pulling me in for a real kiss. "You are."

WE MAKE it as far as Thornborough before it gets too cold to continue. I would have liked to have spent our first night together in Brahm's estate, but the trip is just too long. After all the traveling, I'm so tired I don't even care.

The inn we find is small and quaint, and we stand outside a tiny room on the second level.

My nerves nearly get the best of me as Brahm unlocks the door and pushes it open. The room stretches before us, roughly the same size as the stamp pads at the stationery shop.

The bed is narrow and small, with one pillow and several heavy blankets. There's a chair shoved under the tiny table, but it's so close to the bed, it would be impossible to pull it out. A washing bowl rests on a petite cupboard under the window, and a hand-sized mirror hangs on the wall.

All in all, it's a sad sight, though I know I should be thankful it's clean and tidy. It could be worse.

At least, that's what I keep telling myself.

Brahm clears his throat as he steps inside, avoiding my eyes as I follow him in. "Would you like me to take this room, or..."

Darren comes in behind me, setting down my trunk.

"This is fine." I cross my arms when I realize my fingers keep fidgeting at my sides.

We didn't tell our coachman what business we had with the magistrate in Davon, though I think he suspects.

But the fewer people that know, the better—that's why Brahm secured us two rooms for the night. We'll continue the charade until we return to Brahm's estate.

It's a depressing thought, but I'm not sure I want to spend our first night here anyway.

"Good night, Alice." Brahm hesitates in the doorway before he steps into the hall. "Sleep well."

"You too," I murmur.

After I lock the door behind him, I open my trunk with a sigh, wondering how I'll ever get to sleep. I dress for bed, taking my time as I brush my hair, running the day's events through my head.

I smile when I remember how confidently Brahm said his vow.

We're married.

I press my hand over my mouth, trapping in a girlish squeal. Tossing back the covers, I crawl into bed and stare at the ceiling, willing myself to sleep.

But I lie here, thinking about Brahm...wondering what he's thinking about. Is he in his room, staring at the ceiling, too? Does he wish he was with me?

I sigh, spreading my hands to either side of the mattress, easily touching both edges. I don't even know how we'd fit. Brahm isn't a small man.

The idea makes my cheeks heat, and I fan my face, laughing at my ridiculous thoughts.

Every minute stretches longer than the last. I count backward from a hundred, but I'm still awake. I close my eyes, breathing evenly, telling myself I am very sleepy, but that doesn't work either.

My eyes fly open, and I press my head back into the pillow with a groan.

Maybe, if I knew what room Brahm is in, I could—no.

"It's one night, Alice," I scold myself. "You've been

sleeping by yourself for a lifetime. Surely you can manage this."

I fluff the pillow several times, roll onto my side, and bunch the blankets against me. I close my eyes, sternly telling myself that I really will go to sleep this time.

And then there's a knock at the door—the quietest knock imaginable.

I freeze in the bed, my heart thrumming hard enough it makes me dizzy.

All is silent.

Did I imagine it?

Yes, that must be it. Maybe I was closer to dreaming than I realized.

I close my eyes once more, but there—*again*.

I heard it; I know I did.

I throw back the covers and hurry across the room, my bare feet nearly silent on the wooden floor.

"Yes?" I whisper through the door.

"It's me," Brahm says from the other side.

Immediately, I unlock the door and pull it open. He stands in the hall, his hair disheveled and his shirt open and loose. He leans a forearm against the doorframe, and his eyes trail over my nightgown.

Just seeing him makes my knees weak.

"Did I wake you?" he asks quietly.

"No." A delicious chill feathers over my skin, making me shiver.

"I..." Brahm pauses, glancing away. When he looks back, he gives me a roguish smile that makes the cold hall feel like a fiery inferno. "Do you want company?"

I reach for him, and he responds immediately. We

crash into each other, both desperate. Brahm kisses me, his mouth greedy, his hands possessive at my sides. I cling to him, dragging him into the room. He closes the door behind us, fumbling with the lock without breaking the kiss.

I'm on fire, burning with sensation. I tug at the hem of Brahm's shirt, desperate to toss it to the floor.

"Alice," he groans, stripping it over his head.

My hands trail over his bare skin, exploring his muscular stomach and back, roaming where they will.

He sits on the bed and then pulls me onto his lap. I'm taller than him in this position, and I set my hands on his shoulders, cherishing the moment.

"I love you," Brahm breathes, dragging his lips down my neck, peppering my skin with kisses.

I tuck my finger under his chin and tilt his head back. He looks up, his dark brown eyes meeting mine in the dim candlelight of the tiny inn room.

"And I love you, Brahm. With all my heart."

He takes my head in his hands, pulling me down to meet him. He kisses me long and slow, the pace suddenly slowing to a simmer.

"Brahm," I plead against his lips.

He angles his head, deepening the kiss as he lays me on the bed. Then he tilts his head back and brushes his hand through my loose hair. "You're beautiful."

I trail my hand over his chest—down and up, down and up—while letting him drink his fill, reminding myself we're in no hurry.

He glances around, taking in the room before he looks back at me. "We can wait."

"I want you," I say simply, trailing my fingertips over his biceps and forearms, learning all his ridges and soft angles.

"You're sure?" he asks, catching my hand and kissing the silver ring, loving me enough to wait.

I nod, pulling him to me. "I'm positive."

27

ALICE

The air warms as soon as we cross the bridge into Faerie, though it takes a little bit for it to chase the chill from the inside of the carriage. But soon, I'm able to push away the blanket. The smell of the rosy woods greets us, but it's no longer an ominous fragrance.

I belong here now, and I think the woods approve.

We arrive at Brahm's estate just after dark, and I yawn as I step out of the carriage.

No one comes out to greet us, which seems strange. I expected to see Regina at least.

Brahm frowns as Darren tends to the horses, walking toward the door. I take his arm, holding him back.

"Something doesn't feel right," I say quietly.

He nods, pressing his hand over mine.

Just before we reach the door, Regina steps out. Her expression is flat, but when her eyes meet Brahm's, the barest hint of anxiety crosses her face. "Your mother has come for a visit."

Brahm's arm stiffens under my hand, and he gives Regina a curt nod.

We take the remainder of the stairs quickly, entering the foyer together. As I feared, Queen Marison waits for us, with Ian at her side.

At least a dozen castle guards are here as well, standing expressionless in their posts around the room.

Three of them hold Drake, keeping the prince in place.

Sabine sits on the floor next to her mother, face in her hands like a child. When we step inside, she looks up, and I gasp.

She's pale, and her skin shines with perspiration. Dark circles rim her eyes, and her lips are almost white.

"Sabine," Brahm breathes, crossing the room.

"*Stop.*" Queen Marison raises her hand, adding magic to the command. Brahm freezes halfway to his sister, leg stretched oddly in front of him. He should fall, but the spell must be keeping him in place. His eyes blaze, and Regina takes a step closer to me, grasping my arm as she tries to draw me back.

Her fingers tremble, and my stomach begins to roll.

"Do you know what your sister did, Brahm?" Queen Marison asks in a conversational tone that's at odds with her flashing eyes.

Refusing to answer, Brahm stays silent.

Marison's smile flickers. "She tried to lie to me."

A sob escapes Sabine, and the princess clutches her stomach.

"Foolish girl." Marison casts a scathing look at her

daughter. "Perhaps she thought she could hide the pain. She didn't realize it increases as we age."

Regina chokes beside me, trying not to cry as she watches the scene between her aunt and cousins. I grasp her hand, clutching it tightly to offer comfort even though I'm terrified as well.

"Do you know what she lied about?" Queen Marison continues, sounding as if she's scolding a disobedient child.

But again, Brahm defies her by staying silent.

With a flick of her wrist, Marison releases Brahm. He stumbles, nearly falling before he catches his balance. He rights himself, standing tall even as his mother steps up right in front of him. She's far shorter than he is, slender and slight, and yet she's easily the most terrifying thing in the room.

"She lied about *you*," Marison says. "About your whereabouts."

Still, Brahm refuses to answer.

"Tell me, where were you? Why did your sister stoop to such a level?"

Finally, Brahm gives in, but only marginally. "I was in Valsta."

Marison laughs gently. "I see. And why were you outside of Faerie?"

"That is my business," Brahm says through his teeth.

"Prince Brahm and the human girl were married by a magistrate in Davon, Your Majesty," a voice says from the doorway, startling us all. "I have done as you asked and watched your son diligently."

Darren stands in the foyer, clutching his hat in his hands.

I gape at him as Queen Marison makes a choking noise. Violently, she turns back to Brahm.

"Is that true?" Her voice is grating this time, so harsh it shakes with her fury. She clenches her hand in the front of Brahm's waistcoat, wrapping her long manicured nails into the fabric. "Tell me he is *mistaken*."

Ignoring his mother's command even though she practically has him by the throat, Brahm looks at Darren. "Who are you?"

With a low chuckle and a whirl of sparks, elderly Wallen stands in Darren's place.

"Wallen?" Regina exclaims, aghast.

"Not quite," the man says in Brahm's valet's voice. Again, the swirling sparks surround him, and this time, he takes the form of a small man with pointed, folding ears and a sharp grin.

"*Changeling*," Brahm snarls.

It's impossible to discern the man's age, as I've never seen anything like him in my life. He's only as tall as I am, with a face so generic, he looks like a blank slate. He saunters forward, still dressed in Darren's clothes, and bows before the prince. "Took you long enough, Your Highness."

"What did you do with Wallen?" Brahm demands.

"I dug a pit in the woods and threw him in. But don't fret—I killed him first. Otherwise, it would have been cruel."

Regina chokes back another sob, this one shaking her entire body.

"Enough!" Queen Marison jerks on Brahm's collar. "Tell me—did you marry that human girl?"

"I don't see how that concerns you," Brahm says calmly, though I hear the edge of fear in his voice.

"No?" she pushes him away. "Maybe it concerns your dear, sweet Alice."

"NO!" Brahm yells, but the castle guards surround him from behind, taking him by surprise with their sudden attack. "Alice!"

Marison crosses the room, and her red gown sways as she walks. Regina tries to push me behind her, but I stand my ground and pull the small copper letter opener from a deep pocket in my gown. I hold it out like a tiny weapon, perfectly aware of how pathetic it looks against a queen of Faerie.

"Not so innocent now, is she?" Marison swipes the blade out of my hand with no more than the flick of her wrist and a glimmer of magic. "Pathetic."

"Alice," Regina mews, still trying to get in front of me.

Marison raises her hand to strike me, and I brace myself for her attack. Suddenly, the queen hisses, clenching her hand into a fist as she pulls it back.

"You cannot touch her," Brahm reminds his mother, the muscles in his jaw clenched as he continues to fight the guards. "You saw to that yourself when you agreed to the illanté tether."

Marison's eyes narrow on me. Her nostrils flare, making her look mad.

She whirls around to face her daughter. "Alice is not the only one you care about in this room."

Though Sabine whimpers, her eyes flash. She looks like an injured, cornered animal about to attack.

"Get up," Marison commands, flicking her fingers into the air.

Like a marionette moving against her will, Sabine rises. She cries in pain, gasping as she writhes back and forth, trying to fight her mother's control.

Brahm and Drake yell, dragging their guards forward to intervene, but the men catch their footing and pull them back.

"Look what you did to her, Brahm," Queen Marison says, holding her daughter hostage by magic.

The princess trembles with agony, but her sobs are pure anger.

"You're just like your father—turning your back on your family for a human." Queen Marison shakes her head and walks up to her daughter. "It hurts, doesn't it? Do you regret protecting him now?"

"No," Sabine snarls, still fighting her invisible bonds.

"Then I don't believe you've learned your lesson." Turning her back on Sabine, the queen walks toward Regina and me. She stoops low before she reaches us, using a corner of her skirt to protect her hand as she picks up the letter opener. With a sickeningly sweet smile, she asks, "May I use this for a moment?"

"No!" I yell, but Regina yanks me back.

"Take it," Marison says to the princess.

Sabine cries, shaking her head violently even as her hand reaches for the small tool. She screams when her fingers wrap around the metal handle, and both Brahm and Drake roar with anger.

"That's enough," Marison finally says, and Sabine opens her hand.

The letter opener falls to the ground with a clatter.

"What about now?" Marison asks. "Do you regret lying for Brahm?"

Tears stream down Sabine's face, and she shakes. Blood drips from her hand, falling onto her ivory gown. Even still, the princess's face scrunches with unadulterated loathing as she barely manages a whispered, "*No.*"

Marison's eyes narrow, and something chilling crosses her face. Too calmly, she says, "Very well." She looks back at Brahm. "This is your fault, do you understand? Just as it was your father's fault that Drake betrayed me." Then, to the guards, she says, "Don't let them turn away."

Regina whispers a frantic, "*Please, no.*"

As if she's bored of a game and no longer wishes to play, Queen Marison says, "Sabine, I have no use for you anymore, and I cannot allow such a pathetic creature to inherit my throne. Pick up the letter opener and stab it into your heart."

Too many people yell at once, but it all becomes a blur. I yank from Regina's hold and run across the room, snatching the letter opener half a second before Sabine can take it.

I whirl around to face the queen, prepared to fight even though I know I can't win. But I'll die trying—for Brahm. For Regina and Drake and poor Sabine.

And for Eleanor, my parents, and everything my family has been through because of this woman's wickedness.

"ALICE!" Brahm yells, fighting like a caged bear.

But it's too late for him to save me. Marison surges forward, gathering magic like a sickly cloud around her. Voices scream, dark things that lurk in nightmares.

I lunge forward, prepared to slay the monstrous woman, when she casts her magic at me full force. The world goes pitch-black as the darkness surrounds me. I scream, never having felt agony like this in my life. The magic rips me apart with its icy tentacles, feeling like it's rooting around in the depths of my being, looking for my soul. I fall to the ground, curling up in a feeble attempt to protect myself.

And then...it's gone. I open my eyes to find I am in one piece, no sign of the attack marring my body.

And the scream is no longer mine.

Gasping, I push myself up on trembling arms, watching in horror as Marison's magic engulfs her. She writhes and yells, and everyone in the room watches, helpless.

Suddenly, the black magic dissipates, and the voices go quiet. The queen falls to the ground, eyes open, crumpling like a discarded doll.

28

BRAHM

The guards drop me as soon as my mother falls, apparently free of whatever bond she has been using on them. Horrified, the changeling edges toward the door.

"Drake!" I yell on impulse, "Catch him!"

Drake races for the changeling, tackling him to the ground. Then he looks up, eyes wide, as we both realize what just happened.

I spoke to my brother for the first time in ten years.

Regina kneels, taking Sabine in her arms, rocking my sister as they both cry.

And Alice.

She sits on the floor, staring at my mother as if in shock. She still holds the letter opener like a dagger, even though the metal shakes in her fist.

I race to her, stumbling to the floor as I grab her shoulders.

"Are you all right?" I demand, looking her over, my hands traveling over her face.

She nods numbly, finally pulling her eyes to the letter opener in her hand. Immediately, she tosses it away, shivering. Her voice wavers as she asks, "What happened?"

"Mother's magic ricocheted back at her," Drake says heavily. He looks at me. "The illanté tether protected Alice."

I look down, realizing the golden band of magic no longer rings Alice's wrist. "It's gone."

She rubs her skin as if somehow sensing it as well. "I was linked to you, but I made the vow with your mother. And now..."

We all turn to the fallen queen.

"Is she...?" Sabine croaks.

Reluctantly, I rise. After a deep bolstering breath, I kneel and press my fingers to Mother's wrist.

"She's not dead," I say wearily.

Suddenly, Mother flinches, crying out in her unconscious state. Her eyes move, unfocused, and her face contorts with horror.

"What's wrong with her?" Alice demands, edging away.

Repulsed, I close Mother's eyelids. "She's suffering the effects of whatever spell she intended to use on you."

The room falls quiet.

"What do we do with her?" one of the guards asks.

I shake my head, choking as I try to control a wave of intense nausea. "Take her back to the castle. She'll pass away, or she'll wake. Only time will tell."

Nodding, several guards step forward, scooping the queen's lifeless body into their arms.

Another guard turns to me, understandably nervous. "Your Highness, we—"

"I know," I say heavily. "We all know. There is no need to apologize."

Solemnly, he nods and joins the others.

I walk toward the changeling, wondering what we're going to do with him. "Where did you leave Wallen?"

"In a pit in the woods." He enunciates the words very slowly as if I'm dimwitted. "Didn't we already have this conversation?"

"How long ago did you abduct him?"

How long have I been blaming Wallen for something he didn't do?

The man looks up at the ceiling, thinking. "A month ago, maybe a little more. About the same time you and your pet got cozy in her family's estate."

I resist the urge to strike him.

"Hold him," I say to the guard. "We'll need his help to locate Wallen. Then we'll deal with him."

Alice slowly stands, though she's wobbly. I take her arm to steady her. Once I'm sure she's all right, I go to Sabine.

I kneel in front of my sister, at a loss for words.

"Stop," she says raggedly. "This was not your fault, so don't you dare apologize."

"Thank you for protecting us." I frown at her hand. Because the tool was copper, she'll bear the scar for the rest of her life. "You are—"

"Brave and strong." She leans against Regina's shoulder. "You've told me."

I try to smile, but it's painful. "I was going to say a fool, but you're those things as well."

"I would have been able to defeat her if I hadn't tried to lie," she says bitterly.

"I know."

Drake joins us, and for just a few minutes, we draw strength from each other.

Alice hangs back, giving us time, smiling as quiet tears roll down her cheeks.

Looking truly terrified, Sabine whispers, "Do you think she'll wake up?"

"I hope not," Regina says darkly.

Until Mother draws her last breath, we will live in fear of the queen.

"Help me up, Drake," Sabine says.

Drake immediately steps in, looking a little overwhelmed. She smiles at him, crying again. "I just said your name—right to your face."

"Sabine..." He looks like he's about to lose his composure.

"I feel just awful." She cries freely now. "But I'm so happy."

Drake pats her shoulder and gives her a tight smile.

"Take Sabine to her room," I say to Regina. "She needs rest to heal."

Regina nods, and the two of them begin down the hall.

I turn to Drake, exhaling deeply. He studies me with a guarded expression, not yet sure what to do with himself. Laughing a little, I clasp his shoulder. "All these years, I've wanted so badly to talk to you. Now that I can, I don't know what to say."

SHARI L. TAPSCOTT

He laughs, trying not to show weakness even though he looks close to his breaking point.

Alice steps up next to me, and I immediately pull her to my side.

"Thank you," Drake says to her solemnly. "You've saved us."

Looking dead on her feet, she answers, "I didn't actually do anything."

"You stood up to her," I say. "Alice, no one has dared do what you did in ten years."

"And we are grateful." Drake bows to her.

My staff has finally dared to enter the room, and they gasp at the gesture.

Though Alice likely doesn't know, a Fae prince bows to no one, and yet Drake is here, showing such reverence to a human girl. They exchange looks, unsure what to make of it.

"Where's Ian?" I ask suddenly, realizing the count has slunk away.

We search for him, but it's to no avail. He likely bolted the moment Mother fell.

"Come on," I say to Alice. "You need to rest as well."

She agrees without protest.

To Drake, I say, "I'll be down shortly. I'd appreciate it if you went with me to find Wallen."

Drake gives me a solemn nod.

As I walk Alice down the hall, she reminds me, "Sabine is in my room."

"I'm not taking you to Sabine's room—I'm taking you to ours."

"Our room." She suddenly smiles and leans against my side. "Doesn't that sound lovely?"

Holding her a little tighter, I finally let myself feel a trickle of relief. "It truly does."

29

ALICE

The Fae of West Faerie don't believe in burying those who have passed. Instead, their ceremony consists of cremation and the scattering of ashes. From the earth, to the earth.

I stand at the edge of a ravine with Brahm's close family, listening as he gives Wallen's eulogy. There's grief in my husband's voice, both due to the passing of a man he was close to and the lingering shame of believing that faithful friend betrayed him.

Regina cries openly, and Sabine and Drake simply bow their heads.

It's a somber occasion, quiet and thoughtful. Even the forest seems to understand we're in mourning. The only sound is the gentle rustling of leaves. The birds, too, are silent.

Finally, Brahm opens the urn and tips it over the ledge. The breeze catches the ashes, sending them swirling in the air as they fall.

And then, they are gone.

Brahm turns to me, offering his hand. We walk back to the estate as a group, not speaking until we reach the entry steps.

"What comes next?" I ask quietly, unsure of Faerie funeral traditions.

Brahm turns to me, giving me a sad smile. "Now we move on."

30

ALICE

"You just yawned," I accuse Brahm, looking at him from the side of the canvas.

We're in my studio in our estate in the Rose Briar Woods, and it's the perfect time of day, when golden afternoon light streams through the large glass windows.

"A yawn? Are you sure?" Brahm grins as he covers his mouth again.

I point my brush at him. "You just did it again!"

He laughs. "How much longer?"

"I'm almost done," I promise.

"You said that an hour ago."

I carefully dip the brush in cerulean and then dab it onto the canvas. "And an hour ago, I truly believed that's all it would take."

But now—now it is finished.

I step back, critiquing my work. I've gotten a little

rusty in the last four months, but I'm happy with it nevertheless.

"All right." I set the brush aside. "Come look."

Brahm steps up behind me, absently brushing my hair aside as he loops his arms around my waist and presses a kiss to my neck. "It's worth the boredom."

I angle my head to look at him. "You like it?"

"I love it." He kisses me before resting his chin on my shoulder.

"I still think you should have let me paint you with your mask."

He chuckles like I'm ridiculous and then turns me in his arms. I melt into him, still feeling a thrill every time he kisses me.

We stay like this until the studio door opens.

Brahm casually steps away when Regina walks into the room.

She carries a letter, and she offers it to me as she stops to look at the portrait. "You're quite talented, Alice. How did you manage to paint yourself into the picture with Brahm?"

"I used a mirror."

"It's very lifelike," she says.

"Who's the letter from?" Brahm asks me, even though I only receive them from one person.

"Gustin," I answer absently as I quickly read my brother's ramblings. "He's in Algora. Apparently, he made a lucky bet at a horse race, and he's 'struck it rich.' He says he'll send me something pretty."

Brahm shakes his head. "Some people never learn their lesson."

I carefully fold the letter and set it aside. "I'm glad he's doing all right."

Maybe someday, we'll make amends. Right now, occasional letters are enough.

"Drake is here as well," Regina says. "He didn't want to disturb Alice while she was painting. He said he'd wait in the conservatory."

"This needs to dry," I tell Brahm. "Why don't we go find him?"

We walk hand in hand through the halls, not bothering to hide our relationship. Enough people in the household heard about our marriage. The news of the handsome prince marrying the human girl who defeated the wicked queen is traveling through West Faerie like wildfire.

I can't say I mind all that much.

When we enter the conservatory, we find Drake standing near a bush filled with crimson roses. He stares at it thoughtfully, only glancing at us briefly as we enter.

"You're early," Brahm says. "Did you leave at the break of dawn?"

Drake nods, keeping his eyes averted. "I did, actually."

He's still not comfortable with people talking directly to him, but he's slowly healing.

"How is Sabine?" I ask.

"She's growing restless," Drake admits. "I believe she knows her coronation is imminent, and she's beginning to panic."

It's been several months, and Queen Marison still sleeps, trapped in the nightmare of her own creation. The

Fae physicians predict that even if she were to wake at this point, her mind would be addled.

The kingdom is in a state of waiting, expecting the golden princess to take the throne any day now. Sabine has already been ruling in the interim, making changes her mother certainly wouldn't approve of—including one dear to my heart.

As long as they secure a traveling permit from one of the Fae border villages, visiting humans are now protected for a week instead of a day. It's a start, though I'm confident the crafty Fae will discover a few loopholes that they love so much.

But because of it, Brahm has been able to retire his mask. There are now Faerie guards patrolling the thoroughfares, assisting travelers when they find themselves in a tight spot.

"When you go back, tell Sabine we'll visit after we return from Kellington," Brahm says.

We're going to spend a week in my family estate, celebrating the Spring's Eve festival that begins tomorrow. It's been a little strange, splitting our time between West Faerie and Valsta, but I appreciate that Brahm is eager and willing to embrace human traditions for my sake.

Not only will I never miss a holiday, but I'll never have to spend one alone.

Drake nods, still looking a bit absent as he runs his finger over a velvet petal. "Do you think..." He pauses, looking like he's not sure he's going to finish the thought. After a moment, he goes on, "Do you think there's a chance Eleanor is out there? Somewhere?"

I share a glance with Brahm.

"I don't know," I say gently.

As soon as his curse was lifted, he began looking for my sister, asking anyone and everyone for information. So far, the search has been fruitless.

"We were so close to the border," he says. "Could she have made it the rest of the way on her own? Is it even possible?"

No one has the answer to his question, but I hope he might find it one day. Even a confirmation of Eleanor's death would give him closure.

Give us all closure.

We study the roses for a time, each lost in our thoughts, and then Drake suddenly looks up. "Oh, I just remembered. Why is there a pile of rubbish outside the front gate?"

"A pile of rubbish?" Brahm asks.

Drake nods. "Random things—old dresses and ribbons, shoes, undergarments. A filthy palette and several ratty-looking brushes."

"It couldn't be," I murmur with a small laugh. I turn to Brahm. "You don't think…?"

He shakes his head as if he has no idea what I'm referring to.

The princes follow me as I hurry through the halls and step into the spring sunshine.

When we arrive at the end of the lane, I grin as I open the gate. Sure enough, the things that were stolen from me the day I first entered the Rose Briar Woods are stacked in a shabby pile.

"Do you know what this is?" I exclaim, nearly

clutching my old palette to my chest before I think better of it.

Brahm scowls at the mess. "I have no idea."

Laughing, I toss the palette back onto the pile. "The goblins returned my belongings."

Drake cringes. "You humans collect lovely things."

Perhaps worried I'm going to ask him to help lug it all inside, he turns toward the manor, leaving us to deal with it.

Brahm eyes my possessions with the same distaste as his brother. "You don't plan to keep those things, do you?"

"No," I laugh. "They're not good for anything now. Besides, I traded them all that day. They aren't really mine anymore."

Looking perplexed, Brahm cocks his head to the side. "Traded them for what?"

I step close and stand on my tiptoes. "A chance to meet you."

He drapes his arms around my back, so handsome he steals my breath. "And would you say it was a good trade?"

I shrug, feigning indifference. "I think it turned out all right."

Brahm scoffs as if offended, and I pull him down for a kiss.

As we walk down the lane to join Drake and Regina, I glance back at the rosy forest, remembering the day Brahm and I met. Though he saved me from the goblins, in many ways, we saved each other.

I think it turned out very well indeed.

ABOUT THE AUTHOR

USA Today bestselling author Shari L. Tapscott writes romantic fantasy adventure and contemporary romance. When she's not writing or reading, she enjoys gardening, making soap, and pretending she can sing. She loves white chocolate mochas, furry animals, spending time with her family, and characters who refuse to behave.

Tapscott lives in western Colorado with her husband, son, daughter, and several extremely spoiled pets.

SHARILTAPSCOTT.COM

Printed in Great Britain
by Amazon

22602696R00182